AF490869

THE
RIVER
OF
FALLEN STARS

FALLEN STARS

BOOK ONE

MADISON MCAULEY

Dedication

To all my honorary siblings who made my childhood less lonely and my adulthood more meaningful

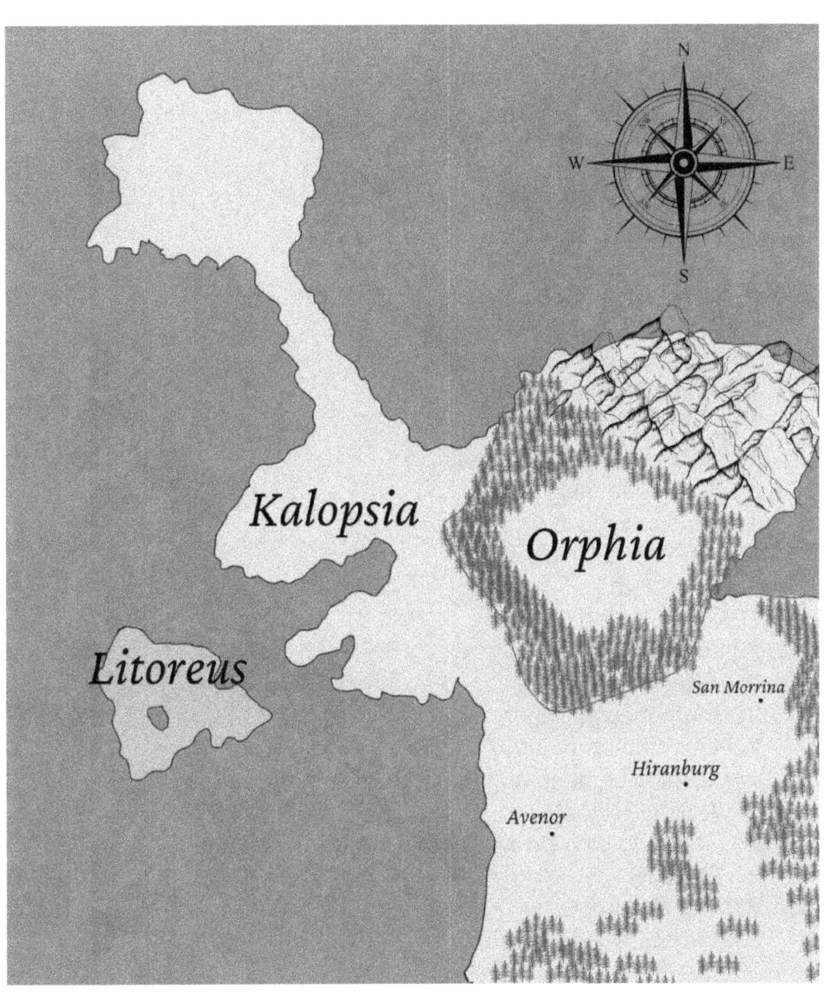

N
W
E
S
Kalopsia
Orphia
Litoreus
San Morrina
Hiranburg
Avenor

Table of Contents

1: A Means of Escape

In Emily's opinion, of all the deceitful words and messages of false hope, perhaps the cruelest was the overused saying "happily ever after." That belief made the friendship with her book-obsessed neighbor all the more ironic.

She had come to her friend's home ostensibly to help tend to the farm. The true reason, however, was that she desperately needed to exert herself and get out of the stifling confines of what was supposed to be her home.

As the workday neared its end and the sun began its descent, Emily's energy remained steady. She wished to keep scrubbing at the mysterious clothing stain, though her fingers already looked like prunes.

"What are you still doing here?" Amira asked. "We're done with chores for the day. Besides, Mother said that stain is never coming out."

The water sloshed as she yanked the clothing out to hold it up in the fading sunlight just to return it to the bucket. She began vigorously scrubbing once more. "It is getting lighter, I swear it."

"I think you're more likely to scrub off your skin than anything." She placed a hand on Emily's arm, stopping the aggressive movement. "Come, let's go inside and rest up before dinner."

"You mean read up before dinner." She glanced at Amira then back to her work. "I saw you sneak a few chapters in while you were pretending to muck the stalls."

She blushed in confession. "Perhaps I did. But I also mucked the stalls and did all the other chores I was assigned. And you did more than your share as always." She grabbed the garment from Emily's hands and hung it up to dry. "So, let us both enjoy a well-earned reprieve, shall we?"

After more discussion, they settled on a stroll about the property. The breeze teased a few strands of hair that had loosened from her bun. It felt most refreshing after being out in the sun most of the day. The gentle rustling of the leaves and the birds chirping above made the scene picturesque. It was so much better than being inside. She was about to say as much when she realized that Amira's library was not left behind, she had instead brought it with her.

Emily lifted her skirt and stepped over a branch in her path. Amira automatically followed suit with her nose remaining tucked inside the latest romance novel she was reading.

Emily rolled her eyes. "How you traverse up this hill blind without injuring yourself must be one of life's greatest mysteries."

"Mmhmm," she replied absentmindedly.

Amira spoke no other words in the minutes that followed. Only a slight gasp here and there and the sound of rapidly turning pages filled the silence.

"You know, if I wanted to be ignored I could've stayed at home," Emily said dryly.

Amira, not even realizing she was being spoken to, didn't so much as flinch.

Emily bit back a sigh. Though Amira grated her at times, she would never wish her away. She had her quirks, but she was a good person and a good friend—something Emily didn't have enough of in her life. They had grown up together and that created a bond that was strong enough to outweigh their difference in personality.

Amira turned the last page and grinned broadly, a characteristic gleeful look in her emerald eyes. She clasped the book shut and held it over her heart as she sighed deeply. "I do love a happy ending." She turned to Emily. "Did you say something earlier?"

"It's irrelevant now."

She offered a bashful grin. "Sorry. I was so close to finishing I couldn't bear to put it off any longer."

"I see."

"Oh Emily, you really should read this one." Amira's voice was naturally a little high, but it rose even more in pitch when she became animated as she was now. "It's the most wonderful story! You see, there's this young lady who —"

"Is some kind of damsel in distress?"

"Well, yes. But then—"

"A handsome hero comes to her rescue, they fall hopelessly in love, he whisks her away and they get married and live out their lives in unrealistic happiness?"

Amira shot her a saucy look. "You know, for someone who never reads these stories you act as though you know very much about them."

The testing of each other's patience was mutual, so she tucked her cynical opinions aside and tried to be a more pleasant companion. "Very well, what is this one about?"

Amira returned the book to her satchel. "Well, speaking in the most generic terms I suppose that is the premise of the story." Her dramatic flair appeared once more. "But there is so much *more* to it than that! The hero is in disguise, so she doesn't know he's her true love. And then they're separated from each other and it all seems hopeless! But in the absolute height of peril he returns! And then..."

Emily listened half-heartedly as her friend continued her detailed synopsis of the story. She never quite understood why Amira was so enamored with these fanciful stories. Even her name sounded like something out of a fairytale, though that was her parents' doing.

Emily supposed there once was a time when she enjoyed such stories. She had memories of sitting on her mother's lap next to a blazing fireplace, listening to her soothing voice read until it lulled her to sleep, granting her pleasant dreams every night. But reality was not so kind to people as the stories were to their characters.

"Shall we take the path around the pond or the forest trail?" Amira interrupted her thoughts.

A faint smile tugged at her lips. "You know I always prefer the pond."

After a few more minutes the water came into view. Emily increased her pace to a quick clip. "Do you think we'll see many ducks today?"

"I hope so." Amira reached in her satchel and pulled out a paper sack. "I brought them a snack."

Emily eased herself down on the grass by the water's edge. She propped her arms behind her to support herself, stretching the sore muscles from today's work in the process.

The reflection of the trees created a green border that encroached on the blue water. Sure enough, their feathered friends were there. One swam right in front of her, moving smoothly across the pond and pausing occasionally to dip its head under for food. It looked effortless, almost as if it were being carried about by the wind.

She found it interesting how different this little animal was above the surface than below. If you looked underneath, she knew you would see its little feet kicking fiercely to propel it forward. Yet, all that people saw was the calm and tranquil scene of it gliding across the shimmering surface of its home. Emily was well aware what that was like.

"Look!" Amira pointed to the far corner of the pond. "They're little babies!"

Her eyes settled on three little ducklings circling each other while a bigger duck, presumably their mother, swam nearby. Her mind flashed back to three dark-haired children, carefree and running about on nearby grounds.

She tore her eyes away and focused on the water itself. It was ridiculous how the most random things reminded her of her childhood. The memories would not bring back her childhood freedom, nor would they bring back the dear friend she lost.

She took a steadying breath, the sweet smell of jasmine tickling her nose. The movement of the ripples in the water slowly gave her a sense of peace. Where life was unpredictable, water was constant and steady. Whether it was the pond, the rolling ocean waves, or the flowing stream of a river, being near the water gave her a sense of stability in her life when she most needed it.

Amira's giggles filled the air as she fed her new friends. "Why hello Mr. Waddles. Care for a snack?" She tossed a few crumbs to the feathered creature and he gobbled them up quickly. She continued tossing more crumbs and soon a feisty crowd of ducks was gathering around her.

Emily watched her friend sit in the dirt with her legs crossed in her lap as she continued calling the ducks by their various names, looking more like a little girl than the young woman she truly was. She often wondered how Amira remained a beam of sunshine in life despite her hardships. Emily never quite managed that, though she had her own methods of coping.

"Oof!" A loud *quack* made Emily jump as one of the ducks stumbled across her outstretched legs. Amira began cackling in laughter and Emily allowed herself a small laugh.

"We should probably start making our way back," Amira said after barely composing herself. "Dinner will be ready soon."

Emily let out a sigh. If only she could remain here forever. "I suppose." She lifted herself from the ground and smoothed her skirts. "Is there anything else that needs to be done first? Any more chores?"

"No. Thanks to your help all of my chores are done. Though I feel you deserve the credit more than I do."

"You know I never mind. Besides, my intentions are not totally charitable. I *need* to work. Sitting idly in Uncle's house all day as a proper lady of leisure would surely drive me to madness."

Her cheerful face fell. "I know. I wish you didn't have to stay there."

"As do I, but you know that I must as long as I am under their guardianship," Emily said without emotion. Amira would never ridicule her feelings, but it had become an ingrained habit over the years to keep them tucked away.

She ignored Amira's concerned glance and diverted the topic. "But that will change soon enough."

Amira perked up a little, as Emily knew she would. "How much longer?"

"Thirteen days and—" she squinted and checked the direction of the sun— "about five hours, I would guess."

"Less than a fortnight and you'll be free." Amira smiled. "Oh, I can't wait!"

Emily stifled a laugh. "Then imagine how *I* must feel."

They crested the hill and the small farmhouse came into view once more.

"Are you staying for dinner?" Amira asked.

"As much as I want to, I can't. I skipped dinner last night because of staying with your family and the two nights before I had a tray sent up to my room. Aunt was sparring with the glares she gave me and I'm afraid I'll receive the full blow if I miss it again." Not that Emily really cared if she offended her aunt and uncle. They never seemed to care much about her. But she had no intention of making her remaining days with them any more miserable than they needed to be.

Thirteen more days, she thought. Thirteen more days and her plan would be put into action. After ten long years, her cage door would finally be open.

2: Averting a Dinner Disaster

Emily snuck up the servants' staircase of her home, her slippers keeping each step silent. She peeked down the hallway to see it blessedly empty and darted into her room. She crossed over to the little golden clock on her bed table to find she was already eight minutes late for dinner.

Drat. Now what? Her aunt and uncle took punctuality very seriously. She was already on their bad side, she doubted they would handle her tardiness with any graciousness.

She would not allow herself to become flustered. She would simply find the most logical solution to her problem and act upon it. The formula had saved her numerous times in the past.

She frowned in the mirror at the muddy streaks on her dress and the same mud-colored hair flying all over the place. She couldn't go back in time—heaven knows she wished to sometimes—therefore she couldn't change the fact she was late. If she rushed down to dinner right away her family would abhor her appearance and that would just give them another reason to belittle her.

Her eyes lit up as an idea sparked. Appearance was just as important as punctuality, if not more so. If she put more than her usual effort into her appearance, she could use that to excuse her tardiness.

She quickly rang for her maid then took a rag from the washbasin and scrubbed the dirt off her skin.

A knock at the door alerted her to Penny's presence. "You rang, Miss?"

"Yes." She tossed the rag aside. "I need to get ready for dinner. Quickly." She pulled the pins out of her bun and released the wild beast that was her hair. She grabbed a comb and began working on detangling the knots. "Please lay out my pink dress. The one with gold trim."

"Yes, Miss."

Penny helped her into the monstrosity of her evening dress, the nicest one she owned. Though even her best dresses were only half as fine as what the rest of her family wore. Aunt always purchased gowns good enough to put on a show of good appearance without spending a coin more than was necessary. Emily never insisted on anything more. Practical, simpler dresses were her preference anyway.

"This gown is so lovely!" Penny remarked. "What's the occasion?"

"Trying to erase my name from Aunt and Uncle's black books."

Penny chuckled despite Emily's dry tone. "Oh dear. I hope it works."

"If it does I plan to sell the dress pattern. I'm sure at least half of San Morrina would be interested."

Penny laughed harder, as she often did at Emily's dry humor. "Either way, it's quite a beautiful gown I'm sure many young ladies would enjoy wearing."

The blush pink and shimmering gold trim was indeed as lovey as it was impractical. The short train was a tripping hazard. The billowy sleeves made it difficult to do much of anything with her arms—she would have to be mindful of that during dinner. And the color made her feel incredibly conspicuous when she was used to wearing dark, plainer colors.

"What about your hair, Miss? Shall I curl it?"

Emily frowned at her stubbornly straight hair. "I'm afraid there's not enough time for that. Something elegant, but nothing too time-consuming," Emily glanced at the clock again. "I'm late as it is."

"I've got just the thing, Miss," Penny said with a smile.

In minutes, she took the wild hair and maneuvered it into several elegant twists and braids, finishing it off with a decorative comb. Emily gazed into the mirror, dumbfounded.

"How are you able to do that?"

"Do what?"

"Take the frizzy mess on my head and turn it into something beautiful."

Penny smiled with unmissable pride. "Practice I suppose."

"Thank you, Penny."

Her skirts swished as she grabbed a pair of gloves to hide her dirty fingernails and then raced down the steps.

She slowed her pace as she reached the base of the staircase. Pausing to take in a breath, she put on a mask of confidence and casual disinterest and sauntered into the dining room.

As she expected, her aunt and uncle's cold eyes bored into her. Uncle looked condescending as always. Aunt looked both irritated and slightly confused. Her younger cousins smirked, eagerly anticipating the rebuke to come.

She curtsied, took her seat at the far end of the table— yet another reminder she was not wanted here—and attempted to look as unaffected as possible.

The table was silent as they waited for Emily to give a reason for her absence and apologize. She simply focused on her soup, which was now cold. If she did not make a fuss over her lateness perhaps they wouldn't either.

"I haven't seen you wear that dress in a while," Aunt Jacqueline said.

"Indeed." Emily sipped from her spoon. "It has been too long."

"Where were you?" Uncle's harsh tone reverberated in the room.

Emily gave him her sweetest smile. "I cannot wear a fine dress like this without the rest of me in an equally fine state." She gestured to herself. "It requires a great deal of time, but appearance is everything for a young lady, is it not?" She looked to her aunt in hopes of a supportive reply. Emily didn't believe the words one bit, but she had heard the lecture verbatim many times from Aunt Jacqueline.

"So is punctuality," Uncle grumbled. "See to it that you plan your time better in the future to allow you both."

Emily nodded. "Yes, Uncle."

Her aunt and uncle ignored her for the rest of the meal. Emily vaguely listened to their conversations between the clinking of cutlery on plates. Uncle spoke of business with the tenant farms and how the new tax law was making things difficult for him. Aunt spoke of the new dress she procured as if she had money to burn. And the twins, well, the twins tried to irritate her by tossing grapes at her when no one was looking.

Any onlooker would only see Emily eating her chicken. They could not see that in her mind she was slamming her head into the table. *Thirteen. More. Days.*

The minute dinner was over she fled to the relative sanctuary of her bed-chamber and changed into something more comfortable. Itching for something productive to do, she sat at the small desk and pulled out the leather-bound notebook to review her plans and see if she needed to make any necessary adjustments.

She would have to meet with Uncle's solicitor to discuss the inheritance from her father and learn exactly how much she would be receiving. Based on her father's employment and lifestyle, she knew she wouldn't be rich, but it should be enough to lease a small home. She put an asterisk next to that line on her to-do list. She would look into other options just in case the inheritance wasn't enough.

She would also need to speak with the landowner of the home she wanted to lease. She had her eye on a small cottage on the other side of the village. It was rather ridiculous that he refused to speak with her presently. No one seemed to take her seriously either because of her youth or her relations. She could not legally obtain her inheritance until she turned twenty and she would not be able to accomplish anything of significance until that day came.

The quill threatened to be crushed under her grip. But getting frustrated wouldn't change anything. She made herself relax and settled on laying out her plans so she could act swiftly as soon as the day arrived.

She already spoke to Penny about possibly hiring her as a maid-of-all-work. Emily did not mind doing the work herself, but it would be safer to have another person in the home with her. Penny was as trapped here as she, and Emily began to view her as something of a friend. Whether or not she had enough to pay her, somehow she would find a way to free them both.

Next on her list was packing. She glanced around the room at her few belongings. That wouldn't take long to do. All she had that was truly hers were some clothing items, her mother's jewelry, a few agricultural books from her father's library, and the miniature portraits of her parents.

She had been tempted to get rid of the portraits many times, but could never bring herself to do so. They always brought up feelings she didn't wish to face. Thoughts of her mother brought up the pain of losing the person who meant the most to her. And thoughts of her father brought up emotions she couldn't understand, nor endure. She was resentful of him for his choices that brought ridicule on the family name.

But her anger was always followed by guilt when she remembered her father was not always that way. He had loved her and her mother and provided well for them for a time. But the death of his wife changed everything. It was because he loved her so deeply that he broke so profoundly.

She stood abruptly and opened her window, letting the cold air coat her lungs and the wind whip at her hair. She needed to regain her balance and steady herself.

Just like the portraits that stayed in the bottom of her trunk, her feelings were better left buried. No one could hurt them if they couldn't tell what they were. And you couldn't experience pain if you simply refused to feel at all. It was her only line of defense to salvage what remained of her battered heart.

3: Cracked

Emily headed to the marketplace, though she was not only there to purchase goods as Aunt thought. She was there to make employment inquiries as covertly as possible. Aunt would never let a young lady in the care of her family demean herself by seeking work. How incredulous that she would actually want to do something meaningful instead of embroidering and gossiping all day.

The sounds of haggling patrons, bleating animals, and clopping horse hooves swirled around her. She tried her best to drown out the unintelligible mix of noises and keep focused on her plan. She needed to have work set aside as a backup plan, but unfortunately, she did not have any particular skills worth hiring.

The only thing she was truly good at was drawing, which was less than useless in the village. What she lacked in skill she could make up in willingness and hard work. But she was still a woman—a small and petite woman at that. Though relatively fit, most of the heavy lifting jobs would be too much for her. She spoke to a few potential employers that offered some doable jobs, but they didn't even spare her a second glance.

Her nose caught a whiff of baking bread, a smell so divine that her mouth watered despite the sight of the sweaty, overweight vendor who just denied her work. Perhaps the kitchens would be more willing to hire her. And a bit more sanitary as well.

"Good morning," she greeted an upper-aged woman kneading dough. Though her face was downward, the graying hair and plump figure reminded her of Amira's great aunt. The thought of the sweet lady set her nerves at ease. "Are you in need of any help in the kitchens?"

"Who wants to know?" Her abrasive voice took Emily aback, though she refused to let her face show as much. Not that the woman looked up from her work anyway.

"I do."

"Can you cook 'n bake?"

"I know the basics."

"Nah, don't need amateurs 'round here." She dismissed her abruptly.

"I learn quickly, Miss. I can certainly clean. Perhaps you could use a scullion?"

She turned and shooed her away, flinging particles of sticky dough as she did.

At the marketplace center she passed a variety of people with their stalls and carts, selling everything from vegetables to trinkets to a questionable "cure-any-ailment" medicine that was most likely just alcohol in disguise.

Looking over the crowd of people, her eyes made contact with a familiar woman. The woman turned away sharply the same moment Emily recognized who she was. The two of them used to play together as children in this very market—though they hadn't talked in years. She stopped playing with Emily after she became an orphan. Her one-time friend was now a cold stranger.

She shook off the feeling the strange occurrence brought on and returned to her mission of employment. Unfortunately, conversations with the other vendors were very much the same as before.

"Why don't you keep to your high-and-mighty uncle where you belong?"

"You comin' to pick on us poor folk?"

"Anyone in that family of yours won't be working here."

As usual, no one saw who she really was. When they looked at her, they only saw her snobby uncle or her foolish father.

She paused at the fountain to sit on the stone edge, hoping to find solace in the water and ease the tension in her shoulders.

"Buy a flower, Miss?" A young voice spoke to her.

She stood abruptly and put some distance between her and the street boy. She kept a hand on her pouch to make sure nothing would be pickpocketed.

The sight before her saddened her. He had a thin frame, pleading green eyes, and dirt under his nails and all over his clothing. A strong enough wind would likely topple him over. He seemed harmless, likely an orphaned street urchin, trying to get by on selling whatever goods he could find.

Though life with her family was unpleasant, she could've had it much worse. This could've been her, living on the street, trapped in the workhouse, or hauled off to the orphanage in Hiranburg like—

She cut off that thought before it finished. Her childhood friend whose name she refused to recall was gone. Thinking of him didn't bring him back from the orphanage and it surely wouldn't bring him back from the dead. She could do nothing about him, but this hopeful boy in front of her she could do something about.

Focusing again on the half-wilted daisy he held out to her, she offered the kindest smile she could, the one only the most innocent and deserving ever saw. "Here." She pulled out her remaining coins and placed it in his bony hand. "Keep the flower and the change."

He looked at the money wide-eyed as if he'd just been given a fortune. "You're not funnin' me, are you? Is there a catch?"

"No catch."

"Thank you, Miss." He gaped at her. "You sure you don't want the flower?"

She shook her head. "Give the one I would've gotten to someone who can't afford to buy one. Make their day."

He nodded and then sprinted away.

She watched him go with a weight on her heart. She didn't know what would become of him once that money was gone. Uncle deemed any charity a waste of funds. But she gave him at least his next meal, along with an opportunity to give to another. She hoped it made a difference in his life, even if it was a small one.

Despite all the rejections she faced today, that simple act made her feel that her trip to the market was not a complete failure.

***

Emily approached the manor after yet another fruitless job search. The inheritance would have to be enough it seemed. If it wasn't...no. She would not worry over that just yet. Worrying about something she couldn't control accomplished nothing but giving herself a headache. Emily already had one of those and didn't need it to worsen.

Aunt was expecting Mrs. Barnewall to call upon her this afternoon and insisted that Emily be present for her visit. She was the wife of Uncle's main business associate which meant everyone needed to look and play the part of a perfectly behaved family.

She was tempted to skip the visit out of spite, for they only had control over her for three more days. But making herself look like an arrogant and reckless female in front of others would only harm her own endeavors. She must never let her emotions get in the way.

Besides, she actually liked the Barnewalls. Despite their business connections with her horrid uncle and the great influence they had in their village, they seemed to be decent and kind human beings. If it weren't for the deceptive hypocrisy of her family she would actually enjoy the visit.

She meandered down the stone path leading up to the home, not in any hurry to get there. Radcliffe Manor was a grand and stately home that was meant to impress. A tall set of double doors flanked by columns reminded anyone who entered of their relative inferiority. The family within the walls was no different—equally as cold as the stones holding the manor together.

A whinnying horse paused her step. She turned towards the sound to see Mr. Carvey approaching. He was Uncle's solicitor, the exact person she needed to speak to regarding her inheritance.

"Good afternoon, Miss Radcliffe," he shouted and dipped his head.

Emily curtsied. "And to you, Mr. Carvey. Have you come to see my uncle?"

"Indeed." He tied the reigns around a nearby tree branch. "He said he had an urgent need to discuss something with me."

She tilted her head and furrowed her brows. What was so urgent that Mr. Carvey was called nearly the same time as Mrs. Barnewall's visit?

"Forgive me, I shouldn't have said that." He looked flustered as he adjusted the top hat on his bald head. "Much in regard to business is of an urgent nature. I'm sure it's nothing out of the ordinary."

He joined her on the steps and they ascended them side by side. "I understand," she replied. "I will not keep you, but please send for me before you depart. I have an important matter I need to discuss with you as well."

"You do?" He gave her the same look of surprise most people did when she acted as the adult she was.

She bit back a sigh of exasperation. "Yes. Regarding the inheritance left for me from my father."

His brow came together. "Your inheritance?"

"Yes." The butler opened the doors for them. "I understand I will not be able to claim it until I become twenty but I'm hoping we can go ahead and discuss the necessary legal arrangements since that is only a few days away. You already being here makes it more convenient for both of us."

The confused lines in his forehead deepened but Uncle's entrance to the foyer cut off any reply he might have made. He glowered at Emily and she took her leave before he could start spitting venom at her. "Pardon me, I will leave you two to your business." She curtsied again and went up the stairs to prepare for their guests.

She opted for her dark green day gown. Aunt liked to keep the parlor windows open in the springtime, so the thin wool should be just enough to protect her from the cross breeze.

She glanced at the clock to see she still had half an hour until tea and decided to spend it in the music room. She would enjoy playing her family's harp while she still had access to it. Though she was not skilled, she always found the gentle humming of the strings quite beautiful.

As she passed by the door to her uncle's study she heard his raised voice. She looked at the closed door and shook her head as she imagined poor Mr. Carvey. Whatever reason her uncle was yelling at him, she doubted it was his fault. She took two steps forward when Uncle's words made her freeze.

"That girl knows nothing about handling finances! Why on earth does she have a need to speak with you?"

"Sir, as her guardian you have been granted authority over the inheritance until she is of age. But once she is twenty years old the legal right is transferred to her."

They were speaking about her and her inheritance without her. Why was she being left out of her own life? And why was her uncle so angry? It's not as if he didn't know she would be claiming her money soon. The two of them never spoke of it explicitly, but as the only male relative of her father, he had been entrusted with his affairs and therefore was informed about what she was to receive and when.

She strained to listen but could no longer make out the words after their volume lowered. She glanced back and forth to make sure no one was watching and backed up to press her ear against the door.

Mr. Carvey was speaking. "...does not seem like the squandering type—"

"She is not your problem, she is mine," Uncle interrupted. "I have been the one responsible to care for her all these years, and I have used the money to do so as I see fit. You have no right to judge me for that, you understand?"

"Of course, Sir. I did not mean to overstep my place. I just assumed that she was already aware that she would not be receiving any inheritance."

Not receiving any inheritance? Emily brought her hand to her mouth as a slight gasp escaped her lips. It could not be true. She had to have misheard—the voices were muffled after all. Or she misunderstood the words out of context. It wasn't possible that she would not receive what her father's will stated she would.

She pressed herself deeper into the door to catch any remaining snippets of conversation. Then it opened and she nearly fell sideways as she caught the men's eye. Mr. Carvey was as wide-eyed and pale as Uncle was red and livid.

"What are you doing here?" Uncle's tight voice demanded.

Emily opened her mouth but the words caught in her throat. Her mask was slipping. She needed to regain control if she was going to get through this.

She put it in place one more. "I was on my way to the music room—"

"I don't believe you," he snapped.

Emily concentrated on maintaining her composure and went straight to the matter at hand. Ignoring her uncle and looking at Mr. Carvey she asked, "What of my inheritance?"

She had done no wrong and had every right to know what they were discussing.

A bead of sweat trickled down Mr. Carvey's ample forehead. "Miss Radcliffe...I'm afraid...well..." he stammered.

"You presumptuous child!" Uncle barked, making Mr. Carvey jump. "You have no inheritance."

Her fingernails dug into her palms. "You sir, are a liar." Hang her manners, she would be gone in three days and meant to put Uncle in his place where this was concerned. "We both know for a fact that my father left me an inheritance to gain once I become of age."

"Your father was a foolish man. He did not take care of you and I was forced to take on that burden. Am I to be expected to do so without compensation? Even a servant receives his pay."

She clenched her teeth but did not flinch at his speech. His words should have pained her, but she had taught herself long ago how to numb herself to his remarks. She was angry but kept herself poised—though only just. "I do not disregard that you have fed and clothed me. I am only asking for what has been rightfully given to me."

"Given to you." He scoffed and pointed his finger accusingly. "Why should *you* expect to be given anything more for you to indulge yourself in? *I* am the one that has fed and clothed you and yet nothing is given to me. I have taken what is rightfully *mine*, you ungrateful girl."

"Indulge myself?" Her voice raised on its own accord. "I have strived my entire life to be agreeable to you. I was only a child who wanted nothing other than the essentials of life!" She turned back to Mr. Carvey. "You were saying?" He would contradict her uncle. Tell him he was wrong.

The silence hung heavy in the room, with only the sound of her own heartbeat to break it.

"Sir?" She prompted him again.

He fingered his hat brim in his hands, avoiding eye contact and looking decidedly uncomfortable. The sick feeling in Emily's stomach increased.

"It cannot be," she said in the faintest of whispers.

He let out a breath. "Your uncle is correct. There is no inheritance for you to gain. All the money has been withdrawn."

All the blood drained from her face. It was gone. All of it. Her inheritance, her freedom, her life—gone. As if in an earthquake, her carefully constructed plans that seemed so solid crumbled to ruin in an instant. It crashed down upon her and left her suffocating.

She stumbled back and leaned heavily against the wall. Her eyes blurred, unfocused. She forced herself to breathe and tried to process what was happening. She tried to form a plan, but the wheels in her mind jammed and it took all her energy just to keep herself from imploding.

"Good heavens child! Control yourself!" Aunt said. Apparently, she had gained an audience.

"Is she gonna cry?" one of the twins mocked.

"Boohoo!" the other added.

Her uncle had just accomplished something he had failed to do her whole life: crack her armor. She gulped down the lump in her throat and blinked away tears that were forming, but they were bubbling up more rapidly than she could control.

The only clear thought she could form was that she would *not* give her selfish family the satisfaction of seeing her break. There was only one option before her.

She had to run.

She gripped tightly to her skirts and darted out the door as though her life depended on it. She didn't know where she was going, she just needed to get away. Away from the manor, away from people, away from the world if she could. For the first time since childhood, she was acting irrationally and she did not even care.

She aimed for the property line and ran past servants. Her tears blurred her vision to the point she could only make out shapes and outlines. The world around her was nothing more than indistinct speech and noise. Only her pounding footsteps and heartbeat filled her ears.

She made it to the forest but did not slow down. She would take no chance of anyone following her. She needed to be completely alone, as far away as her feet would take her.

She wiped the tears away on her sleeve to make sure she did not run into a branch or trip over any roots. She was able to keep a quick pace for a while. When her racing heart protested she slowed her pace but kept going. She gulped in deep, heaving breaths of air and kept moving until her legs and feet ached. Finally, not able to bear anymore, she collapsed under a tree.

As her knees hit the ground, she allowed herself to feel every emotion she had so carefully hidden for years. Fear, anger, resentment, heartache, and humiliation combined in a heavy lump in the back of her throat.

With the trees as the only witness to her outburst, she let her tears soak the earth beneath her face and her sobs and screams fill the air with only the silence of the forest to console her.

4: A Lone Treehouse

A rushing sound filled Emily's ears as a cold wind whipped around her and sent a chill through her aching body. It stung her dry, puffy eyes as she opened them. Apparently she had fallen asleep, but she felt anything but rested. She slowly pushed herself into an upright position, her muscles protesting every move.

She took a moment to collect herself and take in her surroundings. She was unsure how long she had been asleep or how deep into the forest she had gone. Her flight was a bit of a blur, but even on an adrenaline high she could not have gone too far.

She brushed at her dirty skirts in vain. They were covered in grass and dirt stains. Penny would have a fit over it. Perhaps she'd be better off dying it all brown once she arrived home.

Her stomach twisted. She had no home. Radcliffe Manor never was one, and the home she'd planned for herself would not come to be without her inheritance.

She could not return to her family, not yet. Her armor only went so far, and she knew she wouldn't be able to bear them just now. She would go to Amira's home to form a plan and reassemble herself before facing her family.

With that decided she stood, wincing as she stretched her legs, and started towards the village.

Except...she didn't know which direction San Morrina was.

She looked for her footprints to follow but could not see them in the grass. The thick treetops above her prevented her from using the sun as a compass. And it wasn't as if people ran into the woods every day where she could just ask someone for directions.

Standing around woolgathering would do no good either. She huffed in frustration, made an uneducated guess, and began walking.

Her throat burned from lack of water. Muscles she didn't even know existed ached more than she thought possible. And as minutes turned to hours, she struggled to keep her equilibrium.

Don't panic. Panicking accomplishes nothing, she reasoned with herself. Still, she couldn't fully extinguish the unsettling feeling in her gut.

When she finally resigned herself to the fact that she was lost, a wooden structure in one of the trees caught her eye. As she approached it, relief filled her as she searched for an adjoining house or family.

"Hello?" She shouted as best she could. "Hello? Is anyone here?"

She was met with silence.

Surely someone must be around.

She inspected the treehouse closely. It was quite well constructed to only be a child's play spot, yet a bit small to be someone's place of residence.

She wandered through the thick vegetation around her, still searching for civilization. There was no indication of her being near another village or even someone's property. So why a lone treehouse? Perhaps it was a sort of shelter.

She returned to the riddle of a building wondering if she should climb the wooden steps and try to enter. Her body would protest, but if there was food or water inside—

Without warning, a strong arm tightened about her waist yanking her back as another hand covered her mouth. Her heart jumped and she immediately realized the folly of her actions. Being lost was bad, but being found by the wrong person could be her demise.

She kicked and twisted violently in an attempt to free herself, but to no avail. The mysterious man—surely it was a man based on the size and strength of the arms—pulled her to a more secluded part of the woods. Rough tree bark collided with her back as she was turned and pushed against the trunk of a tree.

The tight grip he had on both her shoulders meant her mouth was unhindered. She opened it to scream, but it fell silent on her lips. For now that they stood face to face, her attacker was nothing like she envisioned.

For one thing, he was quite young. His freckles gave him a boyish look, though he was likely closer to her own age. His eyes were dark in color, but not at all in malice. Nothing about his demeanor gave even the slightest hint of evil intentions. Instead, she found his expression mirroring her own—a mixture of shock and fear.

She kept telling herself to scream, kick, throw a punch, or do something to escape his unyielding grip. But she couldn't move, and it seemed he couldn't either. They stood stunned, neither able to look away from each other.

Finally, he found his voice. "How did you find me?" There was no anger, just genuine surprise in his voice.

When she didn't answer, he repeated his question. "How did you find me? Is anyone with you?" His eyes darted back and forth as if expecting to find someone else.

The wheels in her brain began turning again, quite slowly, as she went through her options. Though he seemed more frightened than one to fear, he had still assaulted her. She would be very cautious in what information she disclosed to this stranger who hadn't yet loosened his grip on her.

And yet, there was something about those brown eyes that seemed kind. Her intuition told her there was a reason to trust him. But to trust a complete stranger, in the deep forest at that, was utterly ridiculous. And Emily hated being ridiculous.

It seemed he wasn't going to let go until she made some reply. "Sir," she began cautiously, "I did not even see you, nor was I looking for you. It seems *you* are the one that found *me*."

Relief flashed in his eyes and his grip on her shoulders finally relaxed. He let go as he hung his head. "I suppose I have scared you. I'm sorry. I've just never..." He shook his head and he met her eyes again. "It doesn't matter. My apologies, Miss..." He looked at her expectantly, evidently wanting her name.

I don't think so.

She dipped her head. "Thank you." That reply would suffice. She had no intention of answering his implied question, though she had many of her own. Who was he? Why was he in the forest? What scared him? Who was he hiding from? But her logical side scolded her curiosity and told her to ignore such questions. She was unharmed for now but needed to leave before anything changed.

But her burning throat reminded her she also desperately needed water. Those few brief sentences were painful to voice. "Do you have some water by chance?" She choked out. "I'm afraid my canteen is rather dry."

He hesitated only a moment. "Oh, here." He pulled out his own and gave it to her.

The water was cool and refreshing as it went down her throat, giving it much needed relief. "Thank you." She dabbed at her mouth with the cleanest part of her sleeve. "Now, if you'll excuse me I must get going."

She began walking away but paused as she took in the identical looking trees in every direction. She had not the slightest idea where to go. The sky had darkened and night was approaching. She did not want to admit as much, but the risk of wandering the woods alone for several more hours was higher than telling the stranger she was lost. He may very well be the only person who could help her.

"It seems I got a bit distracted on my walk. Could you point me in the direction of San Morrina?"

"San Morrina?" He squinted slightly as he looked her over as if trying to ascertain her identity. "You are quite a ways from there. It must've been quite a walk you were attempting."

Emily learned that if you did not receive the answer you wanted to a question, the best thing to do was remain silent and wait expectantly. It was a look she had perfected over the years. Most people, uncomfortable with the silent stare, would keep talking. She quirked one brow up slightly, the final touch to her mask, and let it work its magic.

"Um...that way." He gestured behind her "Several miles southeast."

Works every time.

She meant to voice her thanks to him but a loud growl emitted from her instead.

The man smiled with amusement. "Would you like some nourishment before you go?

Goodness, she was hungry. But it would be dark soon. And though the stranger was being polite, something about the way he eyed her made her uneasy. She could endure hunger a bit longer.

"That will not be necessary."

"It will only take a few—"

"I will eat when I arrive at my destination," she interrupted and quickly turned on her heel. "Amira will have my favorite foods anyway," she muttered to herself.

"Wait, what did you say?"

Apparently she didn't mutter quietly enough. She glanced over her shoulder to see him moving towards her. It was time to go. "Nothing of consequence. Good day," she said casually. She picked up her pace as she heard his footsteps getting closer.

"Wait! Did you say Amira?"

"A friend!" Emily replied, not stopping or even looking back.

"Amira Elford? Hyacinth's daughter?"

She halted her steps. How did he know that?

"Do you know her, Sir?" If he was acquainted with them then perhaps she need not fear him after all.

He did not answer, but fixed his wide, calculating eyes on her once more. She tensed when he came right up to her, but one word kept her from fleeing. "Emily?"

She sucked in a breath. He knew her name, but she had no guess as to his identity. She was sure they had never met before.

"Emily, is it...is it really you?" His tone had softened and his eyes watched her with both disbelief and hope.

Again, something about those eyes seemed somewhat familiar, but she couldn't begin to explain why. He wasn't from her village—it was small enough that she would've recognized him otherwise. And it wasn't as if she ran into the forest on a regular basis.

Unable to puzzle it out on her own, she was forced to ask the question. "How do you know my name?"

A smile broke out across his freckled face. "How could I ever forget the name of my childhood best friend?"

No. It couldn't be. He had the same coloring that Luca did as a child, but Luca wasn't alive. He had been gone for years. This man was mistaken, mistaking her for someone else who happened to have the same name. "What are you talking about?"

He put a hand on his chest. "Emily, it's me. Luca."

That was too coincidental.

"But...how?" She closed her eyes in an attempt to shut out the painful memories being brought up. "That's not possible," she whispered. She wanted to believe it, but her mind couldn't wrap around the possibility because it wasn't a possibility. None of this made any sense.

He tilted her chin up with the gentlest of touches and looked into her watery eyes. "It is me. See?" He rolled up his left shirt sleeve, revealing a long scar on his forearm. "You pulled me out of the rocks when we were children, remember?"

She covered her mouth to stifle a gasp as she stumbled back. "It is you." She had never swooned before but felt very close to fainting at that moment. Before she could steady herself he wrapped her up in a friendly embrace. The sweet sound of his laugh filled her ears.

"I should've recognized you earlier," he said as he released her. "I never thought I'd see you again."

"But, the orphanage. The fire. We received a letter. You...they said you died." Her voice nearly broke on the last word.

"Died?" Luca replied in surprise. "No." He shook his head. "No, I survived the fire."

"But you...you were gone. No one has heard from you or...or seen you since." It took all the energy she had left just to speak. She was emotionally exhausted.

He looked pained at her words. "I'm afraid it's a long story." He sighed. "Come, let's get you some food first."

5: A Familiar Stranger

In all the years Luca had lived here, he had not once come upon another person while making his patrols about the border. The forest was considered a reserve so hunters were never an issue. Neither were travelers, for there was no need to go through it to get to any known village. And there was nothing particularly interesting to see to make one want to venture this far—nothing that people were aware of anyway. Needless to say, he was utterly shocked when he saw someone—a woman—peering up at his guard post. And that someone was none other than Emily.

He clearly remembered the first time he met her as a little boy. She watched him warily with hands on her hips and the most serious expression that made her look like a miniature adult. But soon enough they were laughing and playing together regularly and she became a bright spot of his childhood.

She was no longer that little girl he remembered, running past him with pigtails flapping wildly in the wind. In the eleven years of their separation, she had turned into a grown young lady. It left him with an odd feeling in his heart—a mix of wistful longing and brother-like pride, as well as something else he couldn't quite pinpoint.

He had an arm loosely around her as he guided her up the steps of his post. He felt the slight trembling of her body, though whether it was from the cold or the revelation of him being alive he wasn't sure.

When she said she thought he had died, her eyes held the same look of sadness as they did when he last saw her all those years ago. The day he was taken away to the orphanage when she watched him with a brave face but barely concealed tears. It was an image indelibly etched in his mind.

He had no idea his absence caused her prolonged pain. He had no family to mourn him and he hadn't thought anyone cared enough at the orphanage to inform his friends. He assumed Emily's memory and care for him would've already faded. That someone else would take his place as her best friend. It seemed he had been wrong about all those things.

He put his dredged-up memories aside as he fiddled with the lock. He opened the door and the sparse, dim room greeted them inhospitably. It was anything but comfortable for a distressed lady. He wished he had at least tidied up a little before he left this morning. As he only used the space for brief naps and to store food while on duty, cleaning was never a high priority. It wasn't what she needed, but it was all he had to offer.

He cleared the random clutter off the table and stuffed it in a cabinet to put away later. He grabbed a pillow from the unmade bed and set it on the wooden chair in an attempt to make it more comfortable. Once she was seated, he took the blanket and wrapped it around her shoulders.

"Hungry?" Luca asked, trying to draw her out.

She gave him a weak nod.

He went to the small cabinet and pulled out some nuts and berries. It wasn't much, but hopefully it would give her some energy.

She mechanically took his offering and began eating. She had not spoken a word since they began walking. He assumed she would be brimming with questions about his past. He was not looking forward to answering them, but her current taciturn demeanor was even more disturbing.

He drummed his fingers against the wooden tabletop. "So...what happened, exactly?"

She kept eating with a distant look in her eyes. "I got lost."

"How long were you walking?"

"Hours."

"Why were you out here anyway?"

She shrugged one shoulder.

Something was definitely wrong. She had changed not only physically but her demeanor had also been severely altered. There was something in her eyes he didn't remember seeing as a child.

Back then, he could often find ways to make her laugh and soften her expression with a smile. And when her mother died, he had made it his personal goal to make her laugh as often as possible. But he sensed he wouldn't be able to resolve this situation as simply.

Sitting across him at his little table, stiff and silent, she almost looked broken. He didn't think it was possible to break her, for even as a girl she was strong as iron. Of course, being lost deep in the forest would shake up even the strongest of people. But he had this nagging feeling that there was more to it than that.

Whatever was bothering her, she didn't seem to be in the state of mind to discuss it now.

"Here, come rest." He guided her from her seat to the bed and adjusted the blanket to cover her. She silently obeyed.

He crossed back to the table and kept his back to her. It was difficult to give her much privacy considering the treehouse was one medium sized room. He didn't want to leave her alone but staying just felt awkward.

He silently debated for a few minutes when he heard a snore. He glanced over his shoulder and smiled to see she was already asleep. He pulled out his little notebook, slowly tore out a piece of paper, and wrote a brief note of his whereabouts in case she woke up.

He took one more glance at her as he softly closed the door. Despite the circumstances, he couldn't help the grin that came to his lips. Emily, his childhood best friend, was back in his life. As much as he tried to forget his childhood, Emily always stayed in his mind. But he didn't realize how much he had missed her until now. He sincerely hoped they could fall back into the easy friendship they had before.

Although he shied away from his past, he was nearly bursting with excitement to tell her about his present situation. He wanted to introduce her to his friends, his new family, and all the wonders of his home. She would love it.

He stopped mid-stride when the realization hit him. All of that was forbidden. She shouldn't even be allowed in his guard post. His duty would be to send her on her way back home.

He sighed and mounted his horse with much less enthusiasm. It was probably for the better. She would want to be back in the comfort of her own home with her family. For all he knew she might have a husband or children worrying over her. And even if she didn't, her reticence may not be caused by her being lost.

He never even wrote her those years he was in the orphanage. He thought it was better that way, considering what life was like there. On top of that, he led her on to think he was dead all these years. He really couldn't blame her if she wanted to distance herself from him.

This sweet, unexpected reunion was going to be more complicated than he thought.

6: The Mystery of Home

Emily's eyes fluttered, threatening to open, but she forced them to remain shut. She was never one to waste the day by sleeping it away, but her head ached terribly. Surely the day could wait for her a little longer.

She tried to make sense of her strange dream. She rarely dreamed, and when she did they were never this outlandish. Running away from her home, wandering the woods for hours, and then stumbling across Luca. Complete and utter foolishness.

Leaves rustled and the wind whipped at a branch that thumped against the wall right by her head. She groaned as she pulled the blanket over her face. It seemed even the trees were bound and determined to make sure she awoke.

Trees?

There weren't any trees by her bedroom window. Which meant...

She shot up in the bed. It was still night. And even in the dark, she could tell she was not in her room. No, she was nowhere near Radcliffe Manor.

She flung back the blanket and allowed her eyes to adjust and her heart rate to settle. She moved carefully, aiming for the flickering candlelight barely putting off any illumination in the unfamiliar room. It was only when she had leaned over the table to retrieve it that a note caught her attention. Careful of the dripping candle wax, she held the paper up for closer inspection.

Emily,

I have to make my final rounds about the grounds outside. I will return shortly. If you awaken and I have not yet returned, please don't worry. You're safe here.

Luca

She let the paper fall from her hand, barely making a sound as it fluttered to the table.

It wasn't a dream. All of it was real. Her inheritance was really gone and Luca was indeed alive. The events in between started coming back to her.

She felt for the chair behind her and sat down. *What on earth am I going to do?* she wondered as she thought about the predicament that brought her here. Unwontedly, she had no ready answer, nor any semblance of a plan. She squeezed her eyelids together. No wonder her head hurt.

The only thing she could control in all of this was her emotions. She gave in to them yesterday in a rare moment of weakness but she was determined to keep them reined in from now on.

She scanned the note again. The corner of her mouth twitched upward of its own accord as her eyes lingered on the masculine signature. *Luca.*

The one glimmer of light in all of this was Luca. One of the few people who truly cared about her, her closest friend outside of her mother, the boy whose "death" nearly broke the last piece of her soul, was *alive.*

The revelation made her a walking paradox. Of course, she was primarily happy, being that he was alive and well. But she was also hesitant and, if she was honest with herself, a tad anxious. So many years had gone by—he may not be the kind and caring soul he was in boyhood. After all, why hadn't he come back after the fire? Or told her he was alright? She wanted to trust him, but time and circumstance could change even the most loving of people. Her father was evidence of that.

Preconceived notions were no good. She could not make a judgment of character one way or another without evidence, she reminded herself. She needed to hear his story and observe him to see if he had changed or not.

She stood when she heard footsteps on creaking wood. She smoothed her skirts out of habit—Aunt's voice ringing in her ears about appearance—and watched as Luca entered with a smile on his face.

He held a lantern in one hand and a small burlap sack in the other. "I see you're up."

She confirmed the obvious. "I am."

"Good." He unloaded his burdens on the table. "I brought back some findings in case you're still hungry." He reached in the sack and pulled out an apple. "Your favorite, if I remember correctly. Or at least they used to be."

She blinked at him. He remembered that?

He held out the enticing fruit with an unspoken question in his raised eyebrows. She accepted the offering and took a crunching bite, relishing its flavor. The sweet, juicy flesh tasted all the better considering the meager amount of food she had put in her stomach in the last several hours. "Delicious," she said in between bites.

"They're quite good in these parts." He sat in the chair and she followed suit, wincing as she did at her leg.

"Are you alright?" Apparently, the lantern lit up enough of her face for Luca to take notice of her pain.

"My legs are a bit stiff." She tried massaging the bothersome muscle. "They were not prepared for as much use as they received earlier. But I'm alright."

Though she tried to brush it off as inconsequential his look of concern remained. "What happened to you?"

"I got lost."

"You mentioned that. But why were you here in the forest? By yourself?"

She debated how much she should reveal to him. She decided she would start small and see how he reacted. "I needed to by myself for a little while. I didn't realize I had gone so far. When I took my leave, I couldn't find my way back."

Luca set down his half-eaten apple. "But why the forest? What drove you out?"

"My family," she replied simply.

His eyes widened. "Is something wrong? Did something happen?"

She clasped her hands together to avoid wringing them. This was where the story got difficult.

"Is your father alright?"

She snapped her head up wondering why he would ask such a thing. Then she remembered Luca was taken away before her father's passing. He didn't know what happened to him...any of it.

"Father isn't here. He died nearly two years after Mother did."

He blinked at her. "Oh Emily, I'm so sorry. I know that must've been so difficult—"

She held up her hands and cut off the apology. "I've made my peace with it." She had no desire to discuss him currently.

Luca looked ponderous. "So if not your father then are you...that is, did something happen to your husband? Or child?"

She would've scoffed at that question had it not been asked so gently. Few would be tempted to marry a plain girl like her. "I wouldn't know, considering they don't exist." She attempted a half-smile. She really was making this hard for him. He would keep guessing and hit upon the issue eventually, she might as well tell him now. "It was Uncle Thomas and Aunt Jacqueline."

Understanding came over him as he realized the implication of her answer. "I see. I take it their temperament hasn't changed much." It was more of a statement than a question, for he had seen their harshness as a child.

"I'm afraid not."

His eyes scanned her over. "Did they mistreat you? Did they hurt you?"

"No. Not in the way you are implying."

His stare indicated he did not believe her words.

She had to put forth more effort than usual to maintain an even tone. The recent memory of Uncle's greed combined with Luca's genuine concern was nearly overwhelming. "They've never laid a hand on me—I'm not worth that much effort to them. They simply act as though I don't exist unless someone is watching. They make it clear that I am an unwanted burden in their lives." She looked away as she made the confession. It seemed his kindness was stronger than ever, and her emotions could not bear to see it just now.

"Then why do you stay?"

"I have no choice. They've been legally responsible for me since Father...left." *Left* was a more appropriate word choice than *died*, considering he left her behind emotionally long before his life actually ended. "I had a plan to leave but I recently learned that it was insufficient."

Neither spoke for a long moment. Only the sound of roaring wind that had picked up in intensity filled the room.

"I...I don't know what to say. I'm so sorry. You deserve so much better than that."

"It's not your fault." She brushed the pain off as usual. "I'll come up with a solution, I always do." She forced a breath in and out. "But that's enough about me. Now that my interrogation is over I'd like to begin yours." Though attempting to tease, she didn't have it in her to smile. "What on earth happened after you left San Morrina?"

He picked at his fingernail. "Where do I even start?" His shoulders sagged as he let out a deep sigh. "I was taken to the orphanage in Hiranburg, as you know, and stayed there about four years." A haunted look flashed in his eyes, but he didn't elaborate on any details. "Then one day, when I was fourteen, there was a fire. I don't know how it started, but it spread fast. Everyone was in a panic. Children and adults alike were running and screaming. I was one of the last ones out of the building before it collapsed."

She shook off the images of fiery flames in her head. "We received a letter that you had died in that fire. Did no one see you escape?"

He picked up his unfinished apple and spun it in his hand. "No. I barely escaped as it was. The whole building was engulfed in flames. Ceiling beams were falling. The smoke stung my eyes. I thought I was completely trapped." He shuddered. "Finally, I managed to crawl around the debris and make it out of the back window. But outside the grass was catching fire, burning its way toward me."

Emily put a hand to her heart right where it ached for young Luca. Though her life was far from pleasant, she had never been in any true danger. Never had she come so close to facing her own mortality.

He rose and began pacing in front of the table. "I was terrified." His voice quavered slightly. "So I ran opposite from the fire and into the woods. And I just...kept going. Not the wisest thing to do, but between the inhaled smoke and the sheer terror of nearly being burned alive I wasn't exactly thinking clearly."

"No one came after you?"

He shook his head so weakly it was barely perceptible.

"That's terrible." Her words were so empty, but she had no idea how to respond to such a horror story.

"It was in the moment, but it didn't end so terribly." His disposition lightened. "If I had not fled into the woods that day I would've never found...well," Luca paused, searching for the right word, "home."

She raised an eyebrow. "Home? You mean you've been living in this"— she gestured around her—"all this time? As a recluse?" Her tone sounded judgmental even to her own ears. She should've been more sensitive, but it was such an unusual arrangement that she couldn't help it.

Her comment didn't seem to bother him, for he just chuckled. "Not exactly. This is not my permanent residence. It's more of a shelter while I'm on duty."

"Oh." That made much more sense. "Then where do you actually live?"

She hadn't expected the hesitant look in his eyes as he studied her. It was as if he was unsure how to answer such a straightforward question. But when he smiled, all the hesitancy was gone. He stretched out his hand to her. "Let me show you."

His offer gave her pause. She hadn't intended to actually go anywhere with him. She should be heading back to San Morrina. But though her mind was of a logical sort, it was also filled with curiosity about the world and people. With Luca, every question answered only raised many more. And the current sparkle in his eyes had been absent up until he spoke of "home" which intrigued her beyond control.

She took his hand gingerly and followed him out the door. The lantern light broke through the thick darkness illuminating a black steed that otherwise would've blended into the night around them.

"Good boy, Onyx," he whispered. "Would you like to meet my friend?" Emily rubbed the creature's snout, the air from his nostrils brushing against her arm. "I'm afraid we'll have to share," he said a little awkwardly. "But it's better than walking."

An owl hooted somewhere in the distance. She looked out into the vast darkness, feeling hesitant to go anywhere out of doors. "Are you sure this is safe?"

He shook his head. "There is nothing to worry about. Besides, Onyx and I know the way by heart. We could get there with our eyes closed."

Emily was not convinced. "I hope you do not plan on actually attempting that," she said dryly, though completely serious.

"I do not." He smiled, cupping his hands to boost her up. When she didn't move, he dropped his hands and softened his features. "Nothing will happen to you, I promise. Trust me, please." He gently cupped her shoulder. "I won't let anything happen to you."

That was not an easy request to comply with no matter how gently it was made. Few people in her life gave her reason to trust them, but Luca used to be one of them. The brief time of their reacquaintance had given her no reasons to distrust him. And it was not as if she could return home by herself anyway.

With that reasoned out, she nodded her consent and he helped her mount. He followed behind her, and they plunged deeper into the night around them.

7: A Royal Revelation

Emily's uneasiness did not dissipate on their ride. They were going at a steady canter and she assumed they would be arriving at a clearing soon. After several minutes of riding, they only seemed to be going farther into the forest.

"Are you sure that you know where you are going?"

"I do," Luca said confidently.

"And are you sure where you are going is indeed the correct way?"

He made a small sound of amusement. "Yes."

Her mind spun as she tried to think of nearby villages and towns. She could think of none that required going so deep into the forest.

Disliking the uneasy feeling in her stomach, she started talking again. "You still haven't told me where you reside." She found conversation kept her mind on the objective at hand instead of the potential dangers of the woods.

"Oh, right. Orphia," he replied.

"Orphia?" She couldn't recall ever hearing of that name before. "Is it much farther?"

"It's only a few more miles away."

She rubbed at the goosebumps on her arm. "Hopefully we get there soon," she said quietly. The cold wind whipped her unruly hair and sent shivers through her whole body.

Luca must have noticed because he brought Onyx to a stop. "Here." He leaned away to remove his overcoat and gave it to her. "I'm sorry, I should've thought of that earlier."

"And I should've thought to bring the blanket with me," she retorted. She slipped the oversized coat around her, grateful for the small amount of protection it would offer from cold. "Thank you."

"I can take him faster if you want. We'll get there sooner but I was worried it would be too much for you. Can you put up with it?"

Her stiff legs would protest the change but her chilled body welcomed the prospect of arriving sooner. "I think so."

"Ok, hold on then."

She held on tighter as they rode at a full gallop, weaving through trees and making several twists and turns. Emily closed her eyes and attempted to shut out the dizzying movements.

The clacking of the horse's hooves subsided as their pace slowed. Luca spoke quietly into her ear as if he was afraid of rousing her too quickly. "We're here."

She opened her eyes, letting them adjust to the faint lantern light illuminating the row of large trees in front of them. Rootlike vines hung from them like a heavy curtain, tangled and intertwined with each other. Luca reached out his hand, pausing before pushing them aside.

"Just so you know, this place is a little...different."

"Different?" Emily asked with speculation. "What do you mean by *different*?"

He didn't answer, and he seemed to struggle with how to explain himself.

"Should I be worried?"

"No," he said quickly. "No, not at all. It's a good kind of different. It's just"—he shrugged and smiled—"different."

Though spoken calmly, his words made Emily uneasy. What possible reason did he have to provide a warning if there was nothing to be concerned over?

"You have nothing to be afraid of, I promise. I think you'll like it actually." He must've noticed her body stiffen at his previous words. She had to remember to control her reactions more considering she was sitting so close to him on the same horse.

He heaved the vines aside and they entered a clearing. She looked at the scene before her and was surprised to see, not a village, but more forest. At least that's what it appeared to be.

But as they rode on she noticed it was different from the rest of the forest. The trees were bigger—much bigger in fact—and they sparkled. There were hundreds of fireflies...no, they couldn't be fireflies. These glowing dots were stationary. Upon closer inspection she saw that they were lights from people's homes. They were not tree houses like Luca's shelter, but multiple homes built along the trunk of the tree with steps and bridges connecting homes and trees to one another.

"Well?" Luca questioned.

"It's fascinating," she responded.

"I think so too."

"How is it I have I never heard of this place?" she wondered aloud. "Orphia, you said? I can't recall anyone speaking of it back home."

"Well, it's not under Kalopsia's domain. It's its own kingdom."

Interesting. She had read of such independent kingdoms existing but had never heard of Orphia specifically. "Still, I think I would have heard of it."

She felt Luca shift awkwardly. "Well..."

The uncertain tone in his voice instantly put her on high alert. "Luca," she said with an edge to her voice that made it clear this was not simply a curious request, "why haven't I heard of it? What's wrong?"

"Nothing's wrong...per se." He stammered for an explanation. "It's just...well, as you've seen, we're quite secluded and out of sight here. We don't really get many visitors. Visiting is actually quite...discouraged."

The way he said that last word made Emily extremely uncomfortable. "So what exactly will they think of me, the aforementioned discouraged visitor?"

"Don't worry. They'll love you."

Emily nearly scoffed at that. Very few people in her life felt that way about her. "Luca, be serious for a moment," she said frankly. "Why did you bring me here if I'm not welcome? How do you honestly think people will react to a stranger on their land? We should go back."

"You're not a stranger, you're my friend," he said casually.

"I am a stranger to them."

"As was I when I first arrived, and that turned out well."

Her brow furrowed. That was a semi-valid point, which led her to the question: "How did you find this place, secluded as it is?"

"It found me. Well, Yuni found me I should say."

"Yuni?" Another unfamiliar name. "Who or what is Yuni?"

"Who," he explained. "When I was fleeing the fire, I got lost. No one from the orphanage found me—I honestly doubt they even searched for me. So I just kept wandering around until I nearly passed out from exhaustion. Yuni was out riding and found me. She took pity on me—I was a rather pathetic sight, I'm sure. Anyway, she took me in, let me stay here, and cared for me as I finished growing up."

"I see," she said as his story sunk in. "And she has continued treating you kindly?"

"Very much so," he said in an affectionate tone, obviously very grateful to this woman. "Perhaps a little overprotective at times, but very kind indeed. I feel quite indebted to her."

Emily nodded in understanding, though she never experienced such a thing herself. Luca had endured more than she would have ever imagined and was quite fortunate in the result. Not only did he survive a fire and being alone in the woods, but he was found by a perfect stranger who was kind enough to take in the poor orphaned boy.

And then there was her, grudgingly taken in by her family who barely tolerated her.

"It all turned out well." He broke her musings. "So as you see, not all strangers are turned away. Yuni is more like a mother to me now. She'll be happy to meet you." He twisted around to look her in the eye and give her a reassuring smile. "You won't regret coming here. Please, trust me."

Her silent nod satisfied him, and they continued making their way through the village. Her curiosity brought her mind back to the treehouses flanking her, though they were distant enough she could make out very little detail in the darkness.

The stretch of grass beneath them ended and converged to a low, winding tree branch. It was of considerable size, large enough to accommodate their horse without being near the edge. A splash involuntarily brought her eyes downward, but she could see nothing underneath but a pit of blackness.

She kept her eyes forward for the rest of the ride. They came to a stop at a set of large wooden doors looming over their heads with torches on either side.

"Where are we?"

"My home," he said matter-of-factly.

The light illuminated the intricate carvings of vines and flowers on the doors. Never had she seen anything so ornate and grand, not even at Radcliffe Manor. She raised her eyebrows in a silent question.

He paused after dismounting. "Did I mention Yuni is the queen?"

"*Queen?*" Her eyes went wide. "And you live here"—she gestured widely to the structure in front of them—"in a castle?"

He shrugged one shoulder with an apologetic look.

Luca was alive, there was a hidden kingdom right outside her village borders, and now he lived with royalty? How much more convoluted could this whole thing get?

"Luca," she brought her voice low hoping no one would take notice of their arrival. "We need to leave. Now."

He gave her a curious look. "Why do you want to leave?"

Where did she even begin? "First of all, I am in no way presentable to be meeting royalty." She gestured to her sullied clothing. "As an unwelcome visitor I'm violating some sort of law or rule and flaunting that to a monarch with my presence. I'm here unannounced in the middle of the night..." How on earth did she let him talk her into this?

Luca rested his hand gently over her own. "I told you, Yuni is practically my mother. She's not a condescending stuck-up royal. And she is nothing like your aunt and uncle."

How did he know she was worried about just that?

"I promise, you have nothing to worry about." He squeezed her hand. "You don't have to leave. But...but if you want to go back, I will not force this upon you."

She should leave. She should grab the reins this very moment and ride off without turning back. But she knew she wouldn't get very far. Despite her misgivings, she didn't truly want to leave. The more she saw the more her curiosity pulled her in.

"Well, I suppose since I let you drag me into this I should see it through."

A genuine smile swept over his face. "I was hoping you'd say that." He helped her down. "Don't worry, you won't be in any trouble. I on the other hand will probably receive a lecture about arriving back so late and scaring Yuni half to death."

A footman opened the door almost instantly after knocking. "The queen has been waiting for you. She is in the parlor." He eyed Emily a little warily but said nothing about her.

"I will be there directly. Have someone see to Onyx for me, please."

With a crisp nod he marched off through the entryway and they entered the great hall. Her eyes were drawn first to the large tapestries on either side depicting nature scenes, then upward to the arched ceilings featuring more wood carvings. A large, golden chandelier hung as the crown of the room. All of this she took in simultaneously during the length of a few breaths as she followed Luca at a quick clip before turning out into a hallway placing them at the closed parlor door.

She began to shrug off the coat Luca had lent her but one look at the dark splotches on her dress made her keep it on. She smoothed back her hair and readjusted the pins of her bun, attempting to put it into some semblance of order. Goodness, she was going to regret agreeing to this.

"Wait here. I'll explain what happened and then introduce you," Luca whispered.

He rapped on the door before pushing it open and then strode in with confidence. It seemed he had none of the nervousness Emily felt.

"Luca!" A female voice, presumably Yuni's, shouted. "Are you alright?"

"I'm fine, Yuni." He chuckled. "Don't make such a fuss. I'm perfectly alright."

"Where in heaven's name have you been all this time? Xanth hasn't pulled you into some sort of mischief again, has he?"

Xanth? Yuni? These people had the most unusual names.

"No, none of that. I did my patrol as usual. I just had something unexpected come up that delayed me."

"Unexpected?" She sounded concerned, as she should be. "What happened?"

Luca's voice remained perfectly calm and unaffected. "Well, I was making my rounds when I heard someone speaking—"

"Someone was in the forest?" Emily couldn't see Yuni or Luca from her vantage point tucked behind the door, but she imagined Yuni's face was tight with her jaw set, given the stern quality of her voice just now.

"Yes." The word emerged slowly. "But it's nothing like you're imagining. This is a good thing as you'll see for yourself." Luca stepped back into view and glanced in her direction.

"You brought them here?" She dropped her voice lower and Emily had to strain to listen. "You know the rules. Strangers are forbidden to enter Orphia, and you very well know the reason why."

Forbidden. She swallowed, hoping the unsettling feeling of the word would go away. She remained glued to her hiding spot contemplating a potential escape route.

"I know, but—"

"Do you grasp what could happen, Luca? This is serious. I'm surprised it would even occur to you to bring a stranger here!"

"But Yuni, she's not a stranger."

Emily waited anxiously to see what she made of this piece of information.

"*She?*" Yuni finally said.

Luca motioned Emily over. She put on the best dignified facade she could manage in her disheveled state and slowly stepped into view. Her feet felt like lead and Luca had to come and nearly pull her forward.

"Yuni, may I present my friend, Miss Emily Radcliffe."

Emily sank into the lowest curtsy she could offer. "Your Majesty," she whispered.

Even in a night wrap, Yuni displayed a grace and strength one would expect from someone of royal blood. She was a middle-aged woman. Her hair was down, long and wavy, so blonde it was nearly white. Her dark eyes stood in stark contrast to her creamy complexion. They were nearly the same shade of brown Luca's were, though they lacked the warmth that his contained.

It was those eyes that were scrutinizing every inch of her. She reminded herself to stand tall and look confident even though she didn't feel it.

"How do you know her?" Yuni addressed Luca but kept watching her.

"She is my childhood best friend. She had gotten lost in the forest and I stumbled across her."

More like dragged me around and gave me a heart attack.

Yuni knit her brow and her gaze lost some of its intensity, though she still looked speculative. "Emily? The same Emily in the story about that scar on your arm?"

Luca grinned with pride. "The very one who saved my life when I got this scar on my arm."

Emily fought back an eye roll. She could hardly claim such a heroic act. She treated his wound when he injured himself on the rocks and then assisted him home. Although it was a nasty cut, his life was never in any real danger. But as it was a point in her favor she kept that to herself.

She could almost see the debate behind Yuni's eyes as she processed the information. Emily held her breath, then released it when Yuni's expression softened. She gave a small smile, though it did not quite reach her eyes.

"In that case, that kindness alone tells me much about your character. In fact, I feel there is a debt owed to you, Emily. No matter the passage of time, I am grateful to you for taking care of Luca."

Emily was shocked at the bit of praise, especially from someone who moments ago seemed close to throwing daggers at her.

"You must forgive my scrutiny, but maternal instincts make me rather cautious of strangers. But Luca knows you and I trust his opinion." She nodded in his direction. "So, welcome to Orphia."

"It is an honor. Thank you."

Yuni summoned a servant to see her to the bedroom she would occupy. Luca started as if he intended to accompany them when Yuni interrupted.

"Luca, please stay a moment. I still need to speak with you."

He gave Emily an apologetic look. "Of course. Forgive me, Emily. Sleep well."

"Goodnight," she replied quietly before being whisked out of the room.

The maid took her down the long hallway and she caught a glimpse of a spiral staircase up ahead. Upon rounding the corner, however, her attention was captured by a large tree trunk encompassed by glass in the middle of the room.

She tried not to gape at the impressive centerpiece. It was a real, living tree in the middle of a room. Inside a castle. A castle Emily was now a guest in. Goodness, how many things would leave her stupefied before the night was over with?

Somehow she made it up the stairs in her addled state without stumbling and was deposited in her bedroom.

"Here you are, Miss," the maid said. "Do you have any bags?"

She gave the room a quick once over. "No."

"Ok then, we'll see what we can do for you. I'm sure you can borrow some things for your stay."

When the door shut behind her she let her jaw drop. She was staying here in the castle. Though it was likely more humble than her own kingdom's, it was still the fanciest, most luxurious thing she'd ever seen.

Again, there were arched ceilings and intricate detail on the wood bedposts. The smooth silk bed cover was the color of a clear blue sky. She traced her finger along the swirled pattern of the white embroidering, admiring the detail. The bed cover along with the white window curtains presented a nice contrast that brightened the room amid the dark wood furniture.

Within a quarter of an hour the maid returned with a small variety of dresses and nightgowns. "I don't know how long you'll be staying here and how much you'll need, but this should give you a start."

That made two of them. She would likely just stay the night, but until she formed a plan she didn't know anything for certain. The staff had already gone to much work on her behalf, she might as well make it worth their while and enjoy the luxury for a few days.

After helping Emily dress for bed, she thanked the maid —whom she finally remembered to ask and found out her name was Jayla—and settled in.

She laid in the finest nightgown she'd ever worn, on the softest feather stuffed mattress she'd ever slept on, in one of the loveliest rooms she'd ever seen. She hoped that was enough to overpower her racing mind so she could get some sleep.

8: Learning to Fly

Luca made his way to the breakfast table, the plush blue carpets silencing his footsteps in the empty room. He made his plate from the sideboard and dug into breakfast as usual.

His introduction of Emily to Yuni went pretty well, though Yuni was far more scrutinizing than he would've thought. He just assumed Yuni would be drawn to her and welcome her as heartily as he did. He probably should've known better, considering Yuni's past. Just because he knew Emily would be no danger to their community didn't mean Yuni did. He was grateful she trusted him enough to let her stay, though he noticed she had stationed a few more guards around the castle.

He never saw the need for as many guards as they had anyway. Orphia had its issues in the past, but its citizens now were kind and peaceable people. Being a guard was almost ridiculously easy. No outsiders knew about Orphia. No one inside Orphia left or caused trouble. So his job consisted of nothing more than riding around the forest on his favorite horse. That was why he was so disturbed when he found Emily before knowing her identity—he had never really considered what to do if he did encounter someone while on duty.

"Good morning."

Emily entered looking like a new person in the light of day. Her previously windswept hair was smoothed back in a simple bun at the nape of her neck. She held her head up higher, her posture perfect. And the lighter color of the violet day dress gave her a brightness that suited her. He recognized the gown as one that had belonged to Yuni—she must have lent it to her. The hem dragged the floor, understandably so considering Emily was a bit on the short side. But it looked nice on her nonetheless.

"Someone's up early," he replied. "Good morning."

She smiled. It was small, but it was the first real smile he recalled seeing since their strange reunion. He liked seeing her smile and hoped he could coax a broader one out of her.

"Did you sleep well?"

She gathered a small helping of food on her plate. "I slept here and there."

Luca frowned. "I'm sorry. Is there anything that would make you more comfortable?"

"Oh no, it's not that at all." She thanked the footman that pulled out her chair. "The bed was far more comfortable than my own. My mind just wouldn't let me rest very much. It's been quite a busy twenty-four hours after all."

"I understand." Luca raised the fresh fruit juice to his lips and tried to squelch his disappointment. She would need to rest today, which meant he wouldn't be able to show her around Orphia as he wished to.

She eyed his fuchsia-colored drink with intrigue.

"Would you like some?" He gestured to the pitcher of juice on the table.

"What is it?"

"Mora juice."

"What is mora?"

He began pouring a glass for her. "It's a type of berry that grows here. Try it."

She reached out but paused just before making contact with the glass as if it were forbidden fruit not to be touched.

"It's quite good," he assured her. "It looks and tastes somewhere between a blackberry and a raspberry."

Her fingers finally clasped around the glass and she took a small sip. Her eyes widened in delight. "It's delicious."

"I said it was, didn't I?" he replied before taking another sip himself. Despite all the years that had passed, conversation flowed easily, much as it did when they were younger. Though there was still something about her calm and collected demeanor that didn't quite ring true. "There's a garden as well as an orchard nearby that supplies our fruit. I'm sure you would like to rest, but perhaps if you're up to it I could show you."

She waved her hand dismissively as she chewed a bite of food. "Resting is the last thing I'll be doing. I refuse to lay about in bed all day like an invalid. Besides, even if I wanted to rest, my mind won't allow it. I need to figure out what to do upon my return home." She sighed. "Unfortunately that's going to be complicated."

Luca watched her studiously. People had always fascinated him, even as a little boy. He made a habit of studying them. He would pick up on little things in their behavior and try to decipher their meaning. A change in their tone of voice, the direction they shifted their eyes, the various affectations they put on. Emily was his current subject of observation—and a puzzling one at that.

Though she sat up straight her shoulders fell ever so slightly at the mention of going back. She kept her eyes on her plate, avoiding eye contact with him. If this was a small glimpse of what she was truly feeling, he didn't like it at all.

"You look heavy," he thought aloud.

She coughed on her eggs and her head shot up. "I beg your pardon?"

"I mean, you don't look *heavy*." He gestured to his stomach immediately realizing the implication of his words. "I mean you look weighed down. Burdened."

She made no reply of censure or agreement but looked down at her lap. He would bet she was wringing her hands as well, though he couldn't see them under the heavy wooden table.

He had definitely hit upon something. "What can I do to help?"

"There's nothing you can do. Besides, it's not your doing to be concerned over."

Whether it was his doing or not he would be concerned, and he would find a way to help. He hadn't been around the last several years to help Emily with her family, but he was here now. He wanted to do something for his friend.

She smiled again though it was somehow smaller and less satisfying than the first. "I'll be fine, really. I just need to clear my head and think things through. I'll find a solution eventually."

"The best way to clear one's mind is through sleep. You really should rest."

"I will not rest," she said firmly. "I do far better when I busy myself."

"Ah, well that's something I can help you achieve." He pushed his plate aside and stood with chin held up high, looking the picture of formality. "Miss Emily Radcliffe, I am taking you on an adventure today."

She made a sound of amusement, as he hoped she would. "You mean dragging me through the woods and bringing me to a castle wasn't adventurous enough? I have a hard time envisioning how you can top that, Sir."

Oh, this was going to be fun. Little did she know what he had in store for her. "That is only a minuscule part of what Orphia has to offer. I beg for the honor of being your tour guide today." He offered his hand to raise her from her seat. "You will be busy, as you wish to be, and I will wear you out so much that you will have no choice but to sleep tonight, clearing your head."

She chuckled. "Very well then. I could use a respite."

"Then it's settled. Meet me at the stables in an hour." With a flourish of the hand and an overly formal bow, he left the room to prepare for their outing. She rolled her eyes at his absurdity, but he could see a glimmer of amusement in them.

This would do her good. It would get her mind off of her troubles for a while. And he was more than a little excited himself to spend the day showing Emily just what made Orphia so special.

***

Emily was fortunate she had a riding habit included in her selection of outfits from Queen Yuni. Despite her initial skepticism, she was proving to be a very generous host that made sure Emily had all that she needed.

She had hoped to thank her at breakfast but she never came down. Luca assured her that was normal and that she often had a tray brought to her room. Considering the late night their arrival caused her she could understand the appeal even more so. But Emily didn't want her to think she was ungrateful. Her parents raised her better than that.

She walked to the throne room—at least that was her intent. Getting lost seemed to be a habit of hers of late. Somehow she ended up in the kitchens instead.

She stood a moment in astonishment, for the kitchen here seemed gigantic. Servants hustled everywhere—stirring, chopping, pouring. Trying to find a servant that would be the least inconvenienced by her interruption, she asked for directions.

"You should've turned the other way when you exited the great hall," he said. "Go down the hallway and it will be on your right."

"Thank you. By the way, whatever you all are making smells incredible."

She swept past the double spiral staircases where she had just come and turned right at the hallway, but the door opened to the Great Hall again. Backtracking, she realized which hallway the cook meant and finally reached her desired destination.

The throne room, however, was empty. Another servant told her the queen was unavailable at the moment and had no indication of when she would be returning.

Well, she needed to meet Luca soon, so she returned to her room and penned a note of thanks and asked for it to be delivered to Queen Yuni.

Descending the stairs again, she realized she had no idea where the stables were on the property. Fortunately, she passed a maid who was willing to walk with her to the right place.

"This way," she said curtly.

"Thank you." Emily stifled her irritation the servant's tone caused. She thought of all the extra work her stay was undoubtedly causing for her and the other servants. Had Emily been in her place, she may have been even less civil in her response.

"What is your name?"

The maid eyed her a bit nervously, probably wondering if Emily planned to report her bit of cheek to her mistress. "Delilah," she said cautiously.

"What a lovely name," Emily replied. "Miss Delilah, I must thank you and the rest of the staff for your efforts. I know my visit was unexpected and probably increased everyone's workload, but everything has been more than pleasing thus far. Queen Yuni must be proud to have such competent staff."

Delilah sent her a surprised look over her shoulder. "Oh. Thank you, Miss. I'm glad to hear it."

Emily smiled at her, and Delilah's expression relaxed. She had seen how Uncle's servants were often overlooked and under appreciated and she always made an effort to commend and thank them whenever she could. Though Yuni seemed like a kind and fair mistress, she had no plan to cease that habit while she was a guest at Orphia Castle.

Delilah led her out a side door and down the huge winding tree branch. More tree limbs wound around all over at varying heights and directions. In the light of day, she could see that there was indeed a large body of water below the castle. She tried to keep her gaze ahead, careful not to slip as she followed Delilah at a quicker pace than she was comfortable with.

Their path ended at an open expanse of grass and she was grateful to be on solid ground once more. Delilah pointed to a wooden structure in the near distance and let her be on her way.

The thick, lush grass gave Emily a childish urge to remove her boots so she could feel it tickling her bare feet. But she knew better and pushed that notion aside, spurring on until she was inside the stable.

Luca's gelding from yesterday whinnied as she approached. He really was a magnificent creature. A ray of sunlight broke through a gap in the wood, making his black coat shine.

"Hello, remember me?" She spoke softly. What was his name again? Onyx, she thought. She rubbed the snout of the beautiful beast. His ears twitched as she hummed a simple tune, one her mother taught her as a little girl.

Footsteps from behind indicated Luca's arrival.

"Well, you two have become fast friends."

"I believe so." Indeed, Emily loved animals. Another reason why she constantly visited Amira's farm was so she could be around them more often.

He came up beside her and joined in showing the horse attention. The three of them stood in peaceful silence for some moments. Luca looked at his steed affectionately and Onyx closed his long-lashed eyes as he was pet and let out a breath through his nostrils, almost like a contented sigh.

She watched Luca, genuinely admiring his soft and gentle nature. You learned a lot about a person by how they treated an animal.

Luca caught her eye and he made an amused sort of sound. "He was just a colt when I arrived here, so we grew up together in a way. We've been there for each other ever since." He gave him one last pat before stepping away. "I don't go many places without him."

She smiled at him.

"You do ride, I hope?" He asked ponderously. "I didn't think to ask you that first. I realized on my way here that you might not, considering you weren't on a horse yesterday when I found you."

"An insightful observation," she replied. "However, I do ride, I just don't have a horse of my own. Uncle does, but that doesn't mean I have access to it. I ride often when I'm at Amira's."

Luca then asked her about the horse she was accustomed to riding in order to find one with a similar disposition for their trip. He showed her Yuni's docile mare and another horse who had a reputation for its fiery temperament then he finally led her to a white horse at the very end of the stalls.

"This is Pearla," Luca said as he led out the horse.

She flicked her tail as Emily ran her hand down the smooth coat. "How lovely," she whispered. Indeed, this horse was as strikingly beautiful as Luca's but in a completely different way. She was as blindingly white as his horse was ominously black.

He called a stable hand to get Pearla saddled and Luca led out Onyx himself. He explained that he always prepared his horse and preferred to ride bareback on shorter journeys, as he would do today.

"I know I mentioned the orchard earlier, but there are so many more interesting things here to explore. Where would you like to go first?"

"I didn't know this place existed, so I haven't the faintest idea of what there is to see." She was still wrapping her mind around the fact that an entire kingdom, even a small one, could remain as hidden as Orphia was. "Isn't it your responsibility to plan an itinerary, tour guide?"

Luca laughed. "Oh dear, I'm failing already."

"It seems so, and we haven't even begun." She clicked her tongue.

He pressed a hand to his heart in a dramatic gesture. "I am thoroughly ashamed at my ineptitude, but I'm afraid there are no other tour guides. So you're stuck with me."

A laugh crept up her throat. She had forgotten how fun it was to tease him.

"Let's see." He tapped a finger on his lips. "Would you prefer to see cliffs, forests, or caves?"

"Hmm...surprise me."

He flashed a grin at her. "Oh, I can guarantee that." Then he rode off ahead of her without another explanation.

She watched him curiously. Just how many surprises did this intriguing land have in store for her?

They went back across the same tree trunk she had walked on to get to the stables. Though wide and strong enough to hold their horses, seeing the water below made her nervous.

"This seems a rather odd location to build a castle considering all the tree limbs and water," she said, trotting behind him.

"Rather unique though, don't you think?"

"Indeed. But is it safe? I mean, suppose someone slipped and drowned below." She snapped her head up and kept her gaze ahead, hoping that her horse knew not to get too close to the edge.

Luca seemed quite unaffected. "It's not as bad as it looks. The lake is not very deep. Sure, falling in and getting wet wouldn't be pleasant, but there's no danger of drowning. I went wading in it once as a teenager and the water never went past my waist."

Well, that was somewhat of a relief. "Do you make a habit of wading in the waters?"

"No. I only did it because I was dared to and I got in quite a bit of trouble for it afterward. It's meant for looks and a home for the fish, not for play. Or so I was told. Fortunately, there were plenty of other places I could spend my time that were far more interesting."

A palace guard followed behind them to maintain propriety and, Emily suspected, as an added precaution due to her presence, though she didn't say as much. Luca was heartily assured that she would be welcomed, but she was sure there was still a bit of understandable hesitancy on Yuni's part.

She didn't mind too much. The guard was distant enough that she and Luca could converse without feeling as if they were spied upon. Emily was surprised just how quickly they fell back into the kind of easy conversation that was common among good friends.

After passing countless trees and taking in eyefuls of green, she took note of a patch of color in the distance. Once the trees cleared her eyes became riveted to the mountains beyond the edge of the cliff. They were not gray and snow-capped, nor green with vegetation. This was nothing she had ever seen before.

The mountains were striped red, teal, golden yellow, dark purple, and green. It initially reminded her of a rainbow, but the colors were deep and rich, not flamboyant and bright like a rainbow was. It was more like a clothing display, different fabrics hanging in rows stretching across the vast mountain range as far as her eye could see. It looked like something straight out of a fairytale.

"Well?"

She nearly forgot Luca was there, captivated as she was by the phenomena before her. "It's...it's..."

"Different?" He alluded to his earlier warning.

She couldn't help smiling a little at the quip. "Different. Beautiful. Spectacular." Any word that came to mind fell short of what she felt at such a sight.

"I told you it was a good kind of different."

"I've never seen anything like it. What causes the unusual colors?"

Luca cocked his head as he eyed the mountains. "It's the natural color of the soil. I don't really understand it myself. I'm not a scientist I'm afraid."

She would most definitely be searching the library later for a book on the subject. "Are the mountains accessible to get a closer look?"

"Not really. There's no access point unless you dive over the cliffs." He gestured with his index finger. "Which I don't recommend, by the way."

That was disappointing. They were probably even more beautiful up close.

Luca's eyes lit up. "But there is another spot. It won't get you closer but it will give you a different view. Quite a spectacular one, actually."

"Really?" Her tone sparked with excitement.

His tone matched hers as he waved her on. "It's this way."

They rode a few minutes and tied up their horses. He then walked her to a tree with a large limb sticking over the edge of the cliff. Tied to that limb was a swing.

Emily's glee dissipated and was replaced with a weight in her stomach. "You're not suggesting I actually get on that thing are you?"

"I am," he said far too calmly.

After a few steps, he realized she had stopped walking. "Coming?" Luca asked over his shoulder.

"No."

"Come on." He smiled at her and gently grabbed her arm as if to guide her.

She jerked it back. "No," she said firmly. "Absolutely not."

"Why not?"

"What do you mean why not?" She peered over the edge of the cliff while keeping her feet rooted a safe distance away. "That's a two-hundred-foot drop at least. It's not safe."

Luca chuckled—actually *chuckled*! This was not the time for laughter.

"You find me falling to my death amusing, do you?" Emily asked sarcastically. Nothing about the situation was remotely humorous.

He kept on, undeterred. "It's not dangerous. The swing is sturdy. Just hold on to the ropes and you have nothing to worry about."

Emily glared at him. She wasn't the least bit convinced.

"Where's your courage? I've seen it before, I know it's still in you."

She supposed she could consider herself somewhat courageous. Growing up she was braver than most boys in her neighborhood had ever expected. Mostly because she did not go running and screaming at the sight of bugs and snakes as other little girls did. But courage did not mean recklessness.

Luca raised a dark eyebrow and she recognized the look of challenge. She had seen it as a child and never backed down. But she was older and wiser now. This wasn't worth her life.

She matched his challenging look by crossing her arms and lifting her chin.

Luca just smiled that annoying smile of his despite her resistance. "I'll prove it to you," he said. He pulled the swing toward himself and sat facing her, his back to the mountains.

"Luca, don't—"

But he already had. She watched in suspense as he pushed off with his feet and sent the swing in motion over the empty expanse. He swung his legs back and forth, picking up far too much momentum for Emily's comfort.

"Stop that!"

He ignored her and kept swinging higher. The limb creaked in time with the to and fro motion. Although it looked strong enough not to snap easily she was less certain about the rope.

"Luca, I'm serious. You're going to get hurt."

"Come on Em, it's fun!"

Goodness, she hadn't been called "Em" in years. She never understood the point of nicknames when you had a real name, but she had grown accustomed to Luca's insistent use of it. She hadn't realized until now that she sort of missed it.

He kept swinging and his giddy laughter filled the air. He leaned his head back as he did so, the messy black curls bouncing along his forehead. The boyish picture he presented tugged at her memories and, despite everything, warmed her heart as she thought of the little boy she remembered playing with.

But she was upset with him right now. It was not the time to reminisce.

He swung forward, lunging himself off the seat and landing on his feet directly in front of her, a triumphant gleam in his eye. "See? I'm still in one piece." He steadied the swing, stopping its violent motion. He gestured with his free hand. "Your turn."

She put her hands on her hips. "I'm not doing it."

"Since when are you afraid of heights?"

"I'm not afraid of heights," she insisted. That was preposterous. "I am afraid of falling from said heights and causing myself injury or demise." That was a completely rational fear.

Rather than scold or make fun of her, his eyes softened as he held her gaze. "It's not as bad as it looks. I wouldn't ask you to do it if it were truly dangerous. The view is beautiful, Em. You'll love it, I know you will. Please, trust me on this. You have to try it for yourself."

His gentle approach caught her unawares and she couldn't help staring a moment. She hadn't expected his eyes to be nearly pleading as he asked this of her. For whatever reason, her doing this seemed important to him.

She looked back to the swing, barely swaying now as it sat empty. It likely was a beautiful view, but it was such a far drop.

"You don't have to swing as forcefully as I did. You won't fall. I won't let you fall."

She said nothing but stepped closer, looking out over the edge again.

"If you do it, I'll let you tell everyone you're braver than me," he added with a smile.

She let out a very unfeminine snort. She inched a little closer and tugged at the rope. It was thick and nothing was frayed. The knots were tight. That part seemed safe enough.

Was she really considering this?

"You can do this."

Luca wouldn't take no for an answer, and she did not have the energy to fight him right now. She slowly lowered herself into the wooden seat, her heart hammering against her chest.

"Don't you dare push me until I'm ready," she warned.

"I won't."

She clasped a white-knuckle grip on the ropes and held her breath. She nodded and felt Luca's hand gently push against her back as the swing released.

She gritted her teeth as the swing moved her through the air. She concentrated on the motions. Forward, back. Forward, back. Then it dawned on her that keeping her eyes closed was rather pointless considering the whole reason for doing this was to see the view.

Slowly opening her eyes, she could take in the whole landscape with nothing hindering her view. She could see that the colored stripes went all the way down the mountains and across the ground far below her. It was indeed quite breathtaking.

Bird calls echoed in the distance as they swooped down from the mountaintops. With the breeze teasing her hair, she almost felt like one of them. She was flying, light and carefree. She hadn't felt like that in...well, possibly ever.

She swung her legs gently and Luca remained quiet behind her. The swing slowed and he took the ropes and pulled her back to solid ground. He gave her a knowing look.

She tried to match the haughty expression. "I see what you mean."

"It's exhilarating, isn't it?"

She nodded. "Very much so."

They looked at each other seriously, having a brief stare down before they both burst into smiles. It was a beautiful thing, to be around Luca again. He had been a real friend to her, one that she lost far too soon. Everyone she loved had been lost too soon.

And just like that, the joy of the moment died. Like a rock crushing a feather, the weight of reality returned to her. No kind of love ever stayed in her life. She wouldn't be around him forever. She would go back to face her family, her community and their ridicule, and her uncertain future.

She tried to keep a pleasant expression for Luca, but it seemed he noticed her change. He was eyeing her carefully.

"So, where to next tour guide?" She forced the cheer into her voice. She would not give him reason to worry over her. She would never want to take away his joy. She would carry the burden as she always did, making sure no one but her was near enough to be crushed by it.

9: A Peculiar Friend

Luca and Emily made their way to the central market to get some food. Due to the abundance of people, it was decided the guard could return to the castle without compromising propriety or safety. The remaining two now rode in companionable silence which gave Luca a chance to sort out Emily's change in demeanor.

He was glad he had convinced her to get on the swing. It was a bit hypocritical of him to push her to face her fear, but swinging over the edge always made him feel free and alive. He sensed that Emily needed to experience that. And it had worked. Her face lit up more than he had yet seen since her arrival the day before.

It made him feel good, for there were few joys in this world greater than causing someone to smile. She needed to laugh more and he needed to make someone happy just as much.

Then it was gone. A polite smile remained, but the light behind it had vanished like a flame in a rainstorm. She insisted she was fine, but he knew it wasn't sincere. But the question he couldn't answer was: why? Not only why there was a change, but why she felt the need to keep it to herself.

She had been reserved as a child and became even more so when her mother died. Others would comment on how well she was holding up, but he always noticed the moisture in the corner of her red-rimmed eyes. She let herself cry in his presence once or twice and that was something very few people saw. She had felt comfortable enough then to reveal more of herself to him than to others. So it hurt him to see that she now hid behind her mask even in his presence.

He had to remind himself that they were no longer children who played together every day. Years had passed between them, and it sounded like she went through a lot in that time. For heaven's sake, she had been living with a family that couldn't even be bothered to acknowledge her unless it was convenient for them. He couldn't blame her for her hesitancy. She would need time.

He was so wrapped up in his thoughts he didn't realize they already rode past the majority of homes and were nearly at the market. He hoped he had not been silent too long. What if she thought he was purposely ignoring her? No wonder she wouldn't open up to him when he was being an ignorant fool.

He watched her from the corner of his eye. Fortunately, she was paying him no mind. She was busy studying the remaining homes around them with fascination. It struck him as odd for a brief moment until he remembered that they would be unusual compared to what she was used to.

The trees were an impressive sight on their own. They were huge and seemingly touched the sky with their flourishing leaves. Then the houses were built around the massive tree trunks stretching upwards in rows. Wooden stairs and suspension bridges provided the neighbors access to each other. He had been away from society for a little while but knew San Morrina wouldn't have anything quite like *that*.

She craned her neck to look at them as they passed by. People walked across the bridges and went about their business, occasionally waving to them down below. He caught a few people snickering when they took in her expression, unable to hide their amusement as she gazed in awe at what was a normal home for them. He liked seeing her open curiosity.

They reached the market which had a more standard layout. Businesses and stalls remained at ground level spreading out in unorganized rows with people mingling and selling in between. Only a few tree houses remained here and there where the shop-owners would reside.

They tied up their horses and began weaving their way through the crowd wherever there was space to walk. Being peak time, all he saw was heads and faces. So he followed his nose to lead him to his favorite restaurant.

"Those treehouses we passed, do people actually live there? " Emily asked.

"They do."

"Even the ones at the very top?"

"Yes." He grinned. "They don't go to the very top of the trees, but those people still have quite a climb."

They were interrupted by a fruit vendor selling oranges which Luca, not wanting to spoil his lunch, politely declined. He veered off the main junction and took a shortcut behind the bakery where it was a little less crowded.

With the noise and chatter filtered out, Emily picked up their conversation once more. "What kind of trees were those?"

"Great sequoias."

She scrunched her eyebrows in thought. "Fascinating. I've read about them in some agricultural books. From the descriptive wording, I thought I had a good mental image. But actually seeing them"— she gestured widely with her arms—"the immense size is nearly overwhelming."

Luca knew the truth of that. He'd seen them nearly every day for the last seven years but his sense of awe never faded. "Imagine how I felt standing next to them as a scrawny fourteen-year-old. I was sure I had either shrunk or somehow stumbled upon a giant's land."

She let out a small laugh at the comment. "As interesting as the trees are I still can't stop thinking of the houses on them. It reminds me of..." She stopped and shook her head ruefully.

His curiosity was piqued. "Of what?"

"It's a bit silly."

"In that case, you must tell." Though Emily teased, she was far too composed to ever be labeled as silly. Hearing something silly from Emily was a rare thing he wouldn't pass up.

"Well, it reminds me of a fairytale my mother used to read to me. They very much fit the description fairy homes found in the forest." They stepped around a large puddle. "Except in the book they were on a much smaller, fairy-sized scale of course," she added seriously.

He made an exaggerated show of seriousness and tried to mimic her tone. "Of course."

She made a sound of amusement. "I warned you it was silly. I don't even know why my mind went there. It's not as if I make a habit of reading children's fantasies." There was a hint of sadness in her voice, but it dissipated so quickly that he thought he might've imagined it. "The homes are remarkable though," she continued. "How do you even begin to construct something like that?"

He shrugged. "I'm not a builder so I wouldn't know. But the people here posses quite a bit of ingenuity. I'm sure it didn't take much for them."

She tilted her head and watched him with mock concern. "Oh dear. You're not a builder, nor a scientist. Positively shameful. What are you good at?"

He paused his step and made a show of deep pondering, tapping his chin. The impish gleam in his eye matched hers. "Giving tours."

She laughed again.

His eye caught a patch of wildflowers just behind her. "Here." He went and plucked one and handed it to her.

"Please accept this as an apologetic gesture for my inherent inadequacy."

She initially pulled her brows in confusion, but the look dissipated when he smiled at her. She took the flower and placed it behind her ear. "Apology accepted. Thank you."

They arrived at the restaurant and sat at a small table. "You're in for a treat," Luca said. "Davina makes the best soup in all of Orphia." Of course, this was the only place you could order soup in Orphia. Even if it wasn't, Luca was sure it would be the best.

An older woman approached them. "What would you like?"

"Corn chowder for me," Luca said eagerly. It was his favorite.

"Sorry dear, we can't make that. Corn crops haven't fared well and we can't get any."

"Oh, I'm sorry to hear that." Another crop gone bad. That wasn't good for anyone. "I suppose I'll take the special then."

"I'll have the same," said Emily.

She nodded, wrote down what they wanted, and rushed off to the kitchen.

He thought about the bad crops. This had been happening more and more frequently. He didn't know much about farming, but he knew if things didn't start improving soon things would become very problematic for their whole community.

Luca's dejected face must've caught Emily's attention. "Is that a serious issue with the crops?"

He sighed and crossed his arms on the table. "It has been the last few years. Extreme weather has done damage at times. One year we produced so little we had to go on food rations."

"Oh dear."

"We're not at that point yet, but I worry we may be if it continues. Yuni is worried about it and trying to prepare for the worst."

She drew her brows together. "San Morrina relies on trade when our crops do poorly. I'm sure with the unique things I've seen here so far that there is something other villages and towns would gladly take in exchange for produce."

Luca considered the suggestion. He thought it was a good idea, but he knew it would likely never happen. "Orphia has never participated in trade. We live off the land. It's part of the discouraged visitors situation."

She looked at him in surprise. "Even for business matters outsiders are forbidden?"

He nodded solemnly.

Emily looked genuinely puzzled. "Why such strict measures and secrecy?"

"I'm afraid it's a bit of a long story." He rubbed at the back of his neck. "The land has been guarded since its founding. According to legend, the ancient people felt its excessive beauty was too great for just any being to behold. So through select peoples and families, we eventually grew into a kingdom. Things were not quite as strict then as they are now, but the kingdom and its location still weren't publicized. But there was an incident several years ago that changed that."

That was as far as he got into the story when a familiar voice interrupted him. "Well, fancy meeting you here."

Luca started at the greeting. He was so fixated on Emily's concerned expression that he didn't even see his friend approach. "Oh, hello Xanth. It's good to see you."

"Is it?" His voice held an accusatory tone but he kept a lopsided grin on his face. "Well, if you're so happy to see me now then you likely would've been *thrilled* to see me at the castle when I showed up there an hour ago."

"Oh, that's right!" Luca slapped his palm to his head. He made plans with Xanth last week to go riding this morning. The appointment never entered his mind today. "Xanth, I'm so sorry. I completely forgot. I hope you didn't have to wait long."

"Oh no. The staff told me you had slipped off with someone else. I wasn't aware that you had replaced me."

Xanth was definitely put out, but he knew his friend well enough to know he wasn't truly hurt. He learned a long time ago that Xanth did not get offended quickly or easily, but he liked to make a show of things as if he did.

He seemed to just notice Emily out of the corner of his eye. He faced her fully and his fiery brows shot up. Emily remained quiet but drew herself up tall and looked him in the eye as if daring him to challenge her.

Xanth looked back at Luca with a smirk. "And who is that?" He jutted his thumb at Emily. "Surely you didn't just ditch me for some girl."

Luca could've throttled his friend. He knew Xanth meant no insult, but he sometimes spoke without realizing how it might sound to others. Emily had been through enough these past couple of days, Xanth's rude dismissal was the last thing she needed.

To her credit, she did not lash out nor did she shrink back. She drew herself up even taller, back ramrod straight, and tilted her chin up with a confident air. She reminded him of a sword, unbending and unbreakable when faced with an opposer.

If she was the sword and Xanth was the enemy, then Luca would try to provide a peace treaty before the war began.

"Xanth," he said firmly, "I would think with as many sisters as you have that you would know better than to speak that way about a lady."

Xanth's brow furrowed, obviously not expecting a reprimand for what he thought was an innocuous comment.

"Emily, this is my sometimes thoughtless and socially inept best friend, Xanth." He gestured from one friend to the other. "Xanth, this is my best friend from childhood, Emily."

"So you really did replace me." He laughed and then turned to Emily. "Hello my mortal enemy, it's a pleasure to meet you."

Emily looked a bit wary of his odd friend, but she remained polite and dipped her head in acknowledgment.

He invited himself to sit and took an empty chair at the end of the table. "I beg mercy for my comment, Emily. As my friend so clearly stated I don't always think before I speak. May we start over?"

She offered a small smile. "I don't see why not."

"Very well then." He stood and retraced his steps back to the entrance.

Oh goodness. Here we go.

Emily looked between the two men with utter confusion written on her face.

Xanth stopped at the door, turned back around, and walked to the table again. "Hello Luca, it seems you forgot about our appointment this morning." Xanth then looked to Emily. "Oh dear, I didn't realize you had a guest." He bowed deeply. "I am Xanth Odeson of Orphia. Pleasure to make your acquaintance."

Luca laughed at the display, which was now attracting the attention of other patrons. Xanth was never dull. His theatrics were a bit much for some people, but Luca usually enjoyed them.

Far from being annoyed, Emily smiled at the absurdity. It was still small, but it reached her eyes. "The pleasure is mine." She dipped her head again and Luca breathed a sigh of relief that all was forgiven.

Xanth chuckled. "I know that's a lie, but thank you anyway."

"You would dare accuse a lady of lying?" Luca would've been concerned at her tone, but her smile had turned into a smirk and he realized she was teasing him.

"Oh dear, I did it again, didn't I?" Xanth mussed his hair. "Perhaps we could start a third time?"

He began standing again but Emily held her hand out to stop him. "I think I can forgive you."

Xanth let himself fall back into the chair. "Thank you. I am in your debt."

They talked amongst themselves as they ate lunch. Xanth told some embellished stories of his and Luca's antics as teenagers. Luca and Emily shared a few of their own escapades as children, though they mostly consisted of Emily being the voice of reason trying to keep him and Amira out of trouble. But when Xanth asked about her recent life she kept her comments vague.

They exited the restaurant with full stomachs and smiling faces.

"We are still going riding though, aren't we?" Xanth asked.

"Sorry friend, we'll have to reschedule."

Xanth pouted a little. "Come on now, you promised. We haven't been riding in forever!"

"We went riding two weeks ago. That's hardly forever."

"Please," Emily spoke up, "do not let me stop you. Go on and enjoy your ride."

"It's alright, Emily. We see each other all the time, it's not a big deal. I promised I'd give you a tour."

"And you have kept your promise to me, and now you may keep your other promise. As much as I've enjoyed today, I'm afraid I tired more easily than I expected to. I should be heading back."

A twinge of panic hit his chest. Head back where? He hoped she was not thinking of returning home to San Morrina so soon.

"You could always come riding with us, if you'd like," Xanth offered. Ah, there was the good heart he knew his friend had in him somewhere.

"Thank you, but I really should be returning to the castle. I also have yet to properly thank my generous hostess. I have barely seen her since my arrival and I don't want her to think I am an ungrateful guest."

Luca breathed a sigh of relief. She meant to head back to the castle. He wanted to find a way to help Emily out of her situation before she went home. She mentioned she had a plan that fell through but had yet to expound on what it was. Besides, there was still so much of Orphia he wanted to show her.

"Very well, but you are welcome to join us if you change your mind," Luca insisted.

They escorted Emily back to the castle and Xanth was more than ready for their ride. But as Luca watched the door close behind Emily, their ride held less appeal than it had last week when they made the plans.

10: A Turn About the Gardens

Emily looked about her grand room and wondered which of the stone walls would be most obliging for her to slam her head against. Repeatedly.

She had made very little progress in the half-hour she spent at the desk. Note after note, one idea after another, proving fit for nothing but kindling. She crumpled another sheet of paper and threw it away with all the vigor her pent-up frustration could muster.

Despite Luca's efforts, her head was not as clear as it needed to be to remedy her complex situation. She was a bit tired but laid on the bed for no more than a quarter of an hour before she was up again. The urge to busy herself buzzed inside her like a swarm of bees that had been trapped in their hive for too long.

In truth, she wouldn't have minded to go riding and explore some more. But she knew she should not interrupt Luca's riding plans and also knew that he would be too kind to dismiss her if she didn't volunteer to leave. Besides, it would do no good to get attached to anything or anyone here. She rightly needed to step out of wonderland and plan for reality.

If only she could put her brain to good use.

She stood and paced the room. "Think, Emily. Think," she said to herself. "You have faced hardship before. You must find a solution." Unfortunately, that was easier said than done.

She mentally recounted the facts and plausible assumptions of her situation. Her family would expect her to return to their estate, which is exactly where she did not want to be. With no inheritance to claim she couldn't afford to let a house. Her previous attempts at finding employment were spurned, and even if she was hired somewhere, she likely wouldn't earn enough to live on her own. Returning to her family may be her only choice.

If only she could get that inheritance! It all made so much sense now. Her family felt no obligation to care for her—no tender regard. They only kept her around to get her money.

She rubbed at her face and let out a pathetic groan. Why was life so unfair? Nearly everything and everyone that mattered to her had been ripped away in some form or another. If she believed in luck she would've considered herself quite the ill-fated individual.

Now that her money was gone, she was of no use to her family anymore. But they would have to keep up appearances. They were still her guardians after all. They were stuck with each other and as far as she knew there was nothing she could do about it. Absolutely nothing.

She paused mid-step when a horrific epiphany came to her. Her family would only be responsible for her until she married. If they wanted to be rid of her all they had to do was marry her off to any man that would take her.

That thought made her insides squirm in disgust. She had thought of marriage before—it would've been a means to escape long ago. But with her father's tainted reputation, finding an eligible husband would be difficult. As an esteemed businessman, Uncle could probably persuade a gentleman, but he was far too stingy to put forth that kind of effort. And anyone her uncle chose for her would likely be as horrid as he was.

Her lungs constricted. Though in a spacious room, she began feeling claustrophobic as the weight of her problems pressed in on her. She made herself take deep, intentional breaths while tidying up the writing implements on the desk, hoping her own feelings would become organized in the process. *They cannot force you to marry. That choice is not something they can take away from you.*

A knock at the door made her jump and startled her from her stray thoughts. She automatically smoothed her skirts and checked the mirror to make sure she was presentable. "Who is it?"

"It's Jayla, Miss."

She fiddled with a pin in her hair. "Come in."

The maid entered with a missive in hand. "I was asked to give this to you, Miss."

She read the elegant script. It was Queen Yuni bidding her to meet downstairs for a walk in the gardens.

She had inquired about the queen's whereabouts when she arrived but was unable to meet with her. It felt odd, asking for an audience with the queen, but she had yet to appropriately thank her for her hospitality. It seems the message was relayed and she was now available to do so.

"Please tell her I'll be down directly." She placed the note on the bedside table. "Thank you, Jayla."

"Very good, Miss" She bobbed a curtsy and left.

Emily kept on the day dress she had changed into but added a bonnet, gloves, and a shawl for warmth. She caught sight of Queen Yuni at the base of the spiral staircase.

She took a steadying breath before curtsying deeply. The woman made Emily more than a touch nervous. "Your Majesty, I received your note. Thank you for the invitation."

"Thank you for accepting, my dear."

She followed Queen Yuni out the grand oak doors and fell in step beside her. Even though they remained on the castle property, she had a guard trailing several steps behind them. It seemed she was truly of a cautious sort and perhaps was still a bit distrusting of Emily. She hoped this outing would allay some of her wariness, as well as settle Emily's nerves.

"I was told you wished to speak with me and I wanted to get to know you a little better myself." The queen's tone did not indicate any sign of how she felt about the prospect.

"Yes, Your Majesty. I haven't had a chance to truly express my gratitude for your hospitality and kindness. I know I came very unexpectedly, but you and your staff have gone far above and beyond what any guest could hope for. Let alone a complete stranger such as myself."

"I'm happy everything is to your liking." Yuni softened a bit at the praise. "And please, you must call me Yuni as Luca does."

Emily was taken aback. "Would that not be improper?" She immediately bit her tongue. Now she was questioning the queen? That was even worse than calling her by her given name. She was doing a rather terrible job of making a good impression.

Yuni didn't notice, or if she did she did not seem bothered by it. "Not improper at all, at least not when we're in private."

"Of course, then. Thank you Your Maj—Yuni." This would definitely take getting used to.

Their path took them under trellised ivy dotted with pink and tiny white flowers, climbing its way up the sides and onto the roof providing shade and a pleasant floral aroma. It appeared to be *bougainvillea glabra* if she remembered correctly.

"Luca said you two grew up together in San Morrina, is that right?" Yuni asked.

"Yes." Emily pulled her shawl more tightly around her to ward off the chill from the shade. "I was born and raised there. Amira—that is another childhood friend of ours—

Luca, and I were neighbors. As we were all close in age and all without siblings we bonded rather quickly."

"How lovely. Is San Morrina a very large village?"

It felt very strange to be so close to royalty, and even more strange to be making small talk in such a casual setting. "It has grown some over the years, but it is still comparatively small. We will never rival larger towns in the kingdom." Emily was certain the queen would be bored with her monotonous village when she lived in a place as beautiful as this. But she was quite curious about Orphia's history. "I must tell you, your kingdom here is utterly magnificent. But I'm afraid I know nothing about it. Can you tell me a little about it and its culture?"

Yuni hesitated a moment before answering. "The people of Orphia tend to be peaceable, friendly, and affectionate. You will seldom hear someone called by their surname unless they are a member of the aristocracy.

"It is also a land of tradition. Our citizens cherish their history and have great respect for those who lived before them." Yuni spoke with pride and it was clear how much she treasured the land she ruled over. "But through each challenge they go through, they strengthen their character, learning lessons which they can impart to others. That enables the next generation to be even stronger than the last."

She nodded and thought of Luca's brief explanation of Orphia's isolated history and recent crop failures. Traditions had their place, she wasn't discounting that. But did the people even realize what opportunities lay just outside their kingdom? Emily was no expert, but she had learned enough about business from her uncle. She knew things such as trade could truly benefit them. Had Yuni even thought of the idea?

It would be terribly impertinent to suggest as much. Perhaps another time, once she had built more of a rapport with Yuni, she could broach the subject. For now, she would satisfy her curiosity on other matters. "Has your family ruled here for many generations?"

Yuni's posture stiffened and her expression turned a little sad. "It has, though I worry at times about the future. I began ruling after I lost my brother. That was nearly eight years ago." She stopped walking and picked a flower, twirling it between her fingers. "He was all the family I had left."

Emily took note of Yuni's dark skirts. They must have been close for her to still mourn him after so many years. "I'm so sorry."

She didn't look at Emily or acknowledge her comment. "I think that's why I was drawn to Luca and why I worry so much about him. He has become almost like a son to me. We are the only family each other has now."

It appeared Yuni's thoughts had drawn her inward. There was a stretch of silence and Emily wondered whether or not she should break it. She looked away from Yuni, giving her a moment to collect herself, and tried to keep her attention focused on the gardens around her.

Much like the rest of Orphia, it was nothing like she would've expected for a castle garden. Everything was left in a natural-looking state. The bushes that lined the border were large and overgrown, yet not unkempt. Different flowers and greenery were scattered throughout, not grouped by type or arranged in a specific way. The stone path beneath her boots weaved in all sorts of directions around the plants. The design yielded to nature, letting things grow where they wanted and building the man-made path around it. Though it was contrary to her organized nature, Emily liked seeing the beauty in its natural state.

Yuni finally recalled her presence. She quickly pulled herself out of her thoughts and returned to her neutral expression. She tossed the flower aside and took up walking once more. "Well, enough of my sad stories," she said, clearing her throat. "What is your home like? Tell me a little about yourself."

Emily had worn enough masks over the years to know that Yuni was currently hiding behind one. The woman was obviously uncomfortable talking about her loss, much like Emily was when she spoke about her parents. She would let the matter drop, though if Yuni wished to know about her in hopes of a happier conversation she would be vastly disappointed.

"I live with my aunt and uncle. He manages several farmlands and their tenants. Though I am expected to be a lady of leisure I much prefer to busy myself. I usually escape to my friend, Amira who I mentioned earlier, and her family's farm to assist with their chores as well as explore their land." That should be an adequate response.

"And your family, won't they be worrying about you? Luca said you were lost when he found you yesterday."

Of course she had to ask that. "They will not. My absence is likely to be a relief more than a cause for worry." She kept the disappointment out of her voice as she usually did.

Yuni looked puzzled then frowned as she understood the implication. "No one should ever feel so unloved amongst family. I'm sorry."

"Thank you," she said quietly.

Yuni placed a hand on her arm. The unexpected gesture startled her and she had to tell herself to relax.

Perhaps this was a part of the friendly and affectionate culture she had mentioned. That would also explain why Luca had reached for her hand to comfort her yesterday— or she supposed she should say earlier this morning if she wanted to be accurate, which she did. He had always been solicitous and warmhearted by nature, but being immersed in this culture seemed to make his compassionate side flourish.

Still, receiving such a comforting gesture from a stranger who was far above her station felt much more peculiar than from someone she had known since childhood. But she appreciated it nonetheless.

"Will you still return to them? Do you have somewhere else to go?"

That was precisely what Emily had been trying to figure out and she still had no answer. She would not normally open up to someone she knew so little, but Yuni managed an entire kingdom. That had to be far more difficult than her situation. Perhaps she would have some insight that could help her.

"To be honest, I don't know. I do not wish to return but I'm not sure what my other options are. My father left an inheritance for me which I planned to use to secure a living for myself when I became of age. Unfortunately my uncle, as my legal guardian, has had access to the funds until that time. So, on my twentieth birthday tomorrow I have nothing to claim." She felt thoroughly deflated at the admission.

"Oh, you poor child," Yuni said empathetically. "That is quite a predicament. I'm not acquainted with your laws on the matter. What your uncle did was legal?"

Emily wondered the same thing, but his solicitor seemed to confirm it. "As far as I know, it was."

Yuni shook her head. "Disgraceful. The world gives some men far too much power to do as they please, no matter how it affects others," she said in earnest. "I hope you find a way to remedy the situation. But whatever you decide, I hope you enjoy your time here. It sounds as if you need a respite."

When Yuni asked earlier if she had somewhere to go, she thought of Orphia for the briefest moment. But it dissipated almost instantly, for she knew the idea was absurd. No matter her struggles in San Morrina, no matter the beauty of Orphia, she could not leave her entire world behind to be here. And even if she wished to, Yuni's response now, though kind, made it clear she only viewed Emily as a temporary guest. She would have to return eventually, and she would figure things out.

"So, how did you spend your morning?"

Which that welcome change in subject, Emily told her what Luca had shown her thus far. Yuni laughed when she spoke of her introduction to Xanth and supplied her own amusing observations on the young man's character.

She forced herself to enjoy the conversation, but after returning to her room the troubled thought stuck in her mind like tar. Her long-awaited twentieth birthday, her day of freedom, was tomorrow. And she had absolutely nothing to show for it.

11: Crystals and Chronicles

Luca rested his hand on the terrace railing, lingering there as he waited for Emily. His eyes regularly shifted from the back gardens to the base of the stairs. He would start towards them each time he heard footsteps, but was disappointed each time it wasn't her coming down them.

She had yet to make an appearance today and he was getting worried. She requested a tray to be sent to her room for breakfast and he learned from the maid that retrieved it that she had eaten very little.

He drummed his fingers against his leg. Had he hurt her feelings when he left her alone yesterday? He went through all the conversations they had over and over in his mind, trying to find the flaw in his speech or actions. He did that often growing up, but it rarely led him to solutions. Today was no different.

That didn't matter. Whether or not he had caused her distress, he would take whatever steps he could to ease it.

He went upstairs, taking two steps at a time, and brought his hand up to knock on her door.

He paused just before his knuckles made contact with the wood. What if she truly wasn't feeling well and needed rest? The maid had assured him that Emily was not sick, but he already knew she was quite adept at hiding her real feelings.

With quiet footfalls, he went to his room instead. He crossed to his desk in search of paper. He pushed aside the cluttered mess of books, ink blotters, random notes, letters...why was there a sock here? *Gads, I need to clean out this thing.*

He finally found a suitable blank sheet of paper. He wrote out a note with his plans for the day and where Emily could find him should she feel like joining.

He held up the paper and eyed it critically, feeling the inadequacy of his gesture. His arms dropped to his sides and his eyes roved about the room, not looking for anything in particular. But when they landed on the bookshelf across from him he got an idea.

I wonder if she still sketches.

He ran a finger across the spines until it landed on what he was searching for. He pulled it out and couldn't help sniffing the cover. He loved the earthy smell of leather. He unwrapped the cord that held it shut and fanned its pages to make sure they were all blank. Seeing that the notebook was still unused, he wrote an amended note on its first page.

Emily,

A little gift for you in case you want to do some sketching while you're here. And if you feel up to it, I have the perfect place to give you some artistic inspiration.

Luca

He caught a maid in the hall and asked that she bring it to her.

"Of course, Sir," she replied. "I'm also to tell you that Xanth is here to see you. He's in the parlor."

Luca bit back a chuckle. Xanth had become such a regular fixture of the castle that no one bothered with formal introductions anymore. Formality never suited Xanth much to begin with anyway.

"Hello, Xanth," he greeted after making his way downstairs. "What brings you here?"

He leaned casually with one arm against the wall. "Papa doesn't need my help with fishing today. Are you up for another ride?"

"Actually, I was going to show Emily the caves today if she's up to it."

His lopsided smile drooped. "Oh."

As much as Xanth loved his sisters, Luca knew being cooped up in a predominately female household could wear him thin. So he decided to take pity on him. "Do you want to come with us?"

He perked up and pushed away from the wall. "Definitely!" He quickly cleared his throat. "I mean...I suppose I could make the time. You know, if you two really want me to come." He moved in a nonchalant manner to a wingback chair.

Luca laughed. "Please, bless us with your presence."

He chuckled with amusement. "Well, when you put it *that* way then I must come along."

They kept up the banter and talked of horses until he heard light footsteps echoing from the hall. He stood when Emily entered with his gift in her hands. The shadows under her eyes betrayed her lack of sleep, but she had a pleasant expression on her face.

"Hello gentlemen."

"Good morning," Luca replied.

"Indeed it is." She smiled sweetly, revealing a dimple at the corner of her mouth. Had she always had dimples? She must have, but he hadn't remembered noticing them before. "Especially when I am greeted with this nice surprise." She gestured to the book in her hand.

"I was hoping you'd like it," he said with relief, "and that you still draw."

"I do. And as I left my sketchbook behind in my flight this is a very welcome gift." She held the book to her chest with both hands pressed against it. "Thank you."

Though the smile Luca returned was broader than hers, there was no mistaking her gratitude. The gift was supposed to make her happy, but being on the receiving end of her sincere gratitude and joy made his own heart soar a little higher.

"Now what exactly am I going to be sketching? Your note was as intriguing as it was vague. I wasn't sure how to dress."

She wore another day dress, this time in a darker blue. It was still a little long, but he caught the tips of her boots peeking out from the hem. They appeared to be the same boots she wore when he first found her, but now all the mud and grass had been cleaned off of them. He knew absolutely nothing of fashion, but he could think of very few young ladies who would wear sturdy half-boots with such a feminine dress. The thought made him chuckle inside. It was very Emily, lovey yet always practical.

"Do you like my odd choice of footwear? Do you find it amusing?" Emily had her brows raised in a challenge.

"I think they're quite splendid. Don't you, Xanth?"

Xanth was looking boorishly out the window, probably wishing they were already out exploring. "Huh?" He said distractedly.

"Never mind." Luca waved him off.

Emily raised her eyes upward. "I know they don't match but unfortunately Yuni's shoes don't fit me. In addition to being short, I have tiny feet."

"I think they're a perfect choice actually, especially for today's activity."

"Oh, this place is amazing!" Xanth bounced out of his chair to where they stood in one long stride. "We're going to—"

"You'll find out soon." Luca clapped Xanth on the shoulder and cut him off.

"You're not going to tell me where we're going?"

He smiled mischievously. "I"m not." Actually, he had planned on telling her right up until that moment. But now he wanted to keep it a surprise. There was something amusing about keeping the ever organized, ever shrewd Emily in suspense just to mess with her a little.

She let out an exasperated sigh. "Fine, shall we go then?" She stepped towards the door and paused before turning around again. "You are a terrible tour guide you know, keeping your patrons in the dark." Her words would've sounded like an insult given the dry, sarcastic tone, but Luca saw the twinkle in her eyes that told him she was teasing. He was glad for it—teasing meant she was feeling more at ease both in her new surroundings and in his presence.

They went out the door and were greeted by dark storm clouds.

"Oh dear," she said. "It looks like it will rain."

The disappointment in her voice tugged at his heart. They were off to such a good start today, he wasn't going to let a little rain halt that progress.

"It does...let's go."

"Really? You still want to go when it appears the heavens will burst open at any moment?"

"Absolutely."

"But we'll surely be soaked!" She spoke incredulously but not necessarily in protest.

"We used to play in the rain all the time," he countered.

"Yes, but we were children then. Now we're adults with common sense."

"And what adventures came about because of common sense?" He could tell she wanted to go, but her practical side was holding her back. He decided to add a bit of logic to his argument to hopefully win her over. "If we hurry we should arrive before the rain begins. And once we're there we'll be sheltered and it won't matter what the weather is like." He looked to Xanth. "Still coming?"

"Of course! I'm not afraid of a little rain."

He raised his eyebrows at Emily. "And you?"

She stood there silently deliberating. "Ok, fine. But if my sketchbook gets wet and ruined I'm placing the blame on you." She tucked it under her arm.

"I'll accept that. Now come on!" He waved her forward and took off.

They walked at a brisk pace, regularly glancing at the ominous sky above them. They were in sight of the caves when Luca felt a drop of water on his arm. Then his nose. Then his shoulder.

"Hurry!" Luca called as they quickened to a near run, making it inside just as the raindrops quickened their descent.

"Welcome to the Crystal Caves," Luca announced with a grand sweeping motion of his arm.

Emily wiped a few droplets off her face but her arms fell to her sides as her expression filled with absolute wonder. He watched her as she carefully inspected the icicle-shaped formations covering the ceiling like a natural chandelier. It was a shame the sun wasn't out, for when the sun hit the ice-like crystals just right, the whole cave sparkled. But the amazement on Emily's face sparkled enough to make up for it.

She circled about slowly. "Extraordinary," she whispered as she stretched out her arm to touch one. She stood on her toes but they remained just out of reach.

"This way. There are some I can assure you you'll be able to reach."

"This is the best part!" Xanth added as he bounded ahead of them.

They walked through the cave and came to a narrower, tunnel-like section. As the faint sunlight faded behind them, Luca reached for the lantern he kept hanging on the rocky wall. The temperature got warmer and the pounding rain was nearly forgotten as they went deeper into the tunnel before exiting into a large room. He watched her expectantly, and Emily gasped.

The room was filled with crystal beams so big that even Xanth could not wrap his long arms around them. They were jutting out from the ceiling, floor, and walls, in every direction crisscrossing with each other. Even the floors were covered in cut crystal blocks, reminding him of the faceted jewels he had seen many times on Yuni's crown.

"This is magnificent." Emily gazed at a beam towering over her.

"Excuse me," Xanth threw off his coat and began crawling underneath the beams, squeezing himself through an opening.

Emily pulled her eyes away and landed a puzzled gaze on him. "What is he doing?"

"He's looking for treasure."

"There's treasure here?"

He let out an exasperated sort of laugh. "Of a sort. There's an ancient poem about this room..." He cleared his throat and began to recite it with theatricality.

"In the cave, far and deep,
The tunnel's end lies what ye seek.
A crystal treasure for thou to claim,
Its beauty boasts its highest fame.
The few and brave who fight the heat,
Shall find thine riches to make replete."

He gave a small bow and Emily humored him by clapping.

"This"— he gestured around them— "is the crystal treasure referred to." His tone shifted to dry amusement. "But Xanth here has a different interpretation. He thinks there is a hidden treasure chest with gold or jewels and is determined to find it. He's convinced it's hidden deeper here than anyone has yet ventured."

Emily lowered her voice. "But there isn't one?"

"Considering he's been looking for years, I'd say not."

"There is treasure here! Just because it's hard to find doesn't mean I'm giving up on it," he shouted from somewhere behind the beams. "And unless you plan on helping me don't expect me to share!"

"It's all yours, my friend. Search your heart out!" He raised his voice to match, then returned to a normal volume for Emily. "But I'm afraid the smaller crystals will have to do as the model for your sketching. Unless you're crazy like Xanth you won't want to stay here for more than a few minutes. The temperature is much warmer in this room and is nearly unbearable if you stay too long." He felt himself perspiring already.

"I noticed that too." She wiped at her forehead. "Yes, I suppose we should head back."

"Coming Xanth?" His question echoed around the room.

"You two go ahead, I'll find you later."

He chuckled and went back to the tunnel.

"Will he be alright?" A touch of concern entered Emily's voice.

He waved it off. "He'll be fine. He does this every time we come here."

They found a spot near the mouth of the cave and Emily went to work, her hand skillfully tracing the jagged lines of the smaller crystals in front of her.

The rain had become a downpour, turning itself into a waterfall that went over the mouth of the cave and trapped them in. Luca wondered if it was such a good idea to come here after all. They would have to return home at some point. As she finished her sketch, it didn't seem like the rain was going to let up any.

There was another well-intentioned plan that turned into a disaster. He felt the need to apologize but stopped short at seeing her. Her head rested against the cave wall and her eyes were closed with an expression of contented peace. Thunder rumbled in the distance but she did not stir. He had never seen anyone look so calm amid a storm.

"It's soothing, isn't it?" Emily asked, her eyes still closed. "Its steady rhythm could almost put me to sleep."

"I suppose it is. Although it would be just as soothing inside the castle."

"Not necessarily. There's something enrapturing about being so close to the rain. I feel its effect more fully but remain dry. That sounds ideal to me."

He was amazed at her agreeableness. "You know, most people would be complaining about the weather and wishing for sunny skies."

She glared at him with one open eye. "I'm not most people."

He bit back a laugh. *That is most certainly true.*

She sat up and looked at him fully. "As often as people complain about the rain, imagine where we'd be without it. Rain means growth and refreshment. Rain is life. It may not seem as cheery and practical as sunshine, but without it, everything would be dry, barren, and ugly. Rain is invaluable."

He stared at her in amazement. She took something so basic and turned it into something profound. How many young people thought that way, with such insight? "You're right, of course."

She smirked. "Of course." Her wording and tone matched their earlier conversation about the fairy-like tree houses. He couldn't help chuckling at her wit.

His smile drooped as it settled on the rain once more, remembering that it was not always a beneficial thing. "As right as you are, in great quantity it can cause damage." He sighed. "I hope this storm blows over soon and it doesn't waterlog the crops."

There was a solemn silence between them and only the roaring downpour filled it. "You never got to finish telling me the story. Why does Orphia not welcome tradesmen or visitors?"

He shuddered a little but didn't know if it was from the dampness of the cave or from the story he was about to tell. He wrapped his arms around himself.

"When Yuni's father who was king at that time died, her brother Aspen began to rule. As I said before, Orphia has always been a relatively small, secluded community. After the queen mother became ill and passed, he decided it was time to make some changes to the kingdom. He felt a need to modernize the land and learn from our neighbors.

"He disguised his identity and went himself to a nearby land and met an ambassador. He accompanied him back to Orphia and King Aspen revealed his true identity and purpose, to learn from him and see what ideas he had for improving Orphia. Of course, the ambassador loved what he saw here. Apparently too much."

He rubbed at the back of his neck. "King Aspen was thought to be a trusting, altruistic sort of person and had formed something of a friendship with the ambassador—or so he thought. They were walking the grounds discussing plans. There were no guards, no witnesses, and that's when it happened."

Luca swallowed hard and watched Emily for signs of discomfort in case the story proved too much for her. Currently, she watched him with a solemn expression.

"He attacked King Aspen. Yuni was practicing her archery nearby, heard the struggle, and went to them. The man, seeing Yuni armed and realizing he had been caught, fled. She rushed over and screamed for help, but it was too late. He...he went over the cliff and was..."

"Dead." Emily looked grim as she finished for him. "She told me he had died but I didn't realize it was under such tragic circumstances."

"Yuni doesn't like to speak of it. She and her brother were very close. I'm sure she relives that day more often than she wishes to." Luca knew that well. He relived his memories with alarming frequency despite how hard he tried to push them out of his mind. His parents' death, the fire, the horrible days in the orphanage...

"That's why she's so strict about outsiders." He forced himself to continue. "Life has taught her that anyone could be a threat."

"What happened to the ambassador?"

"She sent the guards after him but he was never found. She immediately set up shifts to ensure the land would be constantly guarded. She made sure the kingdom would be protected in case the ambassador or anyone else were to come to do harm. She didn't want the fate her brother met to befall anyone."

Luca sighed with a physical weight pressing on his heart after telling the tragic tale. "They never saw him again. I think she blames herself for not bringing the villain to justice and for not being there in time to save her brother. She tries to conceal it, but there's guilt in her eyes when she speaks of him."

"She has no reason to blame herself."

"I know that. I think she does too. But grief shows itself in strange ways that don't always make sense to us."

Emily looked ponderous but said nothing more. Luca ruminated over his own words in the silence. Emily dealt with much tragedy—how was her grief affecting her? First, she lost her mother years ago. Then her father died. Her remaining family was horrible enough to send her fleeing into the woods. That was enough to shatter a person to their core. And yet, far from being crippled by grief, she had been nothing but calm and composed since they met again. Was her silent composure her way of hiding her pain? And just how many figurative storms had she endured in her life to become that way?

"The rain has nearly stopped." Emily pointed to the opening. The pounding rain had turned into a trickle. "We should probably find Xanth and head back before it starts again."

"Good idea."

They collected Xanth and the three very different friends made their way back to the castle. Luca and Emily were mostly dry and Xanth, drenched in sweat, might as well have been out during the downpour.

12: Know Your Opponent

Emily loved the rain. She appreciated the rain. But that did not mean the rain couldn't be terribly inconvenient at times. It had been raining for several days now and even in a large castle, the confinement was pushing her to madness.

Luca made the most of it and was indeed a faithful and thorough tour guide. He showed her all three stories of the castle from the ballroom to the laundry and everything in between. Even the servants' quarters in the basement weren't omitted. In a few days, she felt that she knew every wall, painting, and corner and every story behind them.

Orphia's castle was not as ornate and grandiose as the Kalopsia castle was rumored to be. It was impressive and spacious of course, but it lent towards natural, earthy tones and wood rather than rich colors and gold. It was designed so that the focal point was the beauty of the land in all its natural splendor.

It's cold, soaked, muddy splendor.

She could not enjoy Orphia in this weather and she definitely could not travel home in such conditions. She should be using her time indoors to plan, but every time she attempted to do so she simply felt overwhelmed. She just couldn't get her mind working the way she wanted it to, the way she desperately needed it to.

She glared out the windows as a steady chorus of raindrops beat angrily against the glass. How unfair, that the sky could simply burst open whenever it wished and release everything it had been holding in with reckless abandon, heedless of how it affected others. If only she could do the same.

But her time with Luca here in Orphia had eased some of the tension she had, up until now, felt constantly. Despite her initial hesitancy, their time together had proven he was still the kind person he had always been. The sketchbook in front of her was proof of that.

She couldn't help but smile as she ran her fingers over the smooth leather. Even after all these years, he remembered something about her, something that was important to her and made her happy. His simple gift touched her more than any expensive present ever could. It was more than a material item—with his thoughtfulness, she received a small piece of his mind and heart that made her cherish the gift all the more. His gesture made her feel valued in a way no other friend or family member had in a long time.

But today she had no desire to sketch more still life of the castle, so she ambled downstairs. The warmth of the fire drew her inside the library where Yuni was reading on the settee.

She glanced at the tall bookshelves but reached for nothing. She had also done quite a bit of reading since the storm. She walked to the other side of the room and the chessboard in the corner caught her eye. She picked up one of the pieces and admired the intricate carving on the small piece of wood.

"Do you play?" Luca asked from the doorway.

"Yes. I love chess." Her father was the one who introduced the game to her as a girl. Playing regularly with him was one of the few memories of that man that she let herself indulge in. "Do you?"

"Sometimes. Yuni enjoys it. Probably because she usually wins."

Yuni chuckled softly, not offering any word of disagreement.

"Perhaps you would like to try your abilities against a new opponent."

"Why not? It's not as though I have much pride left to lose."

Emily observed the board and felt some excitement bubble up inside her. She didn't get to play the game often anymore. Her aunt and uncle wouldn't play with her, the twins would cheat, and Amira would get bored after a few moves and give up.

She, however, loved the strategy chess involved. It was all about planning, thinking ahead, and knowing how to defend your pieces. If only aspects of her life were as easy to manipulate as pieces on a board.

She went first and moved one of her pawns forward. Luca moved his knight. She raised her eyebrows at the unusual opening and he just answered with a customary lift of his shoulders.

Their pieces were interspersed amongst the board with both sides making captures along the way. Luca was holding his own quite well until he captured her knight with his. She hadn't expected him to leave his queen exposed as he did. It was not her exact plan, but ridding him of a high-value piece would give her some leverage. She was not usually competitive, but she allowed the smallest of smirks in triumph as she removed his queen from the board and awaited his next move.

Unfazed, Luca moved his bishop. "Check."

Any temptation she had to gloat was gone as she stared at the board in disbelief. Not only was she in check but her only move was to defend with her queen which Luca took on his next move, placing her in check again. She captured the attacking piece, and now her king was out in the open.

Her brows were drawn together as she watched him take her pieces one by one. "How did you do that?" Emily mumbled aloud. Though internally she was asking, *How did I miss that?*

The triumphant smile that previously sat on her lips had transferred to Luca's, though he was too kind to voice a boast. "The logical choice isn't always the right one," he replied.

His statement gave her pause as it was contradictory to everything she knew. She tucked it away for later evaluation. Right now she had a game to focus on and mistakes to correct.

It was a close game towards the end, but Luca won. She shook her head in mock disapproval as she clicked her tongue. "I do believe you were bluffing when you spoke of your lack of skill."

"I never said I lacked," he defended. "I just said that Yuni excels at the game. She taught me well, but not so well that I surpass her."

"I suppose she has to keep some things a secret from you," she said with a laugh. She glanced over her shoulder to see Yuni peering at them over her book. Though the corners of her mouth were turned upwards, Emily would never call it a smile. It was betrayed by the slight annoyance in her eyes. She realized they had quite thoroughly interrupted the quiet evening she had planned for herself.

"I'm so sorry, Yuni. We are surely disturbing your reading with our jabbering. Forgive me—"

"It's quite alright dear. I was just finishing up anyway." She stood quickly to put the book away before exiting the room.

Emily felt heat creep up her cheeks, a sensation that didn't happen often. "I should have left, not her. I feel terrible."

"Don't trouble yourself so much. Yuni puts up with far worse from me. Besides, I think she enjoys having some female company here. She has become much more withdrawn since her brother...well, you know."

She nodded her understanding and hoped his words were true.

"So, how about another round?" Luca began resetting the board.

"That depends, are you going to teach me your tricks?"

He looked at her in exaggerated disbelief. "A master *never* shares his secrets."

"Which is exactly why I asked you and not Yuni."

He threw his head back and barked a laugh so hearty and genuine that she couldn't help joining him. "For your quick wit, I will share one." He glanced around the empty room and leaned in close, speaking in a hushed tone as if sharing a tremendous secret. "As you already know, chess is about strategy and planning ahead." His breath tickled her skin. "But it's also about reading and adapting to your opponent. So I observed you."

"Observed me?" Emily generally hid herself quite well. "What do you mean?

He leaned back in his chair. "Well, I have a slight advantage because of knowing you since childhood. I know you are a very strategic person and a formidable foe in a game like this. You have a good game face that was impossible to read, but your actions told me you followed very logical gameplay. I figured you would want to rid me of my high-value pieces. I also know you're smart enough to anticipate my next move so I needed to catch you off guard." He held out the queen between his thumb and forefinger. "So I set a trap."

"And I took the bait," she said in near awe.

"You did." He returned the piece to the board with a light thump. "It was a risk, but it paid off."

She twisted a loose lock of hair as she thought. "Know your opponent," she spoke softly. "Know your opponent."

Her mind was suddenly very far from the game in front of her. Could that advice work in real life?

She stood abruptly. "I need to think." She started circling the room, searching.

"Are you ok?"

"Yes. I need paper." She looked at all the tabletops in the room but saw none.

"This way, we can use the study." She followed Luca into the adjoining room and walked past him straight to the large desk. She began moving books out of the way and looking in the drawers.

"Here." Luca came up beside her and opened an ornate box containing writing supplies. She barely noticed how the immense desk swallowed her petite frame when she sat behind it. She dipped the quill in the ink and began making notes.

"What exactly are you doing?"

"Making a list."

"A list of what?"

"Everything I know about my family." She scribbled away. "Anything that might help me know how to play defense, or perhaps offense, and get me out of this situation."

The ink letters started flooding and turning into smudges and she realized the tip was dull. She sighed in exasperation and looked around for something to sharpen it with. Was nothing ever simple? She couldn't even make a list without running into difficulty.

Luca held out his hand. "Allow me." He pulled out a knife and began sharpening the quill himself. "What did your aunt and uncle do?" Luca asked hesitantly. "You never said what happened."

Belittle me. Yell at me. Act as if I don't exist. Complain about what a burden I am. And so many other things she refused to voice.

As if reading her thoughts, his face darkened. "Em, what did they do?" His voice held an almost threatening quality. "What did they do to hurt you?"

He hadn't pressed her about her family since that first day. It was time she told him the whole of it. "Father left me an inheritance I was to gain when I reached my majority. Uncle, being my legal guardian and trustee, had access to the funds in the meantime. He spent every last bit of it and now there is nothing for me to inherit."

Luca's force at cutting the quill was so fierce he just missed slicing his finger with the blade. His jaw was set and there was no mistaking the anger in his eyes. "Of all the conniving, selfish—" He shook his head and cut off whatever other unflattering adjectives he was about to use. He took a breath to calm himself and handed her the quill. "What can I do?"

"There's nothing you can do. I don't even know what to do. That's why I'm making a list, it helps me think."

"I will do something. We can figure this out."

She shook her head. "There's really—" She stopped when he leaned down to meet her eyes. His eyes which were normally warm and kind now held an intense determination that would unnerve even the toughest of opponents. Some of his anger was still there, but it was softened by something else, an emotion she couldn't readily identify.

"He won't get away with this." His voice was quiet, yet full of unwavering bravado.

Luca's fierce protectiveness left her momentarily stunned. Tears threatened to sting behind her eyes. Tears from the girl who never cried. She averted her gaze and blinked rapidly before she replied. "Luca." Her voice wavered only slightly. "I appreciate it, I really do. But it's not your concern to worry over. This is my battle to fight."

He knit his brows as the corners of his mouth fell in disappointment. "You won't let me help?"

She didn't want to upset him, but he would only burden himself with her worries. She could do this on her own. There was no point in involving him in this mess and risk giving her family another person to hurt. He was too sweet and good, she couldn't do that to him.

"You have already helped. You gave me this idea. But I have to figure this out and you don't need to worry yourself over it." She forced a reassuring smile. "I'll be fine."

Luca did not smile in return as she expected him to. His lips parted as he stared at her, concern and disbelief touching his eyes. Her smile slowly slipped as she realized he saw right past her words. He knew she was lying.

"You don't have to fight your battles alone, you know. Not anymore," he said quietly. "I don't know if I can help or not, but you can trust me when I say I will do anything and everything that I can. Please let me try." He grabbed her hand and drew it toward him, and for a confused moment she thought he was going to bring it to his lips. Hesitating, he gave it a quick squeeze before letting it drop. "I have to go to my post now. Goodnight, Em."

She didn't move as he strode out of the room. She rubbed her thumb along the back of her hand, her list all but forgotten as her thoughts went after him.

Her survival had always been dependent on keeping up her defenses, defenses that had already weakened in the time she had spent in Orphia. Luca was a keen observer and saw through her with unsettling ease.

He was sincere, she didn't doubt that. Perhaps she should let him help her. But she was so unaccustomed to putting that kind of trust in someone. It didn't matter that she wanted to trust him, she wasn't sure she was capable of doing such a thing.

13: A Little Competition

The residents of the castle made their way outdoors as soon as the storm cleared, despite the muddy mess left behind. Yuni in particular was eager to escape and participate in her favorite pastime, archery.

She shot arrows with incredible accuracy and speed. But Luca's suggestion nearly made her miss the target.

"A ball?" Yuni said somewhere between disbelief and laughter. "You want us to hold a ball? I've never even seen you dance." She shook her head with amusement. "What's gotten into you lately? You want to throw balls, you go exploring so much that I hardly ever see you in the castle anymore, and even the maid commented that your desk is cleaner than she's seen in months. I hardly recognize you these days."

Luca just shrugged. Maybe he was acting a little different lately, but he didn't think that was a bad thing. He didn't feel like a creature of habit anymore. Emily's curious nature made him more inquisitive and want to try new things. And knowing that the disarray of his room would leave her utterly mortified should she ever see it guilted him into keeping it somewhat presentable.

"Why do you want to have a ball anyway?" Yuni asked.

"I just thought it would be nice. The idea came to me after showing Emily the ballroom. She said how peculiar it was to see such a beautiful room just collecting dust." He drew his arrow back. "It got me thinking, and I thought it might be enjoyable for the people. I mean, why even have a ballroom if it never gets used?" He frowned at his missed shot. Though nowhere near Yuni's level of expertise, Luca could shoot decently enough. But he was off his game today.

Yuni gave him a ponderous look but brushed it off quickly. "I never understood the appeal of balls anyway. It's just hoards of people stuffed into a room meant for half of its occupancy. The din of music and chatter makes it nearly impossible to hold a conversation. A quiet evening in one's home is much more profitable in my opinion."

Luca didn't entirely disagree. He much preferred small, intimate gatherings. But everyone needed a little excitement here and there. And many of the people had never seen the castle. An event like that would be very special for them. It would be a good way to give to the people.

"Besides," Yuni continued, "a ball requires a great deal of work, preparation, and resources. We cannot waste those on frivolous exploits when we may very well need them just to survive."

Her grim expression brought him back to reality. "Is there much damage from the rains?" Luca asked in between shots.

"I sent out some men to do an inspection. They should be returning with a report later today."

"You did?" He let down his bow. "I wish I had known, I could've gone with them." It didn't feel right staying behind on the safety of castle grounds when the land he loved so much could potentially be ruined.

"I know you could have, but you haven't been keeping up with your archery lately. As a guard, that is an invaluable skill needed to protect the people." She fixed him with a look of scolding. "You need to maintain your abilities."

The burning muscles in his back agreed with her chastisement. He had skipped practice most days since Emily's arrival, opting to enjoy her company and traverse Orphia with her. He likely would've skipped it again today if Yuni had not called him down early this morning insisting that he join her.

"I know. It's just..." He chose his next words carefully. He knew he could be open with Yuni, but no matter how close they were she was still the queen and he was her inferior. He didn't want to forget his place. "I just worry, you know? The weather has caused so many difficulties for us before."

She sighed. "I know."

"What can be done if there's damage?"

"I won't know until I get a full report. We'll salvage the food we can. If needed we can ration out what's left to ensure we all have at least something to eat."

Luca shuddered, remembering those hungry days too well. "I hope it doesn't come to that again."

"Me too. But other than that, there's nothing else to be done." She let off a half-hearted shot. "It's not as if we can control the weather."

"Of course not." He remembered Emily's idea and debated how to present it respectfully. Yuni loved Orphia and would be open to any way to help the kingdom. Perhaps she just hadn't thought of it before. "But perhaps we could get food from...other sources."

She paused. "What do you mean by other sources?" Her tone was impassive and he couldn't tell if the question was out of interest or displeasure.

"Well, I don't know. Emily and I were speaking of this the other day and she said San Morrina trades with merchants for their goods. Perhaps we could work out something similar."

"Luca," she said firmly, but not unkindly, "you know why we can't bring people in."

"I know. But perhaps we could go about it more discreetly. Send people out to trade perhaps. I haven't thought through the details yet—"

"Luca." She said firmly again, and he suddenly felt like a little boy who was caught stealing biscuits from the kitchen. "I know this is out of concern and I am concerned as well. But that is not the solution. We cannot risk it. Do you understand?"

He nodded, though he really didn't understand. Perhaps he was naive, but sometimes he felt all the protection and secrecy were unnecessary. He had not yet needed his archery skills to defend the land and he truly doubted he ever would. But agricultural damage resulting from the weather was a recurring problem he felt deserved more proactive attention than it was getting.

Perhaps there was a third option. Or even better, that the damage from the last storm would be minimal and they wouldn't need a solution just yet. He would ask Emily. She was clever, perhaps she had another idea.

They continued practicing in silence, and Luca got back into the groove of shooting. He occasionally glanced towards the castle to see if Emily would join them. He hadn't seen her yet today, but he was sure one of the servants would tell her where they were.

They hadn't had much of a real conversation since that night of the chess game. He hoped she took his words to heart and would let him help in some way. And if she did, he hoped he was truly capable of helping her.

It tore at his heart to see her insist that she was fine when she was so overwhelmingly burdened. He would've almost preferred it if she had cried like she seemed to want to. At least then some of her pain would've been released and he would've been there to wipe her tears. But her silent suffering did nothing but render them both helpless.

A runner, James, was just returning with a handful of arrows when the movement of skirts entered his peripheral vision.

Emily smiled at him, her previous stress undetectable. Hopefully she was truly in better spirits today. She voiced a greeting to Yuni and himself before speaking with James. "Just watching all that running is making me exhausted. You are doing very well, James. I am impressed."

James, who was quiet by nature, didn't respond. But Luca saw his lips quirk up as his eyes wrinkled. Emily had quickly dispelled the initial wariness the servants held of her. She was appreciative and respectful to them and now nearly all of them looked at her with a certain fondness in their eyes.

"I'm glad you joined us today. Do you shoot?" Luca asked.

"I do not. Well, I should say I've never attempted to. But I'll take any excuse to be outside, even if it's just to come and watch."

"Would you like to try your hand at it?" He held out his bow to her hoping she would accept it. He imagined the dauntless Emily with a bow and arrow in her hands would be an impressive sight to behold.

She eyed the instrument with some reluctance, though she stepped toward it. "I don't know. I might hurt someone."

"You'll be fine. Yuni can show you what to do, right Yuni?" He looked over his shoulder at her, knowing she would be more than happy to teach someone the sport she loved.

Her eyes were pensive, her mind no doubt lingering on their recent conversation, but a smile broke through in the next moment. "Of course. I will gladly oblige."

She showed her the basic stance and draw. "Let's see what we're working with. Now focus, aim, and release."

Emily let go and the arrow missed the target, going straight into the ground. She frowned at it and Luca stifled a laugh. It wasn't quite the indomitable picture he envisioned.

"It's alright," Yuni reassured her. "Try again. Keep your eye on the target even after you release."

She did so and the arrow went soaring, this time arching high above the target. Poor James was going to have his fair share of exercise today.

She drew again and Yuni adjusted the position of her hands. "Don't grip too tightly. Rest it against your palm... hold your thumb and index finger here...that's it. Now gently release."

It whooshed through the air at the exact moment Xanth came walking by.

"Am I in time for—*yikes*!" Xanth ducked as the arrow flew over his head.

Emily dropped her bow and clasped her hands over her mouth in horror, though no injury had occurred.

He stood and fingered through his red hair. "I know we're mortal enemies fighting for Luca's friendship, but impalement seems a bit dramatic, don't you think?"

"I'm so sorry!" She glared at Luca. "I told you I was going to hurt someone."

Xanth laughed the whole thing off. "You hit it at least!" He gestured to the outer edge of the target where her arrow had landed. "Don't worry, no harm done. Just warn me before you shoot off the next one, ok?"

To her credit, she did not give up after the mishap. She kept practicing with Yuni and gradually improved over the course of the morning. She even hit the target a few times, though never at the bullseye.

"Well done Emily, especially for your first time," Yuni said. "You have a determined spirit that serves you well. With continued practice, I think you could be quite good."

"Thank you." She looked genuinely surprised and flattered by the praise. "You are a fine teacher."

"Yuni, you should show Emily your trick move."

"Trick move?"

"Oh, don't listen to him." Yuni waved her hand dismissively.

"Oh, come on Yuni!"

"It's amazing, you have to show her!" Xanth added.

"Alright, alright. Very well." She spoke reluctantly but Luca saw the excitement in her eyes. Yuni was so often weighed down by her grief and responsibilities that archery was an escape for her. Everyone should have something like that, a respite that brings genuine joy.

The thought gave him pause. For Yuni, it was archery. For Xanth, it was horseback riding. Emily's was drawing. What was his?

"Is she really going to shoot blindfolded?" Emily whispered, bringing him back to the present.

He watched as Yuni took a handkerchief and tied it around her eyes. She stood closer to the target than she did previously but was still several paces away.

Silence fell over them all as they watched. Even the birds and the wind dared not make a sound to disturb the master. She drew the arrow back, her back straight and stance confident.

As impressed as he was with Yuni's abilities, Luca found it more entertaining to watch Emily gape in awe at her. She so rarely let her emotions show and he didn't want to miss any opportunity to see the real Emily.

With a loud *twang* the arrow left her fingers and flew through the air. Soaring straight ahead, it landed on the board nearly on the bullseye.

They all broke into rapturous applause. Yuni took a bow, laughing as she accepted their effusions.

"That was incredible!" Emily said. "I think it's safe to say I'll never reach that level of skill."

"Nor us," Luca added, gesturing to him and Xanth.

"Speak for yourself!" He placed a hand on his puffed-out chest. "I am on my way to becoming a master."

Luca let out a derisive laugh that sounded more like a snort. "You know I'm a better shot than you."

He looked affronted. "Since when?"

"Now boys, there's no need to argue to try and impress the pretty lady."

Luca hazarded a glance at Emily. She gazed down at her feet and seemed taken off guard by the compliment.

He wasn't sure why. She may not have had the golden hair and tall, willowy frame that most men sought. But anyone with decent eyesight would have to admit she was attractive. With her thick brown hair, hazel eyes that sparkled with intelligence and good humor, and that gentle curve of her slender lips, surely she had heard the compliment before.

But now, why was *he* the one whose face felt flushed?

"It's not about impressing anyone, it's about the truth," Xanth said confidently. "Shall we have a contest, Luca? Say, three shots, fifty paces away?"

Luca returned to the conversation. "Very well, let's do it." He grasped Xanth's calloused hand in his with a firm shake.

Xanth went first, sending off three arrows one after the other. James returned reporting two landed on the middle ring and one in the center, for a total of twenty-six.

Luca took his position. This was not the first time Xanth and he had competed—in archery or otherwise—but it felt different. He reminded himself of Yuni's advice from years of lessons but his mind kept drifting to another person. He was very aware of the fact that Emily was watching him and losing no longer felt like an option.

He was not an impressive person in general. He was not overly tall, not buff, nor swooningly handsome. He was not brave and strong like some knight. He was just...Luca. But Emily was outstanding and had such strength of character. And he also had to agree with Yuni that she was very pretty. He felt like he had to prove himself to her.

Suddenly, this was about more than beating Xanth. This was about winning Emily's favor.

He tried to shake off the sudden nervousness he felt at something he had done a thousand times before. He inhaled a steady breath and tried to focus. He shot off the first arrow. Then the second. He glanced at Emily's reassuring smile and felt a little more confident as the third and final arrow flew from his fingers.

He waited with bated breath as James went to retrieve the arrows and reveal the final score. His face gave away nothing and his voice held all the usual impassiveness of a servant. "One bullseye, a middle ring, and an outer ring, for a total of twenty-three."

He let out his breath in a whoosh. He lost.

Xanth had the decency not to gloat, for which Luca was grateful. He just smiled and clapped him on the shoulder. "Good game."

"Congratulations," Luca returned. He pasted on a smile and nodded, trying to hide his disappointment. It was just a game after all and no one liked a sore loser.

But when Emily shook Xanth's hand to congratulate him, a flurry of emotions settled over him. Disappointment sunk in his stomach like lead. Inexplicable irritation ran through his veins. Even a little sadness tugged at his heart. The uncharacteristic traits sprang up from nowhere and dissipated just as quickly when Emily turned her smile from Xanth to him.

What on earth was wrong with him?

"Well done, Luca."

"Thanks for the pity," he said dryly.

She actually looked offended at the remark.

"I was joking," he amended. "Might as well laugh at myself." Though in truth he did feel rather pitiful.

She shook her head. "Well I am not, and I never give out false praise," she said resolutely. "You may have technically lost, but that doesn't mean you have failed. You've obviously worked hard at this for some time and you are quite good at it. That deserves commendation. Besides, you're far better than I'll likely ever be. So again I say, well done." She put her hand on his shoulder and gave it a gentle squeeze before turning away.

Her approval lifted his spirits tremendously. He didn't move as she left him and kept staring after her as he wondered what it was that made him crave that approval so badly.

When he finally turned his head, he caught Yuni watching him with unusual intensity. He shook himself mentally and strode back into the castle for lunch. He must've been more competitive than he realized. Yes, that was all it was.

With that answer enough to satisfy him, he enjoyed lunch with his friends. The whole time ignoring Yuni's perceiving glances in his direction.

14: An Exchange of Secrets

Luca wanted to show Emily the different types of fauna Orphia had to offer. They traversed the land on foot and she was quickly filling the pages of her sketchbook. They saw some of the familiar things like rabbits, deer, and birds, but there were some more unique creatures to see as well.

They had caught sight of the sunburst squirrel, a small fuzzy animal that was red, tan, and dark purple with an orange stripe that ran down its unusually long tail. Unfortunately, he was not the best model—Emily only got a vague outline of him before he scurried out of sight.

They sat on the rocks to rest their legs for a bit, just enjoying the nature around them. He watched Emily as she sketched a simple wildflower growing in the grass beside her. Her hand glided across the paper almost as if it were dancing. Her eyes were narrowed, shifting from the plant to the page and back again. She was so focused he wondered if she even realized that her tongue protruded out ever so slightly. It was utterly adorable—in a friendly way, of course.

He brought his eyes back to the forest scene looking for the little creatures that tended to nest there. "I hope they show up so you have something unique to add to your collection of drawings."

"And what exactly are we waiting for? A dragon?"

Luca laughed. "Dragons don't exist. You know that."

"I do. But I would've said that rainbow-colored mountains, giant trees, and massive crystals don't exist either, and yet somehow they do."

"True enough. But no dragons, sorry." He stretched out his legs and yawned. "We do have devil-spiked scoundrels though."

She jerked up and her eyes were wide as saucers. "Goodness, that sounds rather frightening."

"They're intimidating creatures to be sure, but they're actually quite interesting looking. I suppose they are what you'd imagine a dragon would look like, scaled skin and covered in thorny spikes. But they're just a big lizard."

"Are they dangerous?"

"They can be when disturbed. They can't fly or breath fire but the spikes are toxic."

Emily's eyes grew wider.

"But don't worry," he added quickly. "I won't be showing you those. Besides, they like to keep to themselves. I haven't come across one in years."

The muscles in her shoulders relaxed. "Well, that's good to know."

She went back to her drawing and he leaned back with his hands clasped behind his head. He closed his eyes to the sun rays that filtered through the trees, enjoying the warmth on his skin.

Neither of them spoke for a while and he loved that they didn't need to. As much he enjoyed their conversations, he also enjoyed the companionable quietude. It wasn't awkward or rude—they could just enjoy each other's company without feeling pressed to speak or do anything. Comfortable silence was a gem that could be enjoyed with very few people.

Leaves rustled ahead of him and he brought himself to a sitting position. He could see movement in the bottom part of the bush just a few paces away. "I think our wait is over."

Emily looked up from her sketchbook as the little rodent-like animal walked across the grass. Within minutes, there was a small group of them varying in age, color, and size. The smallest could easily fit in Emily's small hands and the largest could still fit on his lap. All the furry bodies had a strip of hard shell starting from their nose all the way down their head and back.

Emily laughed at the sight of them. "How can something be simultaneously cute and ugly?"

"They pull that off rather well, don't they?"

"What are they?"

"They're called pancers."

Emily put her pencil to the page but he put a hand out to stop her.

"Hold on, I think I can get them closer." He reached in his bag and started tossing out food crumbs, attempting to lure them to where they sat. Three immediately followed and nibbled voraciously at the food. Another one crept up slowly behind the others and cautiously partook of whatever was left.

Luca tossed out some extra crumbs toward the cautious one feeling it was unfair that he didn't get as much as the others. One of the smallest pancers scurried up to him, squeaking and squealing right before he took the biggest morsel. A bigger one came to take it from him, but the little one squeaked more aggressively until the bigger one gave up and sought for food elsewhere.

"Well, he's a bossy little thing," Emily said. She seemed to have forgotten about sketching and was just enjoying the show.

"Well, he is the alpha."

"What?" She asked in disbelief. "That tiny thing is the alpha? You can't be serious."

"I am."

"How do you know?"

"See how he has a black shell?" He pointed. "From what I've observed with the pancers, and even some other native creatures of Orphia, the alpha is always black even if he's much smaller."

"Interesting." She quirked her head as she watched them eat the last of the crumbs. "What if there's more than one that's black? What happens then?"

"Well, it's not as simple as natural selection. Even if there's only one, just because you're born the alpha doesn't mean you'll continue to be. In order to maintain dominance, they have to stand their ground no matter what. Especially when challenged."

"This little guy must be quite the fighter then." The pancer's nose twitched as he searched for more food. Realizing there was none, he hurried back to his hiding place.

"He is." Luca smiled, though it was a little sad. "He's my favorite in the pack."

"Why is that?"

His voice became more subdued. "Because he reminds me of myself," he admitted. "Or who I want to be, I should say."

Emily turned contemplative. "What do you mean?"

Luca didn't answer right away. He gladly left his past behind when he escaped—at least, he tried to. But the heavy weight of it was always hanging on the edge of his heart, close enough to feel but enough out of reach that he couldn't remove it. Not even Yuni or Xanth knew the full extent of what he went through.

He didn't like to talk about it, but perhaps he needed to. But then, Emily had so many burdens of her own. He was trying to lessen them, not add to them.

He felt the soft, feather-light touch of her fingers on his arm. His eyes followed up her arm to her eyes. They were so sincere, dotted with concern like those little green flecks dotted the caramel ring.

"Tell me about it." Her voice was as soft and gentle as her touch. "Please."

He glanced at the maid sitting several paces away who was focused on the embroidery cushion she brought. He kept his voice low as he started his confession. "I arrived at the orphanage parentless, friendless, and poor. Of course, so had nearly everyone. But when you combine that with my immigrant mother and my small and scrawny frame it gave the other children a lot of projectiles to throw in my direction."

Emily listened, but he couldn't meet her eyes now. He wasn't really looking at anything, his mind's eye only seeing the dark corner he cowered in most days. "The boys would tease me, play tricks on me, and the bigger boys would even roughhouse me." He rubbed at the scar on his jaw, remembering exactly how he got it. "I kept to myself most days, looking for different escapes and hiding spots to use when they were needed. And that doesn't make you great adoption material. I'm disappointed in myself for letting it happen."

Emily wrapped her fingers around his wrist and squeezed it in a thoughtful gesture.

"I see that little guy and wonder if things would've been different had I just stood up for myself. He reminds me that anyone can be brave if they truly want to be."

The wind loosened one of the leaves and it floated down next to him. He watched it as silence fell over them once more.

When Emily spoke, her voice held the perfect balance of gentle and firm. "Oh Luca, you were just a child. A child all alone and facing tremendous loss. You reacted as anyone would. You have no reason to feel guilty because you aren't. You did nothing to deserve being treated that way." She turned towards him, trying to look at his face. "You are one of the kindest people I've ever known. Those other boys abused their power. They will have to live with the guilt of hurting an innocent boy. You can't change the past, but you can learn from it. It sounds like you already have."

Emily spoke from experience, he knew. If only he could be as strong and resilient as she was. He was already on the verge of tears. "I try," he whispered to himself as much as he did to her. He hadn't spoken of the orphanage in years. Though it brought back the familiar pain, the comfort of someone truly understanding him was a balm on his wounded soul.

His watery eyes finally looked into hers and a strange jolt went through his chest. The witty and teasable Emily was gone and a warm and caring one was in her place. He had never seen such a compassionate look on her face before. It communicated a depth of feeling that went beyond words.

It made him feel...strange. Things were far too emotional right now. He needed to lighten the mood for both their sakes.

He took a deep breath in and out and straightened his back. "Well, now you know my deepest, darkest secret." He smiled a little. "Now it's your turn." It felt right to open up to her, perhaps she would let him return the favor.

"My turn?" Emily replied with an incredulous laugh.

"It's only fair. Now, tell me a secret."

After a moment of uncomfortable silence, she looked up at him with a gleam of mischief in her eyes. "Tommy picks his nose when no one is looking."

Luca threw his head back and laughed. That was not the response he was expecting but he appreciated the humor.

"It's true," Emily said in a perfectly serious manner. "He tries to hide it but I've caught him doing it more than once."

"That is your cousin's secret, it has nothing to do with you."

"You said to share a secret. You didn't say whose secret it needed to be."

Oh no, you're not escaping that easily. "Come on now, you know that's not what I meant."

"Well, that's your fault for not being specific."

"Fair enough, I shall rephrase. Please, tell me one of your secrets. Tell me something about the Emily I don't know."

She picked at something on her dress without any response.

"You can trust me. I won't tell a soul." He held up his hand as if swearing an oath. "On my honor. I promise."

She looked into her lap, then up at the sky, anywhere but at him. "You know, it's getting late. We really ought to be getting ready for dinner at Xanth's home." She stood and began walking away.

His heart dropped. She wasn't just teasing him, she really wasn't going to tell him anything.

She looked like a soldier on the march, eyes fixed straight ahead, steps determined. He caught up to her and gently grabbed her arm to look at her face. "Emily?"

She was adept at hiding her emotions. But over the last few days, intentional or not, the walls were slowly coming down. Most often it was her eyes that gave her away. At that moment, behind her aloof expression was fear in her eyes. Did that mean she was afraid...of him? His heart sunk even more.

"Em," he said with a note of distress, "I'm not trying to pry, but I feel like there's still so much of you I don't know. Burdens you bear that I'm willing to help carry, but I don't know what they are. Like there's a whole other Emily I can't see. I want to know her if you'll let me."

Her chin trembled slightly and the muscle of her jaw clenched to keep it still. "But why?"

He gently pushed her hair behind her ear and tilted up her chin, making her look him in the eye. "Because the most valuable treasures are the ones we bury the deepest. And I know yours is well worth seeking."

She turned away again. "Treasures aren't the only thing we hide," she said quietly.

He turned his head to keep her gaze. "You know you can trust me, right?" The question held far more meaning than just if he could keep a secret. Time had not changed how he viewed her, nor had it diminished his trust in her. He knew it was hard for her, but he had tried to give her reason to trust him. To think that she still didn't, or that she was even afraid of him, brought about a pain too deep to describe.

She took a deep breath through her nose, struggling to keep her composure. "Luca, I know you would never try to hurt me. But life has taught me that some feelings are better left hidden. I know I can trust you, but acting on that knowledge is not easy for me. Please try to understand that."

Despite not revealing anything specific, she looked incredibly unguarded right then. She looked so meek, so small, so...human. This was a level of vulnerability Luca hadn't seen in her before. Ever. "Ok," was all he could say in response.

They took up their walk once more, neither saying a word. Luca understood her need for privacy, but it still hurt. Whether the pain was because she didn't trust him as much as he trusted her or because she was fighting a battle all alone and he could do nothing about it, he wasn't sure.

"I'm afraid of spiders," she said as they approached the entrance of the castle.

"Huh?" It was a rather random statement and he wondered if he had heard her correctly.

"I'm afraid of spiders," she repeated. A small smile lit her face, expelling some of the earlier darkness. "It's completely irrational. I try to reason with myself that most of them are harmless and yet I can't help it. Something about all those legs and the way they crawl makes me squirm. I put on a brave face when I see one but inside I feel quite intimidated." She made an amused sort of sound in the back of her throat. "Not even Amira knows that."

Her secret. She told him. Luca smiled and the weight eased off his chest. "Thank you for telling me."

She gave him one last smile before rushing up the stairs to her room.

It was not the burden lifting confession he had hoped for but it was a small token of her trust in him. Perhaps he shouldn't press her for so much all at once. Perhaps this was the first step, albeit a small step, towards regaining the friendship they had as youths.

Whatever it was, one thing was for certain—Emily was a treasure he was not about to give up on.

15: Too Much Insight

Dinner at the Odeson's promised to be an entertaining evening. The lively chatter and joyous sounds of children's laughter exuded from the open windows of their modest home.

Xanth's father, Luca explained, was a fisherman by trade. Instead of living in a treehouses in the heart of town, they lived in a more practical location near the lake. The stone home was quaint and lovely, though Emily was slightly disappointed at not getting to see inside of one of the tree houses.

She quickly forgot her disappointment upon meeting the family, however. They were just as exuberant as she had envisioned based on her brief acquaintance with Xanth.

He obviously adored all of his sisters and the three younger ones practically worshipped him. They hurriedly bounded down the stairs to meet and accost Emily. Once her legs were free of their little arms, proper introductions were made. Eliana, Elodee, and Elora were soon showing her around their beloved home and telling her stories of the memories they made there. Due to the abundance of "E" names, they insisted she call them by their nicknames. For the sake of simplicity, she accepted and called them Ana, Dee, and Lora.

She often wondered if her mother would've had more children had she not died so young. The answer didn't matter, for she would never have a blood sibling like these girls. But that made her all the more grateful that she had Amira and Luca as she grew up.

"Would you like to play a game with us?" Ana asked.

She agreed and Ana excitedly explained the rules of the game—many of which seemed to be made up on the spot—and then dragged her to the living room.

The game ended with Ana as the winner and Dee demanding a rematch.

"Emily, would you like to walk with me to the garden while I gather the strawberries?" Xandria, Xanth's older sister, asked.

"I'd love to."

Dee frowned at her new friend being taken away, but Xanth stepped in. "Don't worry Emily, I will fill your spot on the team." He crouched down to his sister's level and gave her a little nudge. "With me, you can't lose." He winked at the girl, making her giggle.

Luca wagged his finger at him. "Then I shall have to act as judge to make sure you don't cheat."

"Cheat?" Xanth held a hand to his chest as if affronted. "I never cheat, do I, Dee?"

Her big brown eyes looked up at them all. "Well, not all the time," she replied innocently.

They all laughed as Emily and Xandria walked out into the late afternoon sun.

"I hope my family has not overwhelmed you," she said. "We will have a few minutes of peace out here."

"Thank you, although there is no need to apologize. I find the liveliness quite enjoyable."

"You're an only child, I take it?"

"I am. Though I suppose my friends could be considered honorary siblings."

Xandria smiled as another burst of laughter sounded from the window. "I understand. Poor Xanth is highly outnumbered in female company. I know Luca has become like a brother to him and the rest of us."

Emily spotted him through the window, rolling on the floor as he and Xanth tickled the younger girls. She smiled fondly. They could not ask for a better friend than him.

"So, how long have you two been courting?"

"Courting?" She spun to face her so quickly that she nearly lost her balance. "You think Luca and I are romantically involved?"

She raised her eyebrows and seemed to barely suppress a grin. "Are you not?"

"Of course we're not!" Of all the ridiculous notions... "We are only friends. We have been ever since we were four and five years old."

She eyed her curiously, uttering a ponderous "Hmm" before continuing their walk.

They went to the back of the house where a small garden was kept. Varying fruits and vegetables were laid out in orderly rows with small stones creating a rectangular border around them.

"Does Luca know this?" Xandria asked after plucking a few berries.

"Know what?"

"That you two are only friends."

"Of course he does. Why would he think otherwise?" They never talked about romantic feelings. They had an unspoken agreement that friends was all they were. To think they were anything else was completely illogical.

Xandria's eyes filled with compassion. "Emily," she said gently, "as the oldest of five siblings, male and female, I have learned to be observant. I can tell when someone is hiding something, or even pick up on something they haven't even discovered about themselves yet." She placed a hand on her arm. "My dear, friends don't look at each other the way the two of you do."

Emily sucked in a breath and tensed. She was being scrutinized in a way that made her feel very vulnerable and she didn't like it.

"Please, don't think me impertinent for bringing this up," she continued. "I know it's not my business, but as I said, Luca has become a brother to us. I like you too. And though we've only been briefly acquainted, I can make out enough of your character to realize you're a special person. I won't meddle anymore, but I just want to make sure neither of you get hurt."

Emily stood dumbfounded. She needed to squelch Xandria's suspicions, tell her the logical reasons why they were only friends with each other and why that was all they'd ever be. But she couldn't seem to force the words from her mouth.

Xandria just smiled and walked past her to the entrance of the house. "Who wants strawberry shortcake?" A chorus of *me*'s and excited chatter followed.

Like the plants beside her, Emily remained rooted to her spot on the ground. No one could make such a discovery about another after only spending a few hours in their company. If there truly was a connection between her and Luca, they would be the first to recognize it, not Xandria.

Perhaps Xandria wanted to pair them together and so she was just seeing what she wanted to see. That was plausible. But despite her reasoning, deep in the pit of her stomach a knot was forming at the possibility that there was some truth to Xandria's observation.

Emily spoke very few words as she ate her dessert. After making sure Xandria wasn't watching, she would glance at Luca now and again. He didn't seem to treat her any differently than the rest of his friends. He teased, conversed, and gave the same smile to her as he did to everyone else at the table. She never saw the "look" Xandria spoke of. This was how friends interacted with one another. Just friends.

But wait, she mentioned that it was how they looked at each other, meaning she read something on Emily's face as well. What could she possibly have seen? Emily never thought of him as anything more than a friend. Sure, she admired his sweet and kind nature and enjoyed his company. He could make her laugh and she sometimes noticed how his curls bounced along his forehead. But that was all perfectly explainable. It just meant that...she... goodness, what *did* it all mean?

She could not think about this now, not with her emotions flustered and definitely not with so many people around. This was something to be analyzed alone with a clear mind and objective reasoning. Then she would have a perfectly logical answer, she was sure of it.

Emily helped the ladies clean up. They insisted she did not need to but Emily was itching to do some work. She had already spent more than enough leisure time at the castle during the storm. And keeping her hands busy kept her from overthinking Xandria's comments.

They went outside to enjoy the last hours of sunlight before the golden sky turned black. Looking for some peace of mind, Emily sat alone on the stone bench, letting the innocent sounds of laughing children wash over her. She watched the three youngest sisters as they played some made-up game that involved running, spinning, and falling to the ground.

Watching them both made her smile and brought a pang to her heart, creating an emotion she could not name. She was happy to see a family that adored and cared for each other, but there was a gaping hole in that happiness that left her feeling hollow.

Clearly, it reminded her that she had no real family anymore, but that well-worn pain had numbed over the years. She was around Amira's family often. And though she was also lacking a father, she and the other family members always welcomed Emily as an honorary relative.

"Owww!" Dee cried out and stumbled to the ground, grasping her knee.

Before Emily could even react her mother was next to her. "Sweetheart, are you ok?" Ozanne asked with gentle concern.

Dee pulled herself up into a sitting position. "It hurrrrrrts," she drawled.

Her mother kept one arm around her, and carefully lifted the girl's hand from her knee to inspect the wound. Emily could see the bright red scrape from her seat. It was nothing at all serious, but still painful. And for poor little Dee, it probably felt like death.

"Oh, my dear, it's alright. We'll clean it up and you'll be good as new." She placed a gentle kiss on her daughter's head.

Xanth approached and kneeled in front of his sister and wiped a tear from her cheek. "Your eye is leaking," he said with a softness to his tone. He skewed his head. "But you ate happy strawberries tonight, so how can that be?"

"Happy strawberries?" Dee asked between sniffles.

"Yes." The corner of his mouth quirked up. "Because if they weren't happy strawberries, then they'd be *blue*berries."

She wiped at her nose and then chuckled.

"Perhaps a few more happy strawberries will stop the leaking." He leaned in closer to her. "With a little shortcake mixed in." He winked.

She perked up and looked expectantly at her mother, who exchanged an amused glance with Xanth. "I suppose I can allow a *little* shortcake mixed in."

Dee jumped up to take Xanth's hand and skipped inside the house, her tears dry and scraped knee forgotten. Her father beamed at her when they entered and he lifted his daughter in his strong arms and embraced her. She wrapped her little arms around his neck and closed her eyes in a look of pure peace.

And that's when it all clicked into place.

Dee's face blurred until she morphed into a young Emily, letting out a contented sigh as her parents' arms enveloped her in a sense of security and protection. When she was with them in her perfect little world, she was safe.

If only her parents had truly been as safe as she felt.

Because then they were gone, the protection she always knew dying with them. Then she was thrust into the real world where people were unkind, selfish, and cruel. Her only rescuer now was herself.

To protect herself, she had to always be on guard. She remained wary of everyone around her. She was never sure when someone would try to hurt her, take advantage of her, mistreat her, or just abandon her. Never knew if someone was sincere or would simply betray her after getting what they wanted. She missed that feeling of protection, of trusting someone so implicitly that your life felt safe in their hands. She had survived, but never felt truly safe. Because as recent events had clearly demonstrated, sometimes she wasn't enough to save herself—and there was no one else to do it for her.

There had been no magic potion that healed her sick mother, no fairy godmother to reform her father into the man he used to be, and there would be no dashing hero on a white horse to whisk her away from her dragon of a family. She was on her own, whether she was enough or not.

"Emily, you look unwell."

In her evocative trance, she had forgotten that she was among people and her mask had slipped again. Looking into Xandria's concerned eyes, she decided to use the momentary weakness to her advantage. "I'm afraid I don't feel quite right. I may have overtaxed myself considering my recent insomnia. Forgive me, but I think I should be leaving."

Xandria grabbed her hands. "Of course. Will you be alright on the journey home? You are welcome to stay here and rest if you'd like."

The kind gesture and true concern from this woman she had just met made her heart hurt all the more. "Thank you, but I will be fine," she lied. "I thank your family for the hospitality. I did enjoy myself this evening."

"You are welcome at our home anytime, Emily. Anytime at all. I will tell Mamma and Papa about your departure and go get your cloak."

Emily was perfectly capable of getting it herself but didn't object. She looked away from the house and the family inside, closed her eyes, and let out a deep breath.

Upon opening them, she met Luca's unexpected gaze and it made her chest flutter. She wasn't sure how long he had been staring at her, but based on his perturbed expression it was long enough to know something was wrong.

"What happened?" He spoke quietly as he drew closer to her.

"Nothing. I'm just overtired. I believe I shall return early."

He rubbed at his drawn brows. "All right, I'll make our excuses—"

"No." She stood. "Just because I am tired and need to leave doesn't mean you have to as well. Stay and enjoy yourself. I know my way back."

He watched her for a moment. "I don't like the idea of you going back by yourself." The concern behind his eyes shifted to a more scrutinizing look. He studied her as one might study complicated arithmetic. She had come to know that look over the last several days with him. He was looking past her words and trying to see through her mask.

She couldn't have that today.

"I am not a child, Luca." Her tone held more bitterness than she intended. "I am perfectly capable of making my way back."

His jaw tensed and he stepped back. "I know you're capable, I just wanted to help," he said in a slightly defensive tone.

She looked away from him and tried to control herself once more. She didn't mean to hurt him, but the words had to be said. "I know you do." She fought to keep her tone unaffected. "But I don't need you to accompany me back. So you might as well stay here and enjoy yourself." She didn't give him another chance to protest. She needed to get away from all these insightful eyes until she collected herself. "There's Xandria now with my cloak. Goodbye." She deliberately avoided looking at him as she walked past to retrieve her belongings. She nodded to Xandria, used a stone to mount her horse herself, and rode off.

She turned toward the path and saw Luca from the corner of her eye. He stood there bewildered, arms limp at his sides, frowning in disappointment.

Friends don't look at each other the way you two do. She now understood what Xandria meant.

Didn't she just realize she wanted a champion? Someone to save her and care about her? She could see now that Luca had been trying to do just that, and she left him in the dust.

She was just confused...no, overwhelmed by the situation. After all, it's not every day your friend comes back from the dead. Her heart was still trying to figure out how to handle that.

But she could not let him care for her as anything more than a friend. Not when they would inevitably have to part and lead separate lives. And she could not let herself fall for anyone, especially someone like Luca, when she barely trusted herself with her emotions.

She flicked the reins and galloped faster through the forest, trying to outrun the pain as she pictured Luca's sad and deflated form, knowing that she caused it. Yes, love would just leave them both hurt. Because if she felt this way about hurting her friend, it would be nothing compared to breaking the heart of the man she loved.

If her heart could ache any more, she did not know how.

***

"What on earth did I do wrong?" Luca asked Yuni the question he had been pondering since Emily's hasty departure. She was already abed when he arrived home yesterday evening, and he had barely gotten a glimpse of her all day as she requested trays to be sent up to her room. He left her a note inquiring after her and asking if she wanted to go out exploring again, but she returned it with the maid simply saying she needed to rest.

Yuni listened to his concerns as she leaned casually on the settee with her legs tucked up under her, an unread book on the armrest.

"We had been making such headway in our relationship...our friendship, rather. At least, I thought we were." She was showing a little more of her true self day by day. He too was feeling more comfortable in opening up to her. She would still have her moments of reticence, but last night something was different. She did more than simply close herself off, she pushed him away and then quite literally ran from him.

It had to have been caused by him. She had seemed comfortable around the rest of Xanth's family. It was only her conversation with him that seemed amiss. He had thought over every word leading up to her departure, but could pick nothing out of the ordinary.

Yuni's calm expression did nothing to allay his concerns. "I don't know Emily as well as you do. However, I know she has had a rough life and it sounds like she has been very dependent upon herself."

He knew that. Emily told him herself that she did not trust easily. He knew she would need time, but just when things would improve between them she would retreat into herself once more, hiding behind her walls. He wanted to gain her trust but didn't know how.

He stood from the parlor chair and began pacing in front of Yuni. "But I'm only trying to help."

"I know that, but she may not feel that she needs it. She may be afraid to accept it, worried she will be let down by another person who was supposed to care for her."

Luca winced and quickly turned his attention to the hearth. Sparks flew up as he prodded at the logs pointlessly with a fire poker. That was not what he had hoped Yuni would say. Emily had admitted just as much. Her painful words echoed in his mind—*I don't need you.*

She didn't mean them as an insult. No, Emily was too kind for that. She was simply stating what she felt was the truth. But she did need help. She didn't need to bear the burdens alone and Luca wanted to be the one to help her.

Something had changed in him since Emily reentered his life. After those horrible years in the orphanage he had found joy in all that Orphia gave him—the beauty of nature, friends, and family. He had spent so much of his life in the mires of self-pity that he felt his blessings were owed to him and that nothing could make him happier. But he was quickly learning that helping another through hardship, making them smile in the darkness, and giving of yourself for their joy, gave him an inexplicable feeling of contentment he didn't know was missing.

And that was the problem. Maybe she didn't truly want anyone to help her, or worse yet, she didn't want *him* to be the one helping her. She said she didn't need him, but he had begun to realize he needed her.

"Perhaps you should give her some space, dear."

He turned back to Yuni. "What?"

"I know you two are good friends and are happy to be together again, but you are not children anymore. She is a grown woman with a lot to sort out in her life. She may just need some time to figure things out herself. You don't want to smother her."

"But aren't friends supposed to stick with you when you have problems?"

"Of course, and I know you want to be a good friend. But everyone deals with problems differently. Give her some space, let her think things through." She stood and placed her hand on his cheek. "And please remember, you can't fix everyone's problems."

He covered her hand with his. "I know that."

She smiled warmly at him. "I'm off to bed. Goodnight."

"Goodnight," he said as she left the room.

Luca let out a sigh and dropped back into his chair, mulling over her advice. He could see the wisdom in it. In truth, perhaps his helpful attention had been a bit too much. But that didn't mean he had to abandon Emily to fight her battle alone—she had been doing that most of her life. There had to be a balance between the two.

He leaned his head back against the chair and closed his eyes. He tried to imagine himself in her position. What would he need if he were facing a problem like hers?

An idea went off in his head, one he should have thought of before. He shot to his feet, new energy filling him. There was something in Orphia he hadn't shown her yet. Something he hadn't shown anyone. When he felt his lowest or faced a difficult problem, this place was a safe haven for him. If anyone else deserved to see it, it was Emily.

16: A Secret Place

Emily had spent most of the day in her room trying to avoid Luca. She sent for trays to be brought to her, took a brisk walk outside when he left for guard duty, and hurried back up the stairs when it was time for him to return.

Basically, she was acting ridiculous.

She was going to have to face him tomorrow and tell him she was leaving. She could've left while he was gone, but that would've made her more of a coward than she already was. And after all that Luca had done for her during her stay, the least she could do was bid him farewell. And if she was being honest with herself, she wanted to see him one more time. He would never leave Orphia, and she may never be able to return, so it very well might be her last time with him.

It was a shame that this was her reality. She had felt more at home in her brief time here than at Radcliffe Manor where she had spent nearly ten years of her life. The attachment made her decision to leave all the more difficult, though no more unnecessary.

She sat on the edge of her bed, not ready to cut her remaining time short by sleeping. Most in the castle were abed by now, leaving her room still and quiet as she went through her mental list of reasons why she had to return.

She understood and accepted them all logically, but her heart kept trying to dissuade her. Back and forth the arguments went like a ball in a tennis match. The constant tugging between her heart and her mind would tear her apart if she let it go on any longer. She had to leave soon if she was going to survive.

She exhaled deeply and wrapped her arms around herself. A blanket of darkness covered the beautiful land outside her window, hiding it from view. But her mind would remember every detail with great clarity. The rich color of the mountains, the immensity of the sparkling crystals, and the little hard-shelled pancers scurrying across the green grass. And her heart would always remember her faithful tour guide with his ready smile and caring words who was with her for it all.

A knock at the door made her stand. Who was seeking her at such a late hour? Her supper tray had already been picked up. Perhaps it was Jayla returning to bring her some late-night tea. The fill-in maid had been very attentive and seemed genuinely concerned about Emily's increased reclusiveness.

"One moment." She did not want her to have to deal with both the tea tray and the doorknob. Emily donned her wrapper and went to open the door for her.

Except, it was not Jayla on the other side.

"Luca!" She pulled her wrap about her more tightly. "What are you doing here?"

"I have a surprise for you," he whispered. "Meet me by the stables as soon as you're dressed."

In her flustered state, she managed to remember to keep her voice down. "Stables? But it's midnight. What on earth are you thinking?"

He was not the least bit deterred. "You'll see. I have to show you."

"Can't it wait?" Not that she'd have much time tomorrow. But perhaps if she waited one more day...

No. She was being ridiculous. He was being ridiculous. This whole situation was ludicrous!

"No, it can't. I have to show you now."

She threw her hands up. "This is absurd, Luca. Absolutely absurd. Not to mention highly inappropriate."

"Em, there is nothing untoward or improper about this, I assure you." He glanced around the empty corridor. "But it will look that way if I keep lingering here, so we have to get a move on. But I promise you'll want to see this. You need to see this. Please, trust me."

She should've shut the door on him, but her heart betrayed her once more. She stared down at her feet instead. "You've been asking that of me a lot."

"What?"

She peered up at him through her lashes. "To trust you."

He rubbed the back of his neck. "I know I have, perhaps too often. I know that's not easy and I'm sorry if I have been pressuring you too much." He paused, seeming unsure whether or not to voice what he planned to say next. "But, do you? That is...have you been disappointed after listening to me?"

The uncertainty in his tone made her realize why she was more inclined to trust Luca than anyone else—because he genuinely asked her to. He did not just command her as Uncle and Aunt did. He never forced her hand, he always let her make the choice whether to listen or not. True, he was persuasive at times, be he saw her hesitation and prompted her gently. He did not simply want her to do his bidding, he genuinely wanted to earn her trust.

The pleading look in his eyes just now was evidence of that.

"I have not," she answered honestly. "On the contrary, I have been most pleased thus far." She was surprised just how easily that confession came out.

His worry vanished and was replaced with a relieved smile. "Then I beg you to trust me once more. And if you do, I have a feeling you will be more than pleased by what you see tonight." He let go of her hand—when did they start holding hands? Did he reach out, or did she do so subconsciously? "See you at the stables," he whispered, then took off silently down the stairs.

She remained in the doorway and watched him go, wondering what had come over her. She could've told him of her plans right then. It would've been easier. But all her reasoning, all of her logical conclusions of why she had to leave had vanished the moment she saw him. He had that effect on her, which was exactly why she was distancing herself from him, and yet another reason why she had to leave.

And she would leave—first thing in the morning. But dawn was a ways off yet. She would allow herself one more night to be free of her burdens. One more night with the person she most regretted having to leave behind.

***

Luca led Emily through rocky terrain behind a patch of land near the stables. He was so eager to get to their destination that she was hard-pressed to keep up with his quick pace. He was nearly dragging her by the hand so she would not fall too far behind him. He had not let go of it since leaving the stables and she was hoping he wouldn't let go anytime soon.

Only for practical reasons, she thought. I would surely get left behind and completely lost if he let go.

He did not carry a lantern this time. Only the light from the full moon cut through the inky darkness to illuminate the path in front of them, a path that seemed to be getting more indistinct with each step. Where on earth was he taking her?

"Luca, is this safe? Can you even see where you're going?"

"I know the way like the back of my hand. Just wait, we're almost there."

She caught a glimpse of his wide grin, his teeth flashing on his shadowed face. He looked positively giddy—like he was a little boy again on one of their childhood escapades.

He climbed over a larger rock, then helped her as she attempted to hoist her petite frame over it. She stepped carefully, trying to avoid tearing her dress or hiking it up any more than necessary.

Her feet were firmly on the ground once more but he halted their steps. "Close your eyes."

"Seriously?" Emily asked dryly.

He nodded, a wayward curl bouncing as he did.

"But, I can barely see as it is." Not to mention that she already tripped a couple of times while he hauled her to their unknown destination—and that was with open eyes.

"Please?" His voice was softer. "It will be worth it, I promise."

Trust me, he had asked of her. He had done so much for her, she needed to try. She wanted to try.

She rolled her eyes but smiled. "Oh, very well." She shut her eyes. "But you better not run me into anything."

He took her hand once more and led her, at a slower pace, several paces ahead. She furrowed her brow when she heard the faint sound of water.

"No peeking," he insisted.

She held up her free hand in innocence. "I won't." She stopped peeking.

They stopped and he gently grabbed her shoulders to twist her around. The sound of water was very distinct now.

"Ok...open."

As she did so, light immediately captivated her attention. She raised both hands to her agape mouth, her gasp penetrating the quiet night air. She stepped closer to the edge of the cliff to stare at a flowing river below—a river that was literally glowing.

It looked as though the water's surface was embedded with hundreds of glittering diamonds. A steady light emanated from it, such an intense shade of bright blue that the color didn't seem real. For a moment she wondered if it was real or if she was in a dreamlike state. But no, her dreams were never this fanciful. She was certain even the most imaginative person would have a hard time dreaming up such an exquisite sight.

She wasn't sure how long she had been staring when Luca spoke. "Would you like to get a closer look?"

She nodded, not yet pulling her gaze away from the water. The touch of his hand pulled her out of her reverie and reminded her that this was indeed real.

He carefully led her on a steep path down the cliff where the grass had been worn down by footsteps. The glow was even more intense up close. Sitting at the riverbank, she reached out her hand and it hovered just above the water's surface. "Can I touch it?" She needed to determine once again that this wasn't just some beautiful apparition.

"Go ahead."

She skimmed the top of the chilled water with her fingertips, sending ripples through it. "Wow," she whispered.

Luca remained silent as her mind still tried to grasp what she was seeing. It was rare that anything left her speechless, but there were no words to describe how she felt at seeing this. Any words of admiration she had to describe the wonder that was before her eyes would not do it justice. So she just sat there in the silence with him and drank it all in. Like a moth to the light, the sight arrested her whole being.

For the first time, her worries and burdens did not even enter her mind. She did not need to display a different version of herself to hide her true emotions. She felt no need to be on guard against anything. She let the sparkling river wrap her in its beauty, allowing warm contentment to settle over her worn and tired soul in a way that only the natural world can.

"What makes it glow?" Emily eventually asked.

"Well, the answer depends on who you ask. But these little guys are the real cause." With a light splash, he scooped his hand in the water and held out some of the glowing orbs. "They're tiny glow worms called river fireflies. They only come out at nightfall."

Emily stared wide-eyed at the glowing creatures before Luca returned them to their home. Never had she seen anything like it, nor knew it even existed.

Her mind went back to his earlier comment. "You said others would answer differently?"

He wiped his wet hand on his trousers. "Oh yes, some of the older generation like to pass along their folklore."

"And what do they claim the river is filled with?"

"Stars."

She gave an amused snort. "Stars? Do they truly believe such a thing?" While the river did remarkably resemble the starry sky above it, the idea was rather preposterous.

Luca lifted his shoulder. "Probably not, but they share the myth anyway. It's actually quite a touching story."

She looked at him with an arched brow. She was doubtful of the claim, yet curious to hear it.

He understood the question her eyebrows asked. "It goes like this." He cleared his throat and spoke theatrically. "Once upon a time, somewhere high in the heavenly galaxies, the stars were preparing to form into constellations. But there was a problem. The stars, being the argumentative sort that they are, could not agree on who would make up the constellations and what they would look like. Some of the stars claimed that the big dipper's handle was too long, Orion's Belt was too large for his waist, and they made other similar complaints."

Emily rolled her eyes. "Now the stars are talking." Not exactly what she would consider a touching story.

Luca crossed his arms and glared with mock disapproval. "Do you want to hear the rest of your bedtime story?"

She laughed. "Forgive my interruption. Please continue."

"Good." He winked. "Where was I? Oh yes, the argument. Well, they also said that some of the smaller, weaker stars would not provide enough light to be seen. Others were so bright that they outshone all the others, proving too much of a distraction. Others simply were in the wrong place, somewhere they supposedly did not belong. This led to the unfortunate decision that some stars would simply have to be removed, banished from the night sky, forever.

"And so, these misfit stars left the heavens and found the river. They banded together and made it their new home where they could be themselves, just as they were created. For if they could not belong with the others, they would simply make their own unique galaxy."

Emily's amusement faded as a sense of understanding came over her. Her gaze slowly returned to the river, but she saw it differently now. It was not just a delight to the eyes, but it held a greater meaning that struck her heart forcefully. She knew very well what it was like to feel unwanted, lost, and out of place. So did Luca.

"And so the River of Fallen Stars came to be," Luca continued. "A tragedy turned beautiful."

Though the tale was fictional, the story nearly moved her to tears. And yet, there was also a message of hope glimmering in the dark story that made her wonder if there was somewhere out there where she could truly feel she belonged. Was it in her little dream cottage in San Morrina, like she always thought? Or somewhere unexpected, like Orphia? Would she have fellow "stars" to share it with? And did she dare hope that the end of her own story would be something more beautiful than she could even imagine?

She stared in amazement at the twinkling water. How on earth did this farcical story lead her to such a philosophical evaluation?

"So, what do you think?"

"Huh?" Emily asked, somewhat dazed. She truly didn't know what to think of anything at the moment.

"The river, do you like it?"

"Oh." That she knew. "How could I not?" Her voice still held its awe. "It's magnificent."

"Good." He leaned back and braced his arms on the ground behind him. "I'm glad to hear it because it's very special to me."

There was a quality of sentimentality to his voice. She suspected this place was more to him than just something pretty to look at. "Why is that?"

"Well, the river flows for a little ways, so it's not exactly a secret—hence the popularity of the myth. But this section is concealed by all the rock mass nearby. And while the more visible part is pretty, it has only a fraction of the river fireflies. I had not been in Orphia very long when I stumbled across it. I was having a particularly bad day, but being here, quiet and secluded with the glittering water to keep me company, gave me peace I hadn't felt in a long time. This spot quickly became my secret place to go to when I needed to think, to deal with a problem, or to just" —he shrugged—"get away."

She tucked her knees up against her chest. "What did you need to get away from? I thought Orphia was your getaway?"

"It is, but sometimes it's not enough. Though I may be physically away from danger and hardship, my mind replays my past rather vividly." He rubbed the back of his neck. "Memories are rather acute torture sometimes."

Even in the dim glowing light, she could see the dejected countenance on his face. To see such raw pain hurt her deeply. He could always make her smile when she had no reason to. She wished she possessed the same talent at this moment.

She scooted closer to him. "I know exactly what you mean. But I also know that memories fade and lose some of their pain. And you have such a beautiful place to escape to, you can use it to create new memories until they do."

He pondered for a moment, the sound of crickets filling the temporary silence. "I hadn't thought of it like that. Thank you."

"You're welcome." She wrapped her arms around her to fight the chill of the night air. "Sometimes I wish I had a place like this to escape to," she mused aloud.

Despite his pain, he looked at her and smiled. It was not a mischievous or giddy smile, but a sincere, compassionate one. "Now you do."

She had the strangest feeling that he meant much more than just this spot by the river. But he interrupted her before she had time to analyze the suspicion. "You're the only other person I've shown this place to."

"I am?" She dropped her arms. "Truly, no one else has ever seen it?"

He shook his head.

The fact that he trusted her with this place that was so dear to him left her at a loss. "But, why me?"

He grabbed her hand and the chill instantly dissipated. A swarm of butterflies released in her chest and stomach. "Because you are as unique and beautiful as the river itself. There is no one else like you, Em. You are worth sharing it with."

She hadn't realized until now just how close they were sitting to each other. His earnest gaze met her eyes and suddenly she couldn't breathe. She had sat beside him before, looked into his chocolate eyes plenty of times, but this was drastically different.

Her heart hammered in her chest. The river, the moonlight, everything around her froze and time stood still. She only saw him, this man that valued her. She didn't move, breathe, or blink, for fear the slightest motion would unravel this nearly perfect moment.

But...it wasn't perfect. Nothing about her life had changed by sitting here. Her life was not a fairytale, but a tragedy. Reality doused her with all the unpleasant shock of freezing cold water. She was leaving tomorrow—leaving Orphia and leaving him.

With all the strength and self-control she possessed, she leaned away and removed her hand from his. He blinked rapidly as if he was pulled out of a trance and shifted back as well. Whatever spell the river and their hearts had cast upon them was now broken.

She cleared her throat and forced an even tone. "Thank you for showing me this place and trusting me with it." She stood quickly and wiped her hand on her dress, trying to rid it of the sensation of Luca's grasp. "We should head back to the castle before anyone realizes we're missing."

"Right, of...of course," he stumbled.

She keenly avoided looking at him for fear her eyes would reveal too much. She kept as much distance as possible as they walked back, which was difficult considering he had to help her climb up the steep cliff and over rocks. As soon as they entered the castle she bid him goodnight and went up to her room as swiftly as possible without actually running.

She locked the bedroom door behind her and slid down it into a crumpled heap on the floor. This is why she kept her emotions hidden, why she desperately tried not to feel anything too deeply. Because doing otherwise just exposed her to trouble and pain. She failed where Luca was concerned and now they would both hurt because of it.

Without warning, her heart had leaped from behind its stone walls and right into his hands.

17: A Storm is Unleashed

At some point in the early twilight hours of the morning, Luca gave up on the idea of sleep and instead stared out his window. As the sun rose and changed the sky from black, to blue, to a pinkish-orange, he tried to make sense of last night's epiphany.

Sitting by the river with Emily, he realized that he was no longer content with just a friendship. He didn't know when it happened, but it was clear that his feelings had shifted significantly. He had no idea what to do about it.

Even as a child, he had liked Emily. In truth, he had always been somewhat in awe of her. The Emily he remembered from years ago possessed intelligence, strength, and bravery he had never seen in any girl before—or any boy for that matter. She was still all of those things, but since her arrival in Orphia, he had seen another side of her that touched him deeply. Beneath her stoic, emotionally indifferent expression was a heart brimming with gentle kindness.

He brought her to the river in hopes of helping her, but instead, she comforted him when his own emotions resurfaced. The way she looked at him, the softness of her voice that did not deliver empty words of encouragement but instead true concern and empathy, was special.

She really was like the river. Strong enough to be a powerful torrent, gentle enough to be a calm, soothing stream, and deep enough that he could fall very far for her. And he was sorely tempted to dive in.

But how did she feel? They held each other's gaze for what felt like an eternity and yet not long enough. He was trying to see even the faintest indication of her feelings. He thought she sensed the shift too and seemed startled at first, as was he, but for a brief moment he saw a fondness that mirrored his own. It gave him hope, and he had very nearly leaned in to kiss her.

And as if she read his thoughts, she broke away. She put so much physical and emotional distance between them that he wondered if he had imagined everything he thought he saw.

As the sun continued rising his hopes continued fading. After hours of contemplation, he still had no idea how to proceed when he faced her today. Perhaps Yuni would have some advice...no, he couldn't talk to her yet. After all, she told him to give her space and he went and did the exact opposite.

He barely stepped out of his room when he saw Emily coming up the stairs. His heart rate must've tripled in speed. The dark circles beneath her slightly bloodshot eyes were evidence that she did not sleep much more than he did.

But she still looked beautiful. Nothing could mar that. She wore her own clothes, the green dress she wore when he found her in the woods. It brought out the green in her hazel eyes that he was becoming more and more mesmerized by.

"Good morning, Em," he managed to say when he remembered his manners. "I'm...um, headed to breakfast. Would you like to join me?" He figured food was safe territory to begin with.

"Thank you," she said quietly, "but I've already eaten. I just came from the dining hall, actually."

It was not long after sunrise. "You were up quite early then."

"I know," she said flatly. Her posture was stiff and her expression unreadable. That was very inconvenient for Luca who was trying to follow her lead in how to proceed with their relationship—whatever it was.

Perhaps he made her uncomfortable last night and should apologize. But how could he apologize for feelings, new as they were, that he didn't regret? He didn't want to scare her away, but he couldn't pretend that those feelings didn't exist. He couldn't act like things were the same as they had always been. Because no matter how she felt, he knew from last night on that he would never look at her the same way again.

"Emily—"

"Luca—"

They spoke simultaneously, then paused.

He gave her a nervous smile. "Ladies first."

She drew in a breath. "I just wanted to come and tell you goodbye."

His racing heart plummeted to his stomach. "Goodbye?"

"Yes." She shifted her eyes away from him. "I already told Yuni and she has a horse waiting for me, but I wanted to tell you of my departure."

"You mean you're going back to San Morrina?"

"Yes."

No. This couldn't be happening. "You're not going back to Radcliffe Manor are you?"

He saw the slightest glimpse of a grimace pass on her face but she hid it quickly. "I am, though not immediately. I plan to stop at Amira's first to learn what has happened in my absence."

How could she speak so calmly while his head was spinning?

This had to be a nightmare. *Wake up, wake up!* His mind kept shouting the command but nothing was changing. He ran a shaky hand through his hair. "But...but why?"

She held her arms stiffly at her sides with her head held high—a soldier's bearing if he ever saw one. "Because that is where I have to be. I am still under Uncle and Aunt's guardianship, and though my inheritance is gone I cannot help but feel that something about the arrangement is illegal. I deserve justice, and I intend to investigate for myself to see what can be done."

She turned to march down the stairs and Luca leaped forward and laid his hand on her arm. She flinched at his grasp but didn't pull away. He relaxed his touch. He didn't intend to be forceful, but he was in a panic. He had just discovered his feelings for her and she was leaving him behind as if it were nothing. But more than that, she was returning to the life she so clearly hated, one that he feared would one day kill her spirit entirely.

"But, why are you doing it?"

He kept a light touch on her arm and she stared at it, not meeting his eyes. "I just told you of my reasons."

"I know, but...I mean why are you doing this to yourself? Those people treat you with so much contempt that you ran into the woods because you were so distressed. Why put yourself through it again when you don't have to?"

"Because I *do* have to." She sounded exasperated, as if she had already run through this explanation many times. "Thanks to my family my reputation is already questioned. I have no wish to add to it by prolonging my abrupt absence. There are also friends left behind with no clue as to where I am. I don't have another option. I have to—"

"You could stay here," he blurted out, barely refraining from adding *with me* to the sentence. He wasn't ready to expose his heart fully, not when she may very well trample on it in her departure. "I know Yuni would allow it. Or if...if you'd rather have your own place we could find you something. You can start a new life, one free of the people who hurt you." He took both of her hands in his. "Em, I've been there. I've been stuck in a terrible situation with no escape. You have a way out, take it!"

"I can't."

"But you can. We can make it work."

"I *can't!*" Her voice echoed through the empty corridor.

Her tone surprised him and he dropped her hands. She did not exactly yell, but her voice was firm, determined, and no longer emotionally detached.

"And do you know why?" Emily continued with a tremor in her voice. "Because the decisions I make affect more than just me. Yes, I have problems back at home, but I cannot simply run away from them and pretend they don't exist. I will not leave others behind to deal with the aftermath of my choices."

He stared at her, stunned by her sudden transformation. "They would understand."

"They don't even know where I am! I wouldn't be allowed to tell them. I would be dead as far as they were concerned. And though that would likely sadden only a select few, I will not do that to them." A sheen of moisture glossed her eyes. "Do you know how hard it was after you left for the orphanage? And then word came that you died. Dead, Luca, I thought you were *dead*. I was crushed, even after years passed. All of us were. I will not be selfish and cause anyone else that same suffering."

Her words jolted him out of his sympathies and he jumped back at the sudden bitterness in her tone.

"So you're saying I was selfish for leaving?"

She hesitated. "I didn't say that."

"But that's what you're implying." He refused to be misjudged on this account. "So, what, I should've gone back to that grimy orphanage with rodents constantly crawling around our quarters? Where I enjoyed rationed meals and being bullied every single day for four years? I was selfish for leaving that?"

She took a calming breath through her nose but her fists still clenched at her sides. "I don't question why you left that horrid place. But I do question why you didn't come back. You could've returned to San Morrina. You could have at least come to tell us you were alive and unharmed."

"Unharmed?" How could she think such a thing! He still bore emotional scars from those years. Horrible memories started flooding his mind and resentment bubbled up within him. He wanted to be calm, but the mental images addled his resolve. He was angry at the bullies, at himself, at everything that hurt him, and now that anger was transferring to Emily. "You think I survived all of that without any damage? You have no idea the kind of suffering I experienced! I took advantage of my escape because I *needed* Orphia."

She drew herself up. A fire lit her eyes as she pierced him with a glare so intense that it burned him through. The storm steadily brewing inside her was about to be unleashed.

"I watched my mother die before my eyes because she refused to call a doctor. I barely had time to mourn her death when my father turned to alcohol and became the village drunk. I begged him to stop, telling him it wouldn't change anything, that it wouldn't bring her back, but he wouldn't listen." She gestured wildly, growing more and more animated. "More than once I had to drag him off the street where he was passed out while others just laughed at me. He thoroughly ruined his good name and mine all because he chose to numb away his pain at my expense and humiliation. Then, after years of submissiveness to my severe uncle, he spent my inheritance without caring one bit about what it would do to my future.

"One thoughtless action led to another, carrying hurt and pain along the way, all piling up on me. So yes, I thoroughly understand what it means to suffer and be a victim of gross injustice. But I intend for that chain of consequence to stop with me, no matter what I must bear to end it."

Silence hung like a heavy velvet curtain. Luca was stunned, trying to get his bearings in the sudden whirlwind of words and emotion.

Emily breathed heavily and her shoulders sagged as her pent-up emotion seemed to finally be expelled. "I do not wish to leave you this way." Her words barely rose above a whisper. "Forgive me. But please try and understand why I am doing this. Why I have to do this."

How could she render half of him fuming in anger and the other half wanting to wrap her in his arms and protect her from the cruel world she had always known? She had insulted him, but she was also hurting more than he realized. But he was hurting too. He had no idea what to think of anything.

She started to reach for his hand, but she let it fall back to her side. She straightened again, pulling her shoulders back. "Goodbye, Luca."

With those last words, his heart broke, and he heard its cracking in the sound of each of her retreating footsteps.

18: Aftermath

Emily's body shifted atop the horse as it plodded slowly across the forest ground. She forced herself not to look behind her. Her head and eyes listened, but her thoughts were slow to obey.

No amount of forethought and planning had adequately prepared her for this departure. Although she thought Luca might view the situation differently, she had not anticipated such a heated argument between them. But perhaps it was for the best. As much as she hated to leave him in that way, their difference in opinion put some much-needed distance between them, which in turn helped her move forward in her decision to leave.

She needed that push. When he had asked her to stay, all she wanted was to forget her logic and say yes just so she could be with him.

Being in Orphia and being around Luca pulled her emotions to the surface to the point that she couldn't make sense of anything she was feeling. It couldn't be love, not after so many years of separation between them. That was a good thing because love was far too dangerous.

"I hope you enjoyed your time here in Orphia." Yuni's words broke her from her musings.

"I did." She relaxed the white-knuckle grip she had on the reins. "It is a very special place. I will always cherish the time I spent here."

Yuni had insisted on accompanying Emily on her journey home, supplying two guards for their safety that followed shortly behind them.

Between the difference in their stations and Emily's natural tendency to withhold herself from people she didn't know well, she couldn't imagine ever having a warm relationship with her as Luca did. But the woman had been pleasant company and very generous, and for that she was grateful.

"I hope things go well for you back home. You are a clever girl, so I have no doubt that they will and that you will go on to do great things in your life."

If only Emily had as much confidence as Yuni did. She knew the odds of things going well were heavily against her, but she appreciated Yuni's attempt at encouragement, even if they were just empty words.

They made it to a familiar copse of trees where Luca's treehouse was. She glanced at it for the briefest of moments but immediately refocused on the greenery ahead. Luca belonged in Orphia and all thoughts of him would have to stay behind in Orphia as well.

Yuni watched her with a sideways glance and Emily wondered if she noticed the minute movement or detected her inner struggle. Neither of them had mentioned Luca's name since Emily had informed her earlier this morning of her plan to leave.

They brought their horses to a stop. "I'm afraid this is where I must leave you. John will escort you to the forest boundary." She pulled Emily into a one-armed embrace, and Emily tried not to stiffen. The display of affection still felt somewhat foreign to her.

"Thank you again for your hospitality and kindness. I will never forget it."

Yuni gave her a weak smile and Emily started forward. Yuni quickly placed a hand on her arm. "Emily? Before you go, there is one more thing."

"Yes?"

"I know you went on quite a tour here seeing the land and meeting the people in it. What do you think of it all?"

That was an odd question but not a difficult one to answer. "It is the most extraordinary place I have ever seen. I loved everything about it."

Yuni nodded. "So you will do your part in protecting it?"

Emily furrowed her brow, not sure where Yuni's speech was going. "What do you mean?"

She spoke in an authoritative manner that befit her role as queen. "I don't know how much of our history you learned, but Orphia was not always the peaceful land you see now. Its survival depends on its secrecy. And as queen, I am doing all in my power to keep it that way. However, much of its success depends on the cooperation of others. If you truly love Orphia and the people in it"—she flicked her eyes to Luca's treehouse then back—"then you will not risk their safety. You must promise me you will not speak of Orphia, Luca, or your time here to absolutely anyone. It is the best way to protect us all."

Emily sobered at the thought. She knew enough of Orphia's history to understand why Yuni made the request, or rather the command. Part of her longed to tell Amira of the beautiful things she saw here and that Luca was alive.

But she wouldn't. She could never live with herself if she put Luca or any of the other residents of Orphia in danger. "I will say nothing. You have my word."

Yuni nodded crisply. "Very well. Be safe now, Emily."

Emily waved goodbye and she and John continued weaving through the trees until she could see San Morrina before her. She dismounted, thanked John, and looked back over her shoulder as he returned to the castle. Orphia was far behind her, but she could picture it just as clearly as if she were still standing on its soil.

It was just as well that she was forbidden to speak of it, for it would make burying her feelings easier. She said goodbye to Luca and Orphia in her heart and walked towards her previous life, where she belonged.

***

Luca spent the rest of the day replaying his last conversation with Emily. He couldn't believe she thought him selfish for leaving his life in Hiranburg and San Morrina behind. How could she not realize how horrible that time was for him? He had to leave. The fact that she could think him so heartless burned him.

But as he sat in the parlor that night, he tried removing himself from the picture and looked at the situation from her point of view. He tried to imagine going through all the woes she suffered. He had no idea how much she had lost and how much pain she kept hidden just below the surface of calm confidence.

He then analyzed the emotion behind her words. She wasn't bothered with him leaving the orphanage itself. She was hurt at being left behind, hurt he didn't acknowledge how she had been affected by his absence and omission of the truth. All he had wanted to do was heal her pain. Instead, he inflicted more of it. That realization put out any lingering fire and nearly chilled him to his core.

He dropped his face in his hands. What on earth was he to do about all this?

"Luca?" Yuni's voice drifted into the room.

He lifted his head and leaned forward, keeping his elbows on his knees.

She entered and sat beside him. "How are you doing, dear?"

"I've been better."

She placed an arm around him. "I'm sorry things didn't work out the way you wanted them to with Emily."

"I can't believe she left. I just thought..." What did he think? That she would fall hopelessly in love with him despite all the years he had left her behind? Perhaps he was somewhat selfish. "I don't know," he finished.

"I know it hurts, but she has a lot of things she needs to sort out. You have dealt with much yourself. It may not have been the ending you envisioned, but perhaps it's all for the best. Things will turn out well enough, you'll see."

Ending? Was this truly the end for him and Emily? He had been viewing this as merely a rift in their relationship, something that could be repaired. But Yuni was right, this very well might be the sad end to their story.

Suppose he had returned after the fire. He couldn't have done so right away, but perhaps once he was old enough to be on his own. He could've somehow sent word to her in the meantime without revealing Orphia's existence. Or suppose he never found Orphia and went to San Morrina. He could've been beside her all along to help her deal with her problems, and her presence could've been a comfort for his own. He could've found ways to make her laugh, and his days would've been filled with her smiles. He could've discovered his feelings for her earlier, and perhaps she would've returned them. Perhaps they could've formed an everlasting bond, and he could've taken her away from that house, rescuing her once and for all.

How different their ending could've been.

"I'm worried about her." He stared at the carpet, the swirled pattern blurring into an unfocused mixture of colors. "She carries such a heavy burden, one that will likely be even heavier upon her return. She's strong, but everyone has a breaking point." She had already reached it when she ran away. But he was there for her, and he wanted to think he had helped her recover from it. But there was nothing he could do if it happened again.

"I know. But it is up to her to decide how she will live. It's not our place to dictate what she should do or how she should handle matters. She's quite intelligent, I'm sure she'll know how to deal with whatever comes her way." Yuni rubbed small, soothing circles on his back. "I suppose it might ease some of your concern to know that she did make her way back home safely. I saw to it myself."

That temporarily brought him out of his brooding. "You escorted her out?" That was surprising. Yuni tended to stay close to the castle. "Why did you not send for me? I could've gone."

"Do you really think that would've been wise, dear? Especially given your parting words?"

Luca averted his gaze as heat crept up his cheeks. "You know about that?"

"You didn't exactly keep your voices down. Quite the opposite, actually."

"Well, this is embarrassing." How many of the servants heard their emotional outburst?

"Oh, I shouldn't have mentioned it. Please, don't let that distress you. Luca, look at me, dear." She placed her palm against his cheek so that he faced her. "You care about her, I know you do. And that is what makes letting go all the more difficult. But it will do you both good to try and respect her choice, even if you disagree with it." She leaned in and gave him a gentle hug. "Now, come get some dinner. You need to eat."

Luca wasn't hungry. He would much rather sit and continue to brood. But though Yuni meant well, this conversation was draining him and he wanted it to end. If that meant pushing food around on his plate, so be it. "I'll be there shortly."

"Good." She gave him one last squeeze and then left the room.

He stretched his arms before him as he rose and took his time crossing the room. It didn't matter how many what-if scenarios or alternate versions of their conversation he came up with. Yuni was right, Emily was an adult. She made her decision to leave, and she had the right to live her life however she pleased.

He paused at the mirror and spent a long moment analyzing who he was beyond the reflection. There was no reason for there to be fear in his red-rimmed eyes anymore. He was no longer the little boy who cowered in the corner. He was a man that had family and friends where he was and a duty to protect Orphia.

Yes, he had his own life to live. He would simply have to relearn how to do so without Emily in it.

19: Confounded Curiosity

Emily took her time walking to Amira's, taking the longer, unostentatious route where she could easily hide among the foliage. Yuni had also given her a shawl to wrap around her head to make herself less identifiable. She was fairly certain she made it to the farm without being recognized.

Hyacinth was out in the field to the right of the farmhouse. When her back was turned, Emily crept around to the side of the barn and peeked inside.

Empty.

It was nearing lunchtime, and if Amira wasn't in the barn doing her chores then she was most likely in her room washing up before the meal. She knew she wouldn't be in the kitchen, for Amira was infamous for her poor cooking, but hopefully she wasn't at the table already.

She moved stealthily to the back of the house and peered into the bedroom window. Amira sat on the edge of the bed facing her, her long black hair draped over one shoulder. She couldn't actually see her face, but the fact that it was stuck between the pages of a book confirmed her identity more than anything.

She tapped on the glass and moved aside just enough so Amira wouldn't readily see her but so she could still see

Amira. She had no wish to frighten her and she most definitely didn't want her to scream. The foresight, however, was in vain. Amira didn't even react to the sound.

She had to tap two more times to pull her out of whatever fictional world she had immersed herself into. She finally looked up and Emily stepped back to give her a small wave as she approached the window. Amira caught sight of her and gasped. She quickly opened the window and Emily came forward.

"Emi—"

"Shh!" She put a finger to her lips to cut off the exclamation. "Help me through the window, quickly!"

Amira gaped at her like a fish out of water. Finally, her request registered, and she shook off her confusion and did as instructed without question, proving her worth as a good friend.

For once, Emily was grateful for her diminutive size. She just fit through the small window and landed on her feet.

"Emily! What are you doing here?"

"Shh! Keep your voice down."

"Are you in danger?" Amira brought her voice to a loud whisper.

"No. At least, I don't think so."

Amira quickly enveloped her in a hug and Emily returned the gesture with unaccustomed enthusiasm. She was not given to such displays of affection, but she had truly missed her friend.

"If you aren't in danger then why are you sneaking in my window?"

"Because I don't want Aunt and Uncle to find me. If your family knows I'm here, they'll be obligated to tell them."

"Did you come here from your cousin's home?"

She blinked at her. "What cousin's home?" Emily asked, unsure what Amira was referring to.

"I don't know. After your birthday passed and I hadn't seen you, I became worried. I went to Radcliffe Manor and they told me you had left to care for an ailing cousin and didn't know when you would return."

Emily shook her head. "They lied."

An ailing cousin. So *that* was the cover-up story they fabricated when she left. Perhaps there was a smidge of truth behind it, that their plan all along was to drain her of her funds and ship her off to some distant relative.

She knew her family was nowhere near loving her, but shouldn't they have had at least a minute amount of concern for her safety when she didn't come back? At least out of familial obligation? Clearly, they did not, which meant they were even more heartless than she realized. Just thinking of their coldness made her shudder. She couldn't go back to that.

"Oh Emily, you poor dear. Come here." She gestured to the bed and placed a blanket about her shoulders. "What happened? I thought you were to be free on your birthday, but you just disappeared."

"Well—"

Emily was cut off by Hyacinth's voice "Mira, lunch is ready dear. Are you coming?"

They stared at each other with mirrored looks of alarm.

"Um, yes Mother!"

"Please don't tell them I'm here," she whispered. "At least not until I figure out what to do with this wretched situation."

Amira nodded her agreement and slipped out the door.

A quarter of an hour later, she returned and held up some pilfered bread in her hand. "I thought you might be hungry. Unfortunately, stew isn't very easy to sneak away. This is all I could get."

Emily took the offering gratefully. She did not have much of an appetite but her stomach did feel hollow. She knew it would do her good to eat something.

"I will have to get back to my chores soon, but I was able to beg off a few minutes of rest. I told Mother I wanted to finish a story first and she was kind enough to let me."

"Thank you."

Amira sat on the edge of her bed, elbows on her knees and head resting on her fists. "And I am very intrigued by this particular story." She gestured to Emily. "So, what happened?"

Emily had her full attention for a story she wasn't quite sure how to tell. "It's a bit complicated, so I'll give you the summary." She wrung her hands behind her back. "Uncle has had control over my inheritance until I reached my majority, as you know, and he...well, there is nothing left for me."

Amira gasped as a look of horror spread over her face. "How could he do that? Oh, you poor thing! Are you certain there is absolutely nothing?"

"His solicitor confirmed it, though I did not look into it myself. I was so utterly mortified that I was at a loss. I felt like the world was caving in on me and all I could think to do was run."

"You ran away?" Amira had an irritating tendency to ask questions that had already been answered. But Emily indulged her, oddly feeling some relief at sharing her story with someone.

"Yes. In hindsight, it was quite foolish of me." She thought of the sheer terror that spread through her body when Luca grabbed her before either of them knew the identity of the other. If it had been someone else, losing her head could've meant losing her life. It was difficult, but she was making the right decision in leaving Orphia where her emotions bubbled up far too freely. "But I couldn't be in that house or anywhere near it. I needed to be alone until I regained control of myself."

Amira was utterly stunned and apparently at a loss as to how to respond. In the silence, the desperation Emily felt in the moment returned with startling clarity. She was still just as desperate to find a solution to be rid of her family for good. The thought of failing made her physically nauseous.

She stared into oblivion as her thoughts rebelliously strayed back to Orphia. Had Luca been just as desperate to get away from the orphanage and any seeming connection to it? He was only a child, tender and impressionable. He likely was even more traumatized by those events.

"But you didn't return that day." Amira had found her voice again. "Where did you go? Where have you been all this time?"

"I..." She hesitated. "I ran into the woods and got lost."

Amira's eyebrows shot up so high they nearly blended into her hairline. "Lost in the woods! How did you survive? How did you get back?" She quickly clasped her hands to her mouth when she realized her volume had raised. "Sorry," she whispered.

Emily tried to keep her answers as short and simple as possible. "I was lost for several hours and then I was found and given shelter."

Amira went from shocked to intrigued. "Who found you?"

"A kind soul," she replied vaguely. "I stayed there until I could formulate some kind of a plan to enact upon my return."

"And who was this kind soul that helped you? Was it someone from here? Anyone I know?"

Curse Amira and her persistent questioning! She was making it extremely difficult to keep her promise to protect Orphia and not reveal its existence. She would never forgive herself if anything happened to Luca because of a slip of the tongue. Or if anything happened to any of the other citizens, of course.

Amira eyed her impatiently.

"It's a long story."

She flicked a hand towards her full bookshelf, never breaking eye contact. "Those are my favorite kind. I have time."

"You really don't, but that is beside the point." The bed creaked as she shifted in her seat. "I will not lie to you, I value your friendship too much to do that. But as much as I'd like to satisfy your curiosity, I cannot tell you any details."

"Oh, please Emily? You know you can trust me."

Upon quick introspection, she found that she did trust Amira. She knew anything she told her would not go out of her small bedroom. But Emily could not break her promise.

However, telling Amira she was sworn to secrecy would only raise more questions. "I know I can, and I do. But it is not as simple as that. If something changes and the opportunity presents itself where it is safe, I will tell you more. But I cannot do so right now. Besides, I need your help solving a bit of a mystery."

"A mystery?" Her eyes sparkled with excitement.

Perfect. "Yes. Well, perhaps espionage would be a more accurate term. I need to get eyes on my father's will without being seen."

Amira tapped her chin with a contemplative expression so serious it was almost comical. "That's going to be rather difficult." She bounced to her feet and headed towards the door, her radiance returning instantly. "But you know I'm always up for an exciting adventure."

"Let's hope this adventure isn't *too* exciting."

Amira paused as if she had forgotten something. Her plain skirt swished as she spun back around. "Can't you at least tell me who it was that found you?"

Emily grunted internally but was careful not to let the sound escape. Out of all the things she couldn't tell her, that was the foremost. Amira was not as easy to distract as she had hoped. "I told you, I am not at liberty to say."

"But why can't you tell me?" Amira pressed.

"Telling you why I can't tell you would involve telling you."

"But surely you can tell me *something*. Something little at least." She pinched her fingers together, leaving a tiny gap between them. "What harm could come in revealing a name?"

An entire kingdom could be found out and jeopardized and you would probably have a stroke. Not to mention Emily's own heart tore a little each time Luca crossed her mind.

"I can't." She tried, though not very hard, to keep the irritation out of her voice. Being pelted with questions was wearing down her patience. "And it's not relevant to the situation as I do not plan on ever seeing him again." She made herself keep talking so as not to feel the pain of that truth. "My focus now is to find out if what my uncle did was truly legal. To do that, I need to get my eyes on my father's will. Perhaps he's hiding something and I can claim my inheritance somehow."

Amira raised her eyebrows even as a smile tugged at the corner of her mouth and Emily wondered what was so amusing. "So it was a *him*, who rescued you?"

Oh, drat her loose tongue! Now would be an opportune time for the ground to open up and swallow her whole. "Amira, wipe that smirk off your face this instant! I know what you're thinking and it's not like that."

She waved the words away with her smile in place. "But it was a *gentleman* who rescued you, yes? That's quite romantic."

Emily wouldn't dignify that with any response other than an eye roll.

"Is he handsome?"

She quickly pressed her lips together so that the yes on the tip of her tongue wouldn't slip out. "That's an irrelevant question."

"I think it's a very relevant question."

"Fine. I suppose most women would find his features handsome."

"But do *you* find him handsome?"

Emily threw her arms up in exasperation. "Can we please focus? I have far more pressing things to worry about right now."

"Alright," she relented and wrapped her in another embrace. "Still, I'm happy you met someone, even under the unfortunate circumstances."

"I don't think it matters."

"I don't know about that. I think it may be good for you. Besides"—she shrugged—"you never know what could happen." She returned to the door. "I better go see to my chores before my family becomes suspicious. I hope to hear all the details eventually, but for now, I will leave you in peace."

The door clicked behind her, leaving Emily alone with her emotions once more. But peace was the last thing she was feeling.

20: In Repair

"That's the last of it," Coda said as he tossed the last of the ruined crops into a pile that was not as large as they'd feared it would be. "Thanks for your help."

"Of course," Luca replied. Yuni let him have the day off from his guard duties. She said it would be good for him to clear his mind after all that had happened. Though that was true, he found that sitting idle at the castle only provided the opportunity for his mind to wander to more dismal places.

He thought it would be better to do something useful and decided to help the citizens who were still repairing the damage the heavy rains had caused days ago. He spent the day cleaning mud off the vegetation that was salvageable, removing what was ruined, and digging trenches to drain off areas that still had standing water. They had even talked of planting cover crops over the soil after harvesting. It was an idea Emily had mentioned after consulting some agricultural books in the library.

Was this similar to how Emily spent her days when she went to Amira's farm? How she tried to busy herself while avoiding her wicked family?

He scolded himself. *You're not here to think about Emily.* He had quite the opposite intention, hoping that restoring the land would somehow put himself back together. He was already failing on that account.

"What will you do with what we pulled up?" He asked to distract himself more than anything.

Coda adjusted his straw hat. "I suppose I can take it to the barn and use it to feed the pigs. It won't be good for much else, but at least it won't be a total waste." He went to pick up the crops but Luca stopped him.

"Allow me."

"You don't have to trouble yourself, you've helped enough already."

He really did. The busier he was the less he would think of Emily. "It's no trouble at all."

As he went from one home to the next, he began to feel better. Not all his heartache was gone, but it felt good to do work with his own two hands for the place he loved so much. Not that he was usually lazy, he kept up riding and archery after all, but that felt like play. This was work—hard, sweaty, in the dirt, on-your-feet-all-day, physical work. He wasn't used to that but he found it very satisfying.

But the best part was working with the people. He was able to give them more than a passing glance or a greeting on the street. He was working right alongside them, learning about their family, their life experiences, their wisdom, and their humor. It was a camaraderie that you couldn't share with trees and mountains, no matter how beautiful they were.

He was sad to leave them behind as he made his way back to the castle. His boots squished in the still-damp earth. He paused along the trail and eased himself onto a fallen tree branch. His muscles felt instant relief at the reprieve.

Though his spirits had lifted somewhat, he wasn't ready to return to the castle just yet. The still and quiet rooms that used to be peaceful now held an emptiness—an emptiness caused by a single person's absence. He would have to get used to it, but the longer he could occupy himself otherwise the longer he could avoid the dreadful feeling that would bring him back down.

He plucked a leaf next to him. Maybe he could work at chopping and removing the branch. That should occupy him until sunset, at least.

"Luca?" Xandria's figure filtered through the greenery.

"Good evening."

"I was just on my way home from the market and I thought I recognized you. Though you look a little... different." She held back a laugh.

"I likely smell a little *different* too." He didn't need a mirror to know he was completely disheveled. Dirt was trapped under his fingernails, mud and grass stained his clothes, and his curls were likely in a particular state of catastrophe. "I've been working in the fields today, helping the neighbors with their remediation efforts after the last storm."

Anxiety touched her face. "How bad is it?"

"There is definitely some damage, but not as bad as I had feared. The Burroughs family took the worst blow, but they'll still have a harvest from what we salvaged. And they have enough food currently that should last them until then." He let out a breath of weariness and relief. "I think we're all going to be ok."

"Thank goodness," she breathed. "That was kind of you to help. How about a reward for your efforts?" She reached in her basket and held out a treat. "I brought back some mora berry muffins for Xanth and Papa. Would you like one?"

"That's alright, thank you though."

"They won't mind if I share," she insisted and wiggled the muffin in front of him.

"I know, but I'm not hungry."

"Alright then." She tucked it back into the cloth. "Is Emily around? I don't know if she's tried mora berries yet, but she might like one."

"No. She's not here." He paused but quickly decided it was best to get the explanation over with. She would know soon enough anyway. "She's in San Morrina."

Her dark brows pinched together. "She left?"

He nodded.

"The poor dear. I do worry for her. I had hoped she would stay...at least for a while."

So had he.

"Are you disappointed?"

He was about to go into the "I'm fine" speech he had come up with in preparation for these conversations. But one look at Xandria's keen eyes told him it wouldn't work. They were both observant and intuitive and she would see right through his lie. "I am, but I shouldn't be. I mean, we went years without seeing each other after all. I just..." He shrugged, struggling to convert his feelings into words.

"Feel differently about her now than you did the first time you were separated," she finished for him.

He stared up at her. "How did you know? I just found out myself."

"I noticed things." She smoothed out her skirt as she sat next to him. "You look at her with the same fondness in your eyes that Papa does with Mamma."

He sometimes thought he saw a fondness in Emily's eyes too. But he was wrong. "Not that it really matters. She obviously doesn't feel that way."

"Are you certain of that?"

"Well, she left, didn't she?" He left out the part where he asked her to stay and she refused.

"So she did, but perhaps for an entirely different reason. Maybe her feelings aren't so different from yours."

He sat up a little straighter. "Did she tell you so?" He dared to feel hopeful.

"No. She did not. But I have only met her once."

He slumped and cursed that too-eager spark of hope.

"Oh, I'm so sorry Luca." She laid a hand on his shoulder. "Does she know how you feel?"

Did she? Surely she sensed it. He never spoke the words explicitly but surely it was discernible in all he didn't say, in his actions. That night by the river understanding seemed to dawn on both of them. He wondered if his feelings were what scared her off.

But what if she didn't know? If he had told her, would she have returned his feelings? Would she still be here, sitting with him now?

He stood abruptly. "It doesn't matter now." He was tired of overthinking what he couldn't change. He couldn't change the past and he couldn't force her to stay. It was over. They were over.

"You keep saying that," she said gently, "but you act like it does matter. Very much, in fact. It's not too late to tell her. You could go find her and find out how she feels."

Go find her? People didn't leave Orphia. Why would they? Even if they did, he had an obligation to stay here. He could maybe send a letter, but he was too afraid of what the answer would be. He wasn't sure he could bear another rejection. "It might be better this way." That's what Yuni had reassured him. And he felt deeply indebted both to Orphia itself and to Yuni. He could not imagine leaving them behind. "I belong here in Orphia. This place rescued me and I have no desire to live anywhere else. And Emily cannot leave San Morrina. She very clearly gave the reasons why. We cannot be together without making the other person miserable."

Xandria listened calmly, remaining quiet for a ponderous moment before rising to her feet. "You have to do what you think is best. But whatever your choice is, just make sure it's one you'll feel content with without any regrets. If that's talking to Emily, I wish you the best. And if it's staying here, you will heal in time." She hugged him. "And please, come to us if you need anything. You are part of the family and we love you as one of our own."

He swallowed the lump in his throat. "I know, thank you."

She retrieved her basket from the ground and looked back over her shoulder. "Would you like to come over for dinner? I know it's last minute, but—"

"That's alright. I have some more work to do. Perhaps another night."

She nodded and bid him farewell.

Luca went out in search of an axe. The thought of hacking away at a big piece of wood sounded like a great way to expel some of his frustration. He planned on working himself to utter exhaustion so that when he returned to the castle he could simply collapse on his bed, and instantly fall into a deep sleep. Hopefully, without Emily haunting his dreams.

21: Checkmate

Having a selfish uncle had its benefits when it came to finding willing coconspirators to go up against him. Amira had delivered a note to Penny outlining the beginning stages of her plan and she was eager to help—especially since it meant possibly escaping the manor herself. Several other servants were quickly supporting the endeavor, though it had to be done with the utmost caution.

It was amazing, really. Emily could offer them little to nothing, but yet they supported her. Years of her kindness and respect had earned the loyalty that Uncle had failed to attain through simply paying their salary.

Through a series of clever distractions and some late-night searches, they were able to find and read her father's will. Penny met them at the outer edge of the market to relay the news, and Emily suspected to see for herself that she was good and well.

Emily was grateful for an opportunity to get outside. There was a risk of being caught, but she was about to go mad from being confined to a single room that wasn't her own for hours on end, even if it had only been a few days.

"The will is quite clear," Penny said. "It states you are to inherit everything in your father's accounts. And," she added with a grumble, "that your uncle was listed as the trustee and did have the legal right to oversee and withdraw funds until your twentieth birthday."

She nodded. "Well, at least my assumptions have been confirmed. Though it doesn't change much."

"There was something else we found that may be of interest." She glanced around them to make sure no one was near before pulling out a sheet of paper. On it was a list of names and transactions. Emily's eyes skimmed the list and stopped on an absurdly large sum. Amira peered over her shoulder and gasped at the amount. "This was from his ledger. It seems your uncle nearly emptied his coffers to a mysterious *D.S.*"

"And at a very convenient time." She pointed to the date of payment. It was not quite a month after her father's passing. Enough time for the legalities to have been settled and for him to have been granted access to her funds.

"That's not all," Penny continued. "There were some threatening letters demanding payment for a debt. They were all signed by a Mr. Daniel Santis."

"D.S." Amira whispered.

"Precisely."

Emily stared at the ledger in her hand. "A debt for what?"

"It didn't say, but Paul did some digging. Mr. Santis is well known for his skills at the card tables. He played at the same pub where your uncle used to frequent. Paul often drove him there himself, but your uncle was very stealthy about it."

Her mind started working through the facts. "When were the letters dated?"

"I don't remember exactly, but the first ones were a few months before your father died. The last were within days of the payment on the ledger." She cast her eyes downward. "I'm sorry I didn't get the letters for you, Miss. They were filed with some more recent paperwork and I was afraid he would notice if they were missing. I nearly got caught trying to snitch them."

She put a hand on her arm. "Do not apologize. You have been immensely helpful. Thank you and everyone else for your help. I know it's a huge risk."

Penny gave her a determined look. "If it means bringing that money-grubbing uncle of yours to justice after what he did to you, it will be well worth it."

Her plucky dedication brought a smile out of her. "I'm not getting my hopes up, but we will try."

"We'll find a way out of this mess, somehow." Penny's eyes darted around again and she quickly wrapped her arms around her in a hug. She looked a little embarrassed after her uncommon outburst of affection, as it was highly improper for a servant and her mistress. But Emily was grateful for it and gave her a reassuring smile before departing.

Emily recounted what she knew and began threading all the pieces together. Her father did indeed leave her everything and had it legally documented. Her uncle was a gambler, or at least used to be. She had proof of him paying a huge debt at a time he had access to her funds. Was any of that enough to warrant legal action?

"Amira, do you have any legal books at home?"

"I'm afraid not, at least not that I've ever seen."

"Then we'll have to get some."

They scoured the lending library and took any books they could find on legal matters back to Amira's room. Emily pored over the books, desperately trying to find something useful. She rubbed her eyes and wondered if they might shrivel up in their sockets from lack of moisture. How did Amira read for hours on end without taking a break?

It was quite iniquitous of her, but she actually wished her uncle had done something illegal. For if he had, she could hold him accountable. But from what she had read so far, he acted fully within his rights as trustee. It was beyond frustrating.

"Here's something," Amira said. "A trustee's rights may be revoked if he is deemed incapable or becomes unqualified to fulfill his responsibilities as decided by the court."

"Let me see that." She snatched the book from Amira's hands. Her finger followed the words as they entered her mind and ignited a spark of hope in her heart. "He would most definitely be considered incapable due to the gambling debt."

"That's wonderful!" Amira bounced in her seat on the edge of the bed. "We just have to take the paperwork to the courts and all will be settled!"

Emily looked at the torn page from the ledger and frowned. Reality squelched her hope as quickly as it sprung up. "We don't have proof."

"What do you mean?" Amira pointed to the paper in her hand.

"The transaction list alone does not state what the payment was for, nor the full name of the person it was paid to. Uncle could claim it was anything made to anyone."

Amira frowned. "Perhaps if you got the letters?"

"No. It's too risky. I have no wish to endanger the servants any more than I already have. Even if I had the letters in my possession, it only proves my uncle had a debt and it was paid. That's not enough to incriminate him."

Amira's optimism wouldn't let her give up so easily. She opened her mouth to speak but Emily stole her words. "And no, I highly doubt Mr. Santis will testify. And if he did, it's his word against Uncle's. We need proof and we don't have it."

"Then what are we to do?"

"There has to be something else." She kept turning pages, desperately looking for something. Anything. If she were to ever receive one of those miracles people said existed, she would gladly claim one now.

No. She could do this. Uncle was wrong, she was right. There had to be a way to expose the truth.

Know your opponent. Luca's words came unbidden into her mind. The words were helpful, the voice they belonged to echoing in her head was not. What was he doing at this very moment? Was he wondering about her?

She sent the wayward thoughts out of her mind. *Focus, Emily. Focus on the problem.*

She twirled her hair around her finger. *Know your opponent.* It worked for setting up a trap in chess, but...

She shut the book with a loud clap. "Amira, I think I have something that might work. What if—" A knock interrupted her speech.

"Mira," Hyacinth's muffled voice seeped through the door. "Can I come in?"

"Um, just a moment, Mother!" She silently shooed Emily away. She shimmied herself under the bed and had just concealed herself when the door opened.

"Hello dear, how was the market today?"

"Fine. Just fine. Just like any other day." Amira's voice was an octave or two higher than normal. "I brought back the vegetables you asked for."

"I saw that, thank you."

There was a moment of silence, but she heard no retreating footsteps yet.

"Sweetheart, is everything ok? You seem to have been acting a little out of sorts the last couple of days. You've hardly left your room other than when necessary."

"No, I'm fine. Perfectly fine. Everything's just fine," Amira said in her cheeriest voice.

"Is it because of Emily?"

Emily took in a sharp breath.

"E-Emily?" Amira's voice quavered. "What does Emily have to do with anything?"

"I know you're sad that she left. And likely worried too. But I'm sure she'll be back soon."

Emily hoped her pounding heart could not be heard in the silence.

"Oh, come here darling."

They must've sat down, for the bed above her creaked and shifted and nearly smothered her face. She held her breath. *Get her out of here Amira or I won't be able to breathe.*

"Is that a new book?" Hyacinth asked.

"Oh. Yes. Yes it is. I stopped at the library on my way home."

"That is quite a thick one. And it looks like you brought home some others too."

Amira chuckled nervously. "Oh, you know me."

The bed lifted from her face when they stood and Emily could breathe once more.

"And I'd better get started on that new book if I want to finish it. Thank you for the chat."

Emily closed her eyes, waiting to hear the door shut before crawling back out. It was quite dirty under the bed, and there were dust balls everywhere. One of them kept tickling her hand. She attempted to brush it off, but this dust ball had eight legs.

She jerked involuntarily and hit her head on the bed above her. She stifled a groan.

"What was that?" Hyacinth asked. "Mira, what's going on?"

"Um, I...well..."

Emily let out a sigh of defeat. They were caught and there was no point in trying to hide anymore. She slid out from her hiding spot and looked into Hyacinth's alarmed eyes.

She brushed herself off and told Hyacinth of her predicament and presented her idea to both of them. She was not angry at her for her secrecy—she seemed to understand the need for it after all that had occurred.

"Do you think it will work?" Amira asked.

"I don't know," Emily replied honestly. "But it's the only option I can come up with."

"We are here for you," Hyacinth added, wrapping her in a one-arm embrace. "And that will never change, no matter what happens." She placed a gentle kiss on her forehead, much like her own mother used to do when she was a little girl. They were kisses she had not gotten nearly enough of in her life.

She let out a shuddering breath. Before, she would have fought the emotion that bubbled inside her and force herself to be indifferent to it. But this time, she allowed herself to feel. She relaxed her head on Hyacinth's shoulder and melted into her embrace. She pulled her in tighter, and Amira's arm wrapped around her on the other side, enveloping her in a comforting warmth that only love can provide. Emily simply closed her eyes, forgetting her burdens for a moment, and relished in the contentment of being cared for by someone.

Someone she hadn't left behind.

***

"Miss Emily?" The butler greeted her with astonishment. He was one of the few servants that was loyally on Uncle's side, likely because he was nearly as arrogant as his master. In a blink, his surprise left and austerity returned as he put on what Amira liked to call his "butler face." He cleared his throat. "Miss Emily, I was not expecting you."

He had yet to invite her inside, but she pretended not to notice and walked in the door. This had been her home after all, she had every right to be here. "Thank you, Grisby. I have something of interest to speak with Uncle about. I imagine he'll want to see me."

He lifted his chin in the air. "Very well, Madam. Let me show you to—"

"I remember where the rooms are, Grisby. I'll wait in the parlor while you fetch him."

She recognized the exasperated look in his eyes, but he simply nodded and went on his search.

Her eyes traced the pattern of the wallpaper. Over and over she followed its intricate loops and swirls in an attempt to steady her nerves. She knew Uncle's response would not be kind. No one would guess from her calm and unaffected facade that she was trembling inside. But just because one didn't show an emotion didn't mean it wasn't felt with every fiber of their being.

She tried to bury those feelings as she clasped her hands together tightly. If only it was Luca holding her hand, then she might truly feel as calm as she appeared.

She quickly stuffed those confusing feelings away as well, as she did anytime thoughts of Luca brought them up.

The aggravated stomp of footsteps echoed on the marble floor of the hall and she braced herself. It was time.

Her uncle stood erect, his clothing impeccable and his form more imposing than usual. "Emily." He spat out her name in an accusing manner.

They entered a staring battle, sizing one another up. The ticking grandfather clock reverberated in the steely silence of the room.

"Hello, Uncle. A pleasure to see you too. I'm doing well, thank you for asking."

"What are you doing here?" He cut off each word with a harsh bite.

"Why, whatever do you mean?" She feigned a look of innocence. "That seems like a rather odd question to ask someone who has lived here for ten years."

"Not when you ran away."

"Oh yes, that. You mean when I ran off to my cousin's home? How long did it take to formulate that particular lie?"

"You endangered your reputation with your foolish act. That is what we said to protect you," he said through clenched teeth.

Good. She needed to push him to anger for her plan to work. But she had to walk a delicate line to push enough without pushing too far.

"Protect me?" She scoffed. "No. That is what you said to protect *your* reputation. After all, how would it appear to have a young, unmarried woman under your care flee to who knows where doing who knows what?" Was the act working? Was he falling for her confidence or could he tell her heart was threatening to pop right out of her chest and land at her feet? "You are right on one account though, it was a foolish and dangerous act. So how long did you search for me before enacting your cover story? A day? An hour? Or did you forgo the search altogether?"

"You continue to belittle all I have done for you." His nostrils flared. His patience was slipping quickly. He was dangerously close to snapping, perhaps she should back off just a tad.

"But do you deny it?" She removed the sarcasm from her voice, hoping he would take advantage of her seemingly vulnerable state. "You are the closest family I have left. I deserve honesty. Have you ever really cared for my well-being? Or were you just after my inheritance?"

He didn't answer.

"That was the real reason you kept me around, wasn't it? To take what was rightfully mine."

"You are a selfish brat just like your father!" He thrust his finger at her. "He wasted his life on drinking, a foolish pursuit. And yet you are the one who would get the money so you could grow up and do the exact same thing. I knew how to handle your funds properly. It was my responsibility to make sure history didn't repeat itself."

"And what folly would I have spent the funds on? *Gambling*, perhaps?" She emphasized the word suggestively.

He balled his hands into fists at his side.

"Yes, I took meals with you. I have a furnished room and enough dresses to get by. But that would barely make a dent in the inheritance I was to receive. The rest of it went towards your own foolish pursuits, didn't it?"

"You don't know what you're saying."

"Mr. Santis does."

His eyes flashed with an emotion she couldn't place, but it wasn't a pleasant one.

"It was, what, just under ten years ago? Rumor has it you were quite confident in your business endeavors and went off the deep end at the card table."

"How dare you accuse—"

"I can take you to court for that you know," she interrupted. "But I can spare you that if you would prefer to settle now."

He scoffed. "Do you think your word would stand over mine in court, hm? What proof do you have of such an outlandish story?"

He didn't need to know how little she had. "Enough that would surprise you," she said firmly.

She remained perfectly still, determined not to reveal anything as he determined whether or not to call her bluff. *Come on, take the bait.* Her jaw hurt from clenching it so tightly. His burning eyes bore into her, but she stood her ground against the flames.

Then a smirk broke across his face that gave her literal chills. "You're bluffing. You have nothing."

"What I have is nothing to lose." She refused to give in to him. "You, however, could lose a great deal where your reputation is concerned."

He raised his brows. "You think you have nothing to lose?" His voice was calm, yet somehow more menacing than when he was shouting at her. He casually sauntered to the door and shut it with a soft click.

She swallowed and her skin prickled all over. For as much as she disliked her Uncle, she had never been afraid of him before. But the vicious look of greed in his eyes was petrifying.

"I'll tell you something, I did used to gamble. Therefore, I learned a thing or two about risk. And the stakes here are much higher for you than your naive mind realizes."

He strode around the room with an eerie calmness. "Everyone knows of your father's poor judgment in his life. You run off into the woods like a madwoman. You start making baseless, outlandish claims against one of the most respected businessmen in the village. You think that would leave you unscathed?" He looked about the parlor carelessly, almost boorishly. He was trying to toy with her, like a cat playing with a mouse before devouring it. "People have been sent to mental asylums on less evidence."

Her blood chilled even as indignation boiled. She stepped toward him, forcing him to look at her once more. "You would dare do such a thing?" Her voice was not as steady as she had hoped. "You would send an innocent girl to such a place? Are you so greedy and wicked that you would subject your own flesh and blood to such unjust treatment?"

He came forward in two long strides and fiercely gripped her arms, making her gasp involuntarily. "Why would I care for the spawn of my worthless brother who was bound to end up just like him?" She closed her eyes to the spittle that flew in her face. "You listen to me. Even if you do have proof of my gambling, which I don't believe you do, it does not matter. For you will do absolutely nothing about it. Because know that if you dare spread such information I will make sure every minute of your life is miserable. Do you understand?"

"Then perhaps I will accuse you of mistreatment instead." She glanced at the fingernails that were digging into her forearms. He pushed her back as he released her and she stumbled into the table.

He laughed, his words dripping with disdain. "Again, no one would believe you! Where is your evidence? Where are your witnesses?"

When she felt she was far enough out of his reach she let a smirk spread over her face as she looked to the open window on the other side of the room.

He followed her gaze. Outside, behind the billowing white curtain, were Amira and Hyacinth, who had witnessed everything.

He scoffed. "Your friend and her mother? Hardly unbiased witnesses."

"Will the courts feel that way?"

"May I remind you that I am the landowner of their little farm? They could be out on the street tomorrow for any reason I see fit."

"You would blackmail me and them? Just to keep the ridiculous money?"

"I will when I deserve it!"

"And what will you threaten me with, Mr. Radcliffe?" A baritone voice spoke.

Uncle's face blanched as his business partner stepped into view from outside the window. "Barnewall. This, this isn't—" he stammered. "There has been a misunderstanding."

"Oh, I understand quite well. I know what I heard and saw. The threat to the safety of your niece and your tenants as well as your admittance to gambling away Miss Radcliffe's money was perfectly clear."

Uncle stood motionless. His mouth hung open but any words he might've spoken seemed caught in his throat.

"Tell me, will *my* word stand in court? What do you think?"

Emily had never seen her smug uncle look so thoroughly defeated. It proved to be quite a satisfying sensation. She was unsure if he would stay mute, explode, or go into apoplexy.

She would never find out, however. Mr. Barnewall whispered something to Hyacinth and her and Amira walked away. He then looked at Emily and nodded towards the door, indicating she should take her leave as well.

Back outside, the three of them walked back to the farm, relief flooding through Emily's body. The battle was not quite over, but she now had the upper hand. Perhaps it would end with her as the victor after all.

22: Memories in Paper

Mr. Barnewall was just as kind and upright as Emily had perceived and he was adamant about seeking justice for her. He spoke with Uncle in her behalf who agreed to a settlement which meant they would not have to take the time to go to court. Within a week, they signed the paperwork entitling her to the full amount of her inheritance. Half was due immediately and what remained was to be paid within the next year. The money received would be enough for her to let the small cottage she had been looking at. She could scarcely let herself believe such wonderful things were finally happening to her.

"Can you believe it? Your time has come at last!" Amira exclaimed.

"I know. After all these years, I never have to step foot in that house again."

"So, what happens now?" Amira asked before sipping her tea.

"Well, I've already spoken with Mr. Waldron about letting the cottage. Penny has happily agreed to come with me. I'm just waiting on the paperwork to be finalized and then I can move in."

"You will still come and visit me, won't you?"

"Of course." She looked over the top of her sketchbook with a sly smile. "After all, someone has to do your chores."

Amira laughed and Emily sketched the scene out her window. Her nerves were settled enough that she could take pleasure in the activity again.

"What are you drawing?" Amira leaned over the table and Emily held her book back.

"I'm not done yet."

"Oh, come now. I just want to peek."

Emily gently pushed her arm away. "You can wait."

She crossed her arms. "I hate waiting."

Emily rolled her eyes and stifled a laugh. "I know you do, which is why I give you opportunities to practice your patience. You should be thanking me."

"Hmmph."

Leaving Amira to stew along with her tea, she went back to work. Her pencil scratched against the paper as she worked on the tree's shadow.

"Oh goodness!" Amira shrieked. "What is that?"

Emily jumped and the pencil flew from her fingers. "What?" She looked around to see what scared Amira. Hopefully it wasn't a spider.

In one swift movement, Amira stood, snatched the book from Emily's hands, and hurried out of the room.

"Amira!" Emily went after her. "Get back here!"

Their skirts rustled as she chased her through the kitchen, nearly running into her great aunt Eloise carrying the tea kettle. Amira side-stepped her to avoid the collision and Emily paused to apologize. Eloise waved it off and she heard her laugh before continuing the chase.

"Amira!" Emily shouted to no avail. It was too late to abandon the childish game now.

She followed her back into the bedroom where Amira was eyeing the drawing approvingly. "Emily, this is beautiful! Why didn't you want me to see it?"

She shut the door behind her to prevent escape. "Because it wasn't finished."

"Well then, I'll just have to look at some of your finished drawings."

Emily's eyes went wide. She didn't care all that much if she saw her unfinished landscape. But the other drawings...

"Give me back my sketchbook."

Amira was already flipping pages. "I'm not done looking yet."

She crossed to the other side of the room. "Amira," she growled and reached for it but Amira held it high up above her. Curse her and her long arms.

"Is that a squirrel?" She turned the book toward Emily while keeping it out of reach. The page was the sunburst squirrel from Orphia. The sketch was black and white, but the long tail looked unusual.

"Yes. I got my proportions wrong on that one. Now you know why I would like my sketchbook back. *Now.*"

Amira turned the page as Emily jumped to retrieve her stolen property. She held onto one half, Amira the other, as it opened to the exact page Emily was trying to hide.

Drat.

Amira lifted an eyebrow. "Who is this?"

Emily stared at the page. Luca didn't realize at the time that she was drawing his profile. She wasn't sure why she did it, she didn't usually draw people. But she couldn't help trying to capture Luca's likeness on paper. She didn't want to forget the way that one curl hung over his forehead or how his freckles dotted his face like stars. She wanted to immortalize the curve of his mouth when he unleashed his smile so that she could always keep it with her when she needed one of her own.

"He's...a friend," she replied.

Amira's mouth formed a perfect O. "This is him, isn't it? Your mysterious rescuer!"

In her excitement, Emily pulled the book away from her. "It doesn't matter."

"Is it true to likeness? If so he really is quite handsome. He has a familiar look about him, though I cannot quite place where I may have seen him. Perhaps I will make the connection when I meet him."

"Meet him? When and why would you meet him?"

"Surely you will introduce me to the man who saved your life," she stated as if it were the most obvious thing in the world.

"I told you, I don't plan on seeing him again. He found me, gave me shelter, and returned me home. That's it. The end." She snapped the book shut and shoved it underneath the pillow. "Sorry it's not the fairytale ending you're accustomed to."

Amira said nothing but looked at her most inquisitively. Emily had never seen her look at anyone in such a manner before. She sat on the bed and gestured for Emily to do the same. "Tell me about him."

"There's nothing more to tell. I already explained to you that—"

"I know, I know. It's imperative that it remains a secret for some strange reason. You don't have to tell me who he is or where he is. Just tell me what he's like."

She furrowed her brow. "Why?"

"Because I'll just keep pestering you until I learn something about this mysterious gentleman."

Talking about Luca was a horrible idea. She shouldn't say anything considering she was trying to forget him. She kept telling herself that she would rather forget him and wished they had never met again in the first place.

And yet, she kept the sketch of him. And the notebook he gave her. And the wildflower pressed between its pages that he gave her that first day in Orphia. Just like how she claimed to want to forget her parents but couldn't bring herself to throw out the things that reminded her of them.

"What? Does he secretly turn into a monstrous ogre at midnight or something?"

Amira's comment caught her so off guard that Emily threw her head back and laughed. She appreciated the momentary levity.

She was surprised to see, upon recovery, that Amira looked completely shocked at her outburst.

"What is it?"

"You...you laughed," she said incredulously.

"Of course I laughed. How could I not laugh at such absurdity? You intended to be humorous, not to receive a legitimate answer, did you not?"

"Of course, it's just..." Goodness, Amira looked positively emotional now. "I've missed hearing you laugh."

Whatever did she mean? "I laugh."

"No, you really don't. You get amused sometimes and maybe let out a light chuckle here and there. But you haven't truly laughed like that in years."

Emily was stunned. Had she been so burdened that she stopped laughing without even realizing it? Had she stuffed even her pleasant emotions inside?

"But since you've gotten back you've been different," Amira continued. "I can't say how exactly, but you just seem more genuine. You smile more readily despite what you've been through. You're more like the Emily I met as a child." She smiled with a tear in her eyes. "I've missed her."

Emily suddenly felt choked up but she kept the tears at bay. She had no idea how to respond to that.

Fortunately, Amira kept on so she didn't have to. "Now, tell me about him. Please."

Emily kept her eyes down, lacing her fingers through each other. Truth be told, she did want to speak about him even though it would likely deepen the pain in her heart.

"He's very kind. He made sure I felt welcome. For once, I didn't feel like I was burdening anyone."

Amira nodded. "What else?"

"He can be quite amusing at times," she laughed lightly as she thought of him teasing her, coaxing her on the swing over the cliff. "He is compassionate and understanding...no, it was more than that. He understood me better than I understood myself." Though difficult to speak at first, the words now seemed to flow with ease. And her heart wasn't constricting like she thought it would. "I don't know how to explain it, but he could sense when something was bothering me and knew what I needed without my voicing it. He continually put my comfort ahead of his own. He is charming, and caring, and..." she paused, as the realization struck her heart like a hammer.

"And what?"

"And I repaid it with cruelty," she admitted. She had accused him of being the exact opposite of everything she had just mentioned. And in the heat of that moment, she had believed it. But those assumptions were about a boy she never met, one who was hurting and unloved. But the man she had come to know while in Orphia was everything a gentleman should be and more. "I was unfair to him. I spoke so foolishly. I feel ashamed of myself for it." She hung her head.

"Oh, Emily." Amira patted her hand. "I don't know what you said, or even the name of the man you spoke to, but I know you and you are anything but foolish." She let out a theatrical sigh. "But alas, we are all fools in love."

"Love?" The mention of the word unleashed a fluttering feeling in her stomach. "I never said anything about love."

"You didn't have to. I think it's rather obvious."

Her friend had many fanciful ideas, but this one was preposterous. She couldn't be in love with Luca. "Amira, the time I spent in his company is not long enough to fall in love. Not in the real world." And yet, just the notion of being in love with him set her heart racing.

"Perhaps not yet, but you may be well on your way to that. Be honest with yourself, listen to your heart."

She let out a short, sardonic laugh. "Following my heart is the last thing I want to do. Losing my head is what got me into this whole mess."

"Hold on, before you start throwing daggers at me let me clarify." She held up her hands in innocence. "I did not say follow your heart, I said listen to it."

That explanation was no clearer than stable muck.

"I may enjoy romance novels, but I am not completely daft. I realize following your heart is not always the answer."

She scooted closer and took both of Emily's hands in hers. "For as long as I've known you, which has been a very long time, you've always used your head. That's not a bad thing, for you're very intelligent. But you have a heart for a reason, and it's stronger than you think. It's not good to go through life constantly throwing your feelings aside. For the first time in a while, it sounds like you've acknowledged your feelings. And though it hasn't gone perfectly, you seem the better for it. So, find out what's in your heart—listen, hear it out. Then use that information and find the balance between what's in there, and what's in here." She tapped her head.

Emily let the uncharacteristic wisdom sink in. "The logical choice isn't always the right one," she said under her breath.

"Exactly."

She narrowed her eyes. "When did you get so wise?"

She shrugged. "I read things other than fiction you know." She hugged her friend. "And if this mysterious hero of yours is in there"— she gestured to Emily's heart—"then I'm sure you'll find a way to work things out. And I hope you do."

Emily thought of her parting words to Luca that night instead of sleeping. She was wrong in what she said, but what could she do? She could apologize, but then what? That wouldn't change their situation. Though the mess with Uncle was nearly behind her, she still had many things that kept her here. She would have her cottage soon. Amira's family was here. She grew up here, she belonged here. And he belonged there, in the world that saved him and made him happy.

Even if they could be together, would he want that? Did she? To love means to be vulnerable, and that leads to pain. Love destroyed her father. She wasn't sure if she was capable of trusting someone enough to let herself love in that way. No, Luca deserved so much more than she was capable of giving.

But as she stared up at the ceiling, the darkness of night shrouding her, she remembered Amira's speech. She could not deny that, despite all those facts, Luca held a significant grip on her heart.

***

Emily sat by the window with tea in one hand and a book in the other. Her things were all moved into the cottage and she was now able to truly enjoy it.

She took great pleasure in running her own home. It was not extravagant like her previous residence at the manor, which made her love it all the more. It was cozy, simple, and comfortable.

It was also very empty.

Penny came with her as a maid-of-all-work, but they were not always in each other's company. She was often left to her own pursuits, especially in the evenings.

Solitude never bothered Emily before—she quite often relished it. Even just moments ago, she enjoyed reading up on gardening and learned several things she wanted to implement. But as she turned the last page and set the book on the table beside her, the stillness of the room came upon her in an unsettling manner. It was like the empty room echoed a void inside of her, a continual reminder of how alone she really was.

Her gaze drifted to the window. The darkness of night had not yet fully settled over the village, but the last remainders of sunlight were hiding behind the clouds. The light spring rain kissed the glass pane, forming little rivulets that slowly made their way downwards. It was this kind of rain that she loved the most, but tonight it seemed more like a gentle weeping.

After years of planning, she had exactly what she wanted. It was everything she had dared to hope for. And yet it felt so...unfulfilling.

Soft footsteps alerted her to Penny's presence. "This came for you, Miss. It's from Mr. Carvey's office. The paperwork you requested along with some things they found while going through your father's records."

Emily took the papers in her hand. "Thank you."

She bobbed a curtsy "Of course, Miss."

She raised her brows and gave her a scolding look. "Penny..."

She smiled. "Of course, *Emily.*"

She smiled back. "That's better." Penny was a true friend to her through the years in her Uncle's home. She very much wished to continue that friendship and insisted they be on a first-name basis.

"I agree," Penny continued. "But old habits are hard to break." She left the room.

Grateful to have something to occupy her mind with, Emily began perusing the papers. There was the lease agreement, a copy of Father's will, her copy of the settlement, more bank papers, and—

Her whole body froze as she uncovered the last paper. This was no legal document. It was folded like a missive with her name scrawled across the front. She could not have been more shocked by the handwriting, though she recognized it immediately. It was her father's.

The crackling fire called out to her, telling her to burn it. She could pretend it never existed and move on. But what if it was important? And even if it wasn't, what on earth could it contain? It had to have been written years ago.

She stared at it for several paralyzing moments before shaking her head. *Quit being such a ninny. It's only a letter.*

She retook her seat with a huff and slid her finger beneath the seal. Her eyes jumped to the date. It was written just a few weeks before his death.

My Dearest Daughter,

I have penned this note more times than I can count trying to find the right words to say to you. Everything I try to say falls vastly short compared to the depth of my feelings. Still, I must try to convey them to you the best that I can, for I am beyond ashamed of myself. This last year, perhaps even longer, I have not been the father I should have been.

You know I am away on business, but there is another purpose for my trip. I am tired of being a slave to my vices. I brought it upon myself and I don't know if I shall ever be fully liberated, but I am trying. I am seeking advice from a doctor here and thus far I have gone three days without a single drink. It is a pitiful victory, but a victory nonetheless. He suggests that I extend my stay at least a few more weeks to reduce the risk of relapse. I want you to know that my prolonged absence is not due to willful neglect. I long to be back with you, the light of my life, though I am not worried. You are more than capable to care for yourself as you are wise beyond your years.

Most importantly, I find the need to make amends with you. In my lucid moments I have realized how much my poor actions have affected those I love, you first and foremost. I know "sorry" is not enough to express my remorse, but my dear Emily, I truly am sorry. I'm sorry for all the pain I have caused you. I'm sorry for not providing for you like a father is supposed to. And I'm sorry for stealing away your innocent childhood. I cannot give any of that back to you, though I wish I could. The past is gone, but I hope I can be a bigger part of your future.

Falling tears soaked into the paper. The words were dredging up so many feelings from her past that had long been forced into dormancy. But she couldn't bring herself to stop. She wiped the blur from her eyes and kept reading.

The day your mother died crushed us both. I was so caught up in my grief that I didn't consider your own, and added to it in the process. Your mother was everything a parent should be, everything I haven't been for you. If I could bring her back, take her place so she could be with you, I would. As it is, I can only offer myself. Do you even want me after all I've done? I cannot blame you if you don't. But maybe it would be good enough. Maybe I can finally start being the father you deserve. For no man on earth could ask for a better daughter than you.

Though I have given you ample reason to doubt it, please know that my love for you has never wavered. I love you, my dear. I always have, I always will, with my whole heart.

Your Hopeful Father,
Benjamin Radcliffe

Memories of the father of her childhood flooded her mind. How he used to carry her on his shoulders. The strong hands that would lift her in the air, but were gentle when he brushed the hair out of her eyes. The softness in his eyes anytime he looked at her and Mother. The bristly feel of his mustache when he kissed her cheek.

She heaved a sob. The letter crinkled in her clutched hand as she doubled over in her chair. She felt the loss of both her parents acutely, nearly as painful as the day they both left her.

She spent so many years angry at her father. She assumed he didn't care enough to even notice he had hurt her. But in his letter, he didn't make excuses or try to justify himself. And he was trying to do what he could to fix his errors. How could that not be sincere?

Do you even want me after all I've done? That one question seared through the ropes that had been holding years of resentment, anger, and pain close to her heart, setting them free and letting them fall away from her.

"Yes," her shaky whisper barely reached her own ears. She would have welcomed him with open arms to have the father she knew as a little girl with her again. She never wanted a perfect father, just one that loved her. All she ever wanted was to see some sign of the man he used to be. And through this letter, she had it.

She retired early, barely having the energy to walk to her bedroom. Though her heart still hurt, she felt as if a weight had been lifted from it. Forgiveness lifted a heavy burden she did not even know she carried.

Perhaps second chances were worth taking. For she would give almost anything to have another chance with her father. But he was gone, and she would never get the opportunity to tell him how she felt.

But somewhere on the other side of the forest, there was someone she cared for. Someone who was not taken away from her life yet. If she stood any chance with him, she was determined not to let it slip away.

23: Decision and Alarm

Luca had another fitful night's sleep and exited the castle before sunrise. He didn't have a route planned, he just wanted to get outside for a while. He barely acknowledged the chirping crickets or the residual dampness in the air from last night's rain. He just kept walking.

He had changed a lot in the month since Emily left. True, he continued his guard duties, riding with Xanth, and his archery lessons just as before. But he had also made an effort to be more involved in the community. He was getting to know the people of Orphia better, their stories, their livelihood, and even their problems.

It opened his eyes and revealed he had been living in ignorance for a long time. Orphia was beautiful, yes, but it was not a magical place that fixed everyone's problems. It saddened him to see the various trials people faced, but he was grateful that the knowledge lent him the ability to help them through it, or at least lend a listening ear to those who needed it. It gave him a greater sense of purpose in his life.

And yet a piece of him still felt empty. He knew it was a piece of his heart that Emily had taken with her.

No matter how busy he was, his thoughts always wandered back to her. Was she safe? Did she resolve things with her family? Did she miss him like he missed her? His feelings for her had changed alright, but only in intensity. They were stronger than ever.

His feet automatically took him to the river. He stood at the edge of the cliff and stared at the sparkling waters below. The perpetual blackness before dawn made the river fireflies stand out all the more. It was as beautiful and serene as ever, but he didn't feel at peace. The last time he was here, he wasn't alone.

He lowered himself into the dirt, sitting with his thoughts for a while as the earliest lights of dawn began to shine through. He could clearly picture the way Emily's eyes lit up when she saw the river. She was just as entranced by the sight as he was, and her wonder-filled eyes outshone the glittering waters.

He didn't regret sharing this place with her, but it would never be the same to him. He no longer thought of it as his place. It was also her place—*their* place. A shared memory that was seared into his mind and heart forever. Much like the myth itself, their story was both beautiful and heartbreaking.

How had she made such an impact on him in that short period of time? The beauty of Orphia, its sights and creatures, used to be all he wanted and more. It used to mesmerize him. But now it felt dull without her to share it with.

He hurled a rock in frustration, sending it into the water with a splash. She wasn't here. She decided to leave and there was nothing he could do about it.

But then again, he could do something. He could not decide for her and force her to stay, but he always had a choice. He had thought about going after her before, but something always held him back. Anxiety, uncertainty, fear. But staying behind wasn't making him happy.

He scrubbed his face. His mind was a complete mess. What did Emily say she did when she felt that way? She made a list. Perhaps he should give that a try.

Lacking paper, he grabbed a stick and drew two rectangular columns in the dirt. On his left would be reasons to stay. To his right, reasons to go.

He started with the left. He would be leaving behind Yuni, his assignment, his friends, and of course the beautiful place he called home. But mostly, it was fear holding him back. Fear of the unknown, fear of failure, fear of running into his old roommates from the orphanage, fear of ridicule after being gone so many years, and fear of rejection. The stick scraped the dirt as he drew his last tally mark. He had at least 9 reasons to stay.

Now why he should go. There was really only one reason: Emily.

He stared at the single line and frowned. If the choice was so clear-cut, why was he disappointed? He amended his list and began to add all the reasons why he wanted to return to Emily.

She had an intelligent mind and a sharp wit. Her dry humor made him laugh. Though she downplayed her looks, he found her quite pretty. He even added an extra tally mark for her adorable dimple.

But there was so much more to her than that. She was kind and selfless. She added meaning to his life, giving him someone to care for and protect. Her reasonableness balanced him out. She was brave and faced her fears in a way that made him want to be stronger. Yes, that's what he loved most of all—she inspired him to try and be a better person. She made him better.

Soon the right column was filled with tally marks that made the other shrink in comparison. The right choice was plain to see. He smiled and silently thanked the river, its sparkles now replaced by the sun's reflection. Coming here always gave him the clarity he needed.

He had wasted enough of his life running from the past. Now, he would run towards his future, towards Emily. Because he knew with newfound clarity that she was his future.

He bolted back to the castle stables and saddled Onyx. He put one foot in the stirrup and hesitated. He should probably tell Yuni where he was going. She would worry about him otherwise and it wouldn't be right to just abandon her. Emily would want him to be considerate. But consideration could be quick.

He left Onyx in the paddock and ran to the front of the castle. He rushed to the doors right as they opened and almost plowed into Yuni.

"Luca!"

"Sorry!" He stumbled back and gulped in a breath. "But I'm glad I found you. I have to go."

"Go? Go where?"

"To Emily."

"Emily?" Her brow pinched in confusion. "Has she returned?"

"No." He rushed through his reply until he was nearly breathless. "Yuni, I've been an idiot. I never told her how I feel. I have to talk to her. I have to see her. It's all so clear now."

"Whoa, now. Slow down." She spoke to him as if he were a runaway horse. "You're saying you're going back to San Morrina?"

"Yes."

"For how long?"

"I...don't know." He hoped he could still return to Orphia. But even if he could not, his decision would remain. He realized now it didn't matter where he was. As long as he was with her, he'd be happy. "If she'll have me, I hope to return with her. But if she can't leave then I'm willing to stay with her there."

"And what if she won't have you? What if she doesn't want to see you after all that transpired? I don't want to see you get hurt."

"I don't know." He paused and sighed, then took up his confident stance again. "But I have to find out one way or another."

He wasn't content to just stand still. Energy pulsed through him, begging him to move. Without really thinking about it, he began walking out the door with Yuni keeping pace with him.

"Dear, you should not do anything rash."

"I'm not being rash. I've spent a whole month waiting to be happy again. I know this is what I have to do."

Yuni placed a hand on his shoulder, halting his progress. His impatience was eating at him, but he tried to be gracious for Yuni's sake.

"You haven't been to San Morrina in years. It sounds like everyone thinks you're dead. What will you say to them?"

"I don't know, but I've been hiding all my life. Hiding from people, from my past, from myself, from everything. I'm sick of it, and I refuse to do so anymore."

Yuni's eyes were wide with panic and he felt a twinge of remorse for causing it. She took good care of him in the latter years of his life, after all. But he was a grown man, and he had to set out on his own path. One, he hoped, that involved having Emily by his side.

He sought to keep his voice gentle. "I know you're concerned, but I have to do this. I need her, I need to see her again. Nothing's been the same...I haven't been the same without her."

Yuni looked at him for a long moment and he resisted the urge to pull away from her. She let out a sigh, resignation in her eyes. "You are quite determined to do this, aren't you?"

"I am."

"I was afraid this would happen someday," she said quietly, almost to herself. "Please, wait here a moment, will you? I...I have something for you before you go."

"Very well."

She gestured to a low tree limb and he sat on it. "Wait here, I'll be back in a moment."

He had no idea what could be so important for him to wait for, but he obeyed. He tapped his fingers on his leg as he waited, his thoughts staying on Emily. He was nervous, to say the least. He didn't know how she would take his arrival, but he was hopeful things would turn out well. It couldn't be too terrible, they were friends after all. Perhaps they could finally be something more.

***

Emily never imagined she would have run off into the woods once, let alone twice. But this time she was equipped with a horse, food, a compass, and a much better purpose.

After half an hour or so of searching, she breathed a sigh of relief upon spotting a lone treehouse in the middle of the woods. She sped up her mare towards Luca's guard post, hoping he was inside.

Her nerves resurfaced as she climbed the steps. What if he wasn't happy to see her? What if he was angry? No, Luca was kind. Even if he was upset with her, he would be kind about it. She rapped her knuckles on the door and waited.

No response.

"Luca?" She knocked again. "Luca, are you in there?" There was still no answer.

He must have been out making his rounds. He would come back eventually and she would be here waiting for him when he did. She only hoped she was not too late to make amends with him.

She climbed back down and found a low tree branch to sit on. For a moment, she just took in the beauty of the forest around her. She admired how the color green could have such a variety of shades. The smell of pine mixed with damp earth saturated her senses. She smoothed her hair back as the charms of nature settled over her and calmed her.

The sound of a galloping horse sent a tingle of excitement and nerves down her spine. She looked expectantly, longing to see Luca's freckled face and chocolate eyes.

Instead, she was greeted with fiery red hair and green eyes.

"Oh, hello Xanth." She hoped she didn't sound too disappointed.

"Emily?" His usually jovial face was replaced with a more solemn expression. "What are you doing here?"

"I came to talk to Luca. Have you seen him?"

He looked at her with confusion. "Wait...you mean he's not with you?"

"No," she drew out the word slowly. "Why would he be with me? He's not at his guard station so I'm assuming he's on duty." The impatient horse beneath Xanth snickered, and she eyed the black steed with alarm. "Isn't that Onyx? Why are you riding him?"

He looked equally alarmed. "I think Luca is missing."

24: Shining Light on a Dark Truth

Emily's blood went cold. "What happened?"

"I went to the castle to see him and was told he left to go to San Morrina."

He was returning? He had seemed adamant about never setting foot there again. Could it be he was returning for her? Did he miss her too?

She gave herself a hard mental slap. *Now is not the time to daydream, you need to focus on the problem at hand.* "So is he truly missing or has he just gone away to San Morrina?"

"I thought he went to San Morrina, but..." His pale cheeks colored. "Well, it's kind of embarrassing now, but I was irritated that he left without telling me or saying goodbye. So I decided to go for a ride and I figured I'd just use one of the castle horses since I was already there. That's when I saw Onyx, saddled in the paddock with no rider in sight."

She reflected for a moment. "Were any of the other horses missing?"

"I don't think so, but it doesn't matter. Luca always rides Onyx. They're practically attached to each other. No one else rides him...until now, that is."

Emily thought it best to keep her ride with Luca on Onyx a secret for the moment. There were more pressing things to attend to. "Well, if he didn't go on horseback then where would he be?" Perhaps someone was mistaken and he hadn't left at all.

"I have no idea. I just started riding kind of hoping I would find him along the way. There's no way he could've gotten this far by walking, but I didn't know what else to do."

"This isn't good." She tried to ignore the panic rising in her chest. She needed to maintain her equilibrium now more than ever before.

She mounted her horse and followed Xanth back to Orphia. "How long has he been gone?"

"I guess not too long. Yuni said he had left just this morning."

"Yuni is the one who informed you of his departure?" Surely she wouldn't be mistaken on his whereabouts.

"Yes."

"Did she see him leave? Did she escort him out?"

"She didn't say. I guess not."

That struck her as odd. "She escorted me out personally when I left. I can't imagine her not doing the same for Luca." He had always said how protective Yuni was of him. Surely, she wouldn't have let him out of her sight so easily. "How did Yuni act?"

"What do you mean?"

"Did she seem upset? Or sad? Or worried?"

He thought for a moment. "Not really. She seemed a little...surprised? Maybe flustered to see me. But other than that, she was normal."

"Hmm." She would've expected a more emotional reaction from Yuni.

Something was bothering her, and it wasn't just Luca's disappearance. Something about the scenario kept nagging at her, begging to be noticed. But she couldn't put her finger on it. "Did she say anything else?"

Xanth ducked under a tree branch. "Not much. I asked where Luca was. She said, *'He didn't tell you?'* and I said, *'Tell me what?'* Then she said he decided to go back to San Morrina to find you and wasn't sure if he would be returning."

Her heart flipped in her chest. He *was* coming back for her. She would've been thrilled by this news under normal circumstances. But he was missing and possibly in danger. And if something happened to him because of her, she would never forgive herself.

Don't let it come to that. Think this through. Emily forced her mental faculties into order. "Ok, let's go back to what we know. Luca intended to ride Onyx somewhere but didn't, which is very odd. He was not riding bareback, so he must have intended to go somewhere fairly distant, presumably San Morrina. No other horses were missing, so we can conclude that Luca did not ride anywhere. Based on that information, we can deduce a few possibilities. Either something happened before he left the castle grounds, he went somewhere within walking distance, Yuni was simply mistaken, or..." Her breath hitched as panic slid over her.

No. It couldn't be. She tried to shake off the treasonous thought but it held fast, clinging to her mind like a wet cloak.

"Or what?"

Or Yuni wasn't telling the truth. She thought back on her interactions with Yuni and some of Luca's comments to see if the possibility fit. Someone lied when they were hiding something. What would Yuni have to hide?

"Hold on, Xanth." She brought her horse to a stop. "How long has Yuni been queen?"

"I think it's been around eight years."

"Immediately after her brother died, yes?"

"Right. She was next in line for the throne. I guess the only one in line, actually."

Dread steadily pooled in her stomach. "Did anyone other than Yuni witness his death? Was a body found?"

"I don't think so. He was pushed off a steep cliff." He furrowed his brow. "What are you getting at?"

Her skin prickled all over with goosebumps. "I..." She forced the words out of her dry throat, "I think Yuni might have lied about her brother's cause of death. Which means she may be lying about Luca as well."

Xanth stared at her, clueless for a moment. But the moment her words registered, his face blanched. "Wait, you don't think that she..."

"I know from experience that even blood family can be cruel if the motivation is strong enough. So yes, I think it's a possibility that she went to extreme measures to secure the throne for herself."

Xanth's jaw hung open as he began to process what she said. "But...but he was her brother! And she rescued Luca and raised him like a son! Why would she...how could she..." He was too stunned, or perhaps too afraid, to finish any of his thoughts aloud.

"I don't know. Maybe I'm wrong. Goodness, I hope I'm wrong. But if I'm not, Luca might be in serious danger."

Xanth spoke in earnest. "We have to save him."

She squeezed her eyes shut. How on earth could they save him? If she was right and Yuni was capable of everything Emily feared she was, what chance did they have of beating her at her own game?

Luca's warm brown eyes flashed in her mind. He didn't give up on her when she needed him, despite her insistence otherwise. Now he needed her. She left him behind once, she would not turn back on him again.

Adrenaline swelled in her as panic turned into determination. "We *will* save him."

***

Luca's head lay against a cold hard surface. The vague sounds of dripping water slowly saturated his foggy mind.

He finally opened his eyes, and a set of iron bars were before him.

He shot up and winced. The back of his skull throbbed and the sudden movement made his stomach turn. He sat still until the wave of nausea passed, trying to make sense of what happened—or rather what was happening.

The last thing he remembered was sitting outside the castle right before blackness clouded his vision. Now he was locked away somewhere, but he couldn't recall how he got here. *Please let this just be a terribly realistic nightmare.*

Once it felt safe to stand, he grabbed the iron bars and gave them a firm tug, then a push. Sure enough, they were very real and unfortunately sturdy. He kept shaking the bars anyway, but it was in vain.

He groaned in frustration as he thrust himself away from them. He wiped his dirty hands on his trousers before placing his face in them. "I've got to get out of here," he mumbled.

"I've been seen saying that for eight years, boy."

The deep voice startled him. Only a few lanterns and torches hanging along the wall lit up the confines. He peered through the gloomy darkness and saw the figure of a man in a cell across from him.

He was probably middle-aged, though his large beard and unkempt hair made it difficult to determine with any certainty. He had a trim frame that, while not scrawny, seemed too thin to be his intended physique given his broad shoulders. His eyes were dark and shadowed and they somehow looked familiar.

"You must be Luca."

The shock at his familiarity cut through any lingering fogginess of mind. "How do you know that?"

"Yuni spoke about you at length."

"You mean, Yuni knows I'm here?" If she knew where he was, why was he still there? Why had she not sought to release him?

"You don't know," he said quietly. No amount of darkness could hide the pity in this mysterious man's eyes. "My boy, Yuni brought you here."

"What?" Yuni did this? Was this some weird punishment of hers, trying to convince him to stay behind? It was a bit extreme. "Where are we?"

"The castle dungeon."

The nightmare was getting worse. "I didn't even know there was a dungeon."

"It's not something that's publicized. Only the royal family knows of its existence."

He snapped his head in his direction again. "Who are you?"

He heaved a heavy sigh. "Yes, allow me to introduce myself. I am Aspen, former king of Orphia."

25: A Story Retold

Xanth and Emily rushed back to the castle and Emily wondered whose heart was beating faster, her mare's or her own. She knew worrying over Luca would not make him safer, but her heart and mind were not listening to each other much lately.

They stopped at a part of the forest that abutted the castle property. "So, what's our plan?" Xanth whispered.

Emily took a few calming breaths before responding. "We find Luca without being discovered by Yuni or the servants, free him from wherever he is, and escape. Preferably unscathed."

He raised his eyebrows and tilted his head. "Ok, I like that plan."

"Carrying it out is the hard part. First, we have to find out where he is." She peered through the foliage, trying to get a glimpse of the castle. "How do we get in there without getting caught?" Emily mumbled. "You know the castle well, are there any secret entrances? Or somewhere else we can slip in discreetly?"

Xanth shook his head. "Not that I know of. There's only the front entrance and a side door. Both constantly guarded."

"Of course." That would've been far too convenient. "Perhaps...no, that won't work either." She was going to suggest some sort of distraction. But the odds of that succeeding were low, and even if it did work they would have to rely heavily on luck to evade all the servants once inside. No, that wouldn't end well at all.

"We could always just walk right in and say 'Good day, Yuni. We think you're lying and possibly guilty of murder and kidnapping. Where are you hiding Luca?'" Xanth said sarcastically.

As ridiculous as the comment was, a light had been lit in her mind, illuminating a possibility that had been hiding in the shadowy recesses of her brain. *The logical choice isn't always the right one*, she remembered. Would it be insane to do that? Absolutely. But...

"You know, I think that could work."

Xanth looked at her as if she had spoken another language. "Pardon?"

"Not the part where we accuse her. But walking right in. Of course, if I were seen it would be a disaster. But you frequent the castle, so your showing up now wouldn't raise suspicion." The fact that Xanth was generally clueless would make the act all the more convincing.

"So...you like my idea?"

The corner of her mouth twitched despite the gravity of the situation. "Yes Xanth, I do."

He grinned triumphantly. "Finally! Someone gets it! No one ever likes my ideas." He softened his smile a little. "Maybe you're not so bad after all."

"Let's just focus on getting Luca to safety. Here's what we need to do..."

With their plan formulated they tied their horses to a tree and set off.

"Are you ready?" Emily whispered.

Xanth saluted. "Of course, Captain Emily."

She gave him a scolding look. She understood the desire to lighten a stressful situation, but she wished he would leave the jesting alone for the time being. Perhaps it was his way of dealing with things, but it only made her more anxious about his capabilities. "Xanth, this is serious."

"Of course it is," he said in complete innocence. "I am being serious. Why do you think I saluted?" He then spun on his heel and marched forward like a soldier headed for the battle.

Goodness, she hoped he could pull this off.

***

No matter how many times Luca pinched himself, he wasn't waking up. It took him a while to get over the initial shock and find his voice. "You're Yuni's brother?"

Aspen nodded.

"Then, why are you here? Everyone thinks you were killed by the foreign ambassador. Yuni thinks you were… said you were…" The room started spinning as he tried to make sense of it all. "This can't be happening," he whispered.

"As I've been without company all these years, I suppose someone ought to hear the real story." Aspen let out a sigh that sounded like it held a thousand sorrows.

"I was twenty-nine years old when my father died and I took his place as king. He trained me well in his ways and while I was taught to respect the laws and traditions that made Orphia what it is, he also expressed his trust in me. He wanted me to really embrace the role I was to inherit and told me not to be afraid to explore where my intuition might lead.

"Orphia has always been a land of tradition. Beautiful and good, but also isolated and lacking growth. By the end of my first year, I felt strongly that change was needed. I didn't want us to be content to just live, I wanted us to thrive. Orphia had so much opportunity to grow and improve, and I felt we could learn a lot from other cultures. In turn, we could share our values and beauty with others."

Even now, sitting in a dark cell, Aspen spoke with deep conviction. He was obviously passionate about helping his citizens. The years of captivity wore on him physically, but his spirit seemed remarkably unbroken.

"Of course, change is hard for people to adjust to. My mother was especially hesitant about my ideas. But I felt certain about them and knew my father would want me to try. After she died, I decided it was time to take action. I wanted to ease the citizens into it, so I took things slow. Without revealing my identity, I made personal visits to a nearby kingdom to see what I could learn. Yuni stayed behind to care for things in my absence."

His shoulders sagged and a shadow passed over his face. "It was then that I fully realized how sheltered Orphia was. So I invited an ambassador to accompany me back to Orphia so that we might learn from each other. Yuni, however, kept trying to persuade me to send him home. She said that things were fine as they were, that it's not want the people wanted, not what our parents would've wanted. But I think her true concern was what the changes would mean for her.

"You see, the ambassador frequently mentioned his unmarried daughter whom I had met. She was quite lovely, and I had mentioned her a couple of times myself. There was no plan of a union, but Yuni knew if I married and produced an heir, she would fall behind in line for the throne. Her brief time as queen regent made her power-hungry."

Was that why Yuni never married? He knew the laws, the right of rule went to males by default. If she married, she would lose most of her authority. Luca initially thought it odd to see a monarch remain unmarried, but as he came to know her, it seemed she was just the type of person that enjoyed solitude. Apparently, he didn't know Yuni at all.

Aspen continued his story. "Under pretense as my messenger, Yuni sent the ambassador away and threatened him into silence. I was appalled by her actions, but I had no wish to embarrass her by publicizing her folly. I confronted her outside and we held our conversation in private. I tried to reason with her, but she was indignant. I had never seen such a desperate look in her eyes."

The conviction had been slowly seeping out of his voice as the subject shifted from his kingdom to his sister. He paused for a long moment before he was able to continue. "I am unaware exactly what happened next. I saw her reach for something as I turned away from her. And then I was here. I surmise that she knocked me unconscious and dragged me here with her horse." He scrubbed at his face. "I had seen her slowly change since our father's death, but I never imagined she would sink so far into treachery. I thought I could pull her out of it."

Luca's heart sunk clear to his stomach. There were no words to form a response. What was he supposed to say when he found out that everything he had known had been a lie?

A slow squeaking of a rusty hinge pierced the air, followed by the heavy thud of the metal door. As if on cue, Yuni walked in with all of her usual grace. Her posture was perfectly straight and her royal finery impeccable. She looked like she should be promenading into a soirée, not a dungeon.

She glanced at Luca with a completely aloof expression. Had he imagined the gentleness he saw in her eyes all these years? The ones that now seemed dull and cold?

"I see you're awake." She placed some food in his cell and then in Aspen's and quickly turned to leave.

That was it? Four words and some bread? The least she could do was give him an explanation of her own. He didn't know whether to think her the cruelest of villains or the weakest of cowards.

"Why?" Luca hardly recognized the stern voice as his own. But his sorrow had become indignation. He had to ask. If she was going to make him sit and rot in prison for the rest of his life, he deserved to hear everything from her.

Yuni paused her step. He waited, but she made no reply.

He ground his teeth and came up to the bars. "Why?" He asked again, harsher than the first time. "Why do this? "What do you gain by hurting innocent people who…who loved you for a crown? Does that make you happy?"

He stared at her back and he felt like he was speaking to a statue. She just stood there—still, stiff, cold, and lifeless.

Then she walked away. His only answer was the clicking of her shoes and the door latching shut behind her.

He vocalized his aggravation with something that was between a scream and a groan. He leaned his forehead against the grimy stone walls. This was his future and he was powerless to change it.

He was grateful now that Emily had left. She would be far away, safe from all of this and unaware of his suffering. No, she likely wouldn't think of him at all.

He, on the other hand, would surely spend every day of his life thinking of her and the future that might have been.

26: The Fine Line Between Brilliancy and Insanity

Emily snooped around outside as much as she dared. But without risking being seen, there was little for her to do except wait for Xanth's report.

When he finally came striding back to her post, he shook his head. "No Luca," he mumbled with his mouth full.

Her heart sank, though she didn't truly expect to find him there. "Did you...wait, why are you eating?" Could the man not complete a single task without getting distracted? So help her if he followed his stomach and did not even look around—

"I needed an excuse to go scope out the kitchens. Asking for Cook's ginger biscuits was as good as any." He popped another sugary treat in his mouth. "I didn't want to raise suspicion by turning them down once I was there, and I most certainly am not going to waste them." He swallowed the last bit in his mouth.

Fair enough. "Thank you for the sacrifice," she said dryly. "But what happened? Did you find anything? Was Yuni suspicious of you?"

"I didn't even see her. I come often enough they don't bother announcing me anymore unless she's nearby. I went straight to Luca's room but it looked unchanged since the last time I was there. I snuck around a few other places and went into the one secret room I know of." His face went grim once more. "He wasn't anywhere."

She felt remorse over her doubt now that she looked into Xanth's eyes. His methods were different than hers, perhaps a little unconventional also, but that did not equate with negligence. No, he was going to give his all to help Luca.

"So it seems he is not in the castle, but I don't think he could be too far away from it."

"But where?"

She rubbed her hair between her fingers. "The only clue we have to his whereabouts is the stables. Let's check there again." Maybe Xanth would see something she hadn't.

They waited behind the trees until the stable hand was long out of sight before they returned to the paddock. There was nothing that Luca left behind. No personal articles, no signs of a struggle, not even a strand of hair could be found.

They went into the stables themselves, hoping Emily would see something Xanth hadn't. She didn't even know what she was looking for, but she was desperate. She fought to keep her head afloat even as waves of hopelessness threatened to drown her. They checked Pearla's stall, then a chestnut stallion's, and finally one that belonged to a light painted horse with clear blue eyes.

"Hello there, Sapphire. You sure look better."

She turned inquisitively to Xanth."What do you mean she looks better?"

"She was smelly this morning." He scrunched his face. "When I came and got Onyx I saw her in the next paddock over. She smelled fishy and her legs were dirty."

Fishy and dirty...had she gotten wet? "Was the rest of her dirty?"

He thought for a minute. "No. Just about up to here." He held his hand against the underside of the mare's belly.

"Why didn't you mention that earlier?"

"I didn't think about it. Why? Is it important?"

Was it? A horse got dirty, something that happens all the time. She had no idea how that would tie to Luca unless—

She gasped as another memory clicked into place. "This is Yuni's horse!"

He stared at Sapphire with drawn brows. "You're right, she is. But what does that mean?"

She pondered. Yuni rode her horse somewhere this morning where she had gotten dirty and wet. Where would the horse have walked through water and why?

She snapped her fingers. "The lake! Are you familiar with the lake under the castle?"

"Not really. We were never allowed to swim in it."

"Does it smell fishy? Is it about waist deep?"

Understanding lit up his eyes. "You know what, it is!"

"Then let's go find out why Yuni wanted to keep you out of there so badly."

***

Emily trudged through the murky waters trying hard to ignore the foul smell that kept creeping up her nose. Afraid the horses would be too conspicuous, they opted to wade on foot. It wasn't so bad for Xanth and his long legs, but the water came up to Emily's torso. As it turned out, she didn't love *all* forms of water.

They stayed along the edges, checking cracks and crevices in the stones. "So what are we looking for?" Xanth asked.

"Anything that might be a hiding place."

They continued their inspection until they were at the back of the castle where a cave-like opening awaited them. She motioned silently for Xanth to follow her as she went inside. They walked along an incline that led them out of the water before plateauing.

The pervasive murk and gloom threatened to suffocate her as she walked along. The air was musky and damp, but she made herself continue to take deep breaths as she tried to discern their location.

"I think we're underneath the castle," she whispered.

"I never knew this place was here," Xanth said, his tone mixed with awe and apprehension.

"It would be the perfect place to hide someone." Her eyes darted all over, noting potential hiding spots for themselves in the alcoves lining the walls. If they ran into Yuni, or anyone other than Luca for that matter, they would need to act fast.

Deeper they went, the sunlight diminishing behind them and torchlight coaxing them forward. At the end of the arched tunnel was an imposing iron door.

She reached forward, slowly wrapping her fingers around the cold metal, bracing herself for who or what might be on the other side. She pulled.

It didn't move.

"Locked," she grumbled. "We need to get it open."

"I have an idea," Xanth said proudly. "We just need some fire."

"No."

"But you didn't even hear what I was going to do."

"Fire is not going to help us with this." She pulled a pin out of her hair and pointed it at him. "But this might."

Xanth crossed his arms. "I thought you liked my ideas," he muttered.

Ignoring his pouting, she fiddled with the lock. The pin was too flimsy to accomplish anything on the bigger mechanism. She needed something sturdier.

She let the pin fall to the ground. There had to be something else she could use. "Do you happen to have a knife or something on you?"

"Actually, yes!" He perked up a little and bent over to pull it out of his boot. "Here."

She tried again, pushing and twisting the blade until it made a satisfying click. With a firm tug, the door inched opened. Her heart-rate picked up speed and she quickly pulled it wider.

She was greeted with a hiss and she stifled a scream. Xanth came beside her, wide-eyed.

"Devil-spiked scoundrels," he whispered fearfully.

They were every bit as intimidating as Luca had described them. Scaled skin, prickly horns along its head and back, and a pleated skin flap around its head that unfurled when it hissed. There were easily half a dozen of them in the small space. All their beady eyes were staring at her and Xanth.

"Now what do we do?" She couldn't help the slight tremor in her voice.

"Uh, how about we run?"

"No. We can't run from this." Behind the foreboding creatures was another door. She could make out a faint light coming through the bars. "Luca might be behind there."

"But how on earth could he get past them?" He thrust his hands out at the animals. "They're dangerous! Poisonous!"

"Keep your voice down! He's got to be behind there. We must figure out a way to—"

One of them darted toward her and she shoved the door closed before it could escape. She leaned her back against it and breathed heavily. *Stay calm. Don't lose your head now.*

"Maybe we could leave the door open so they leave?" Xanth suggested.

"And have them run about loose? I don't like that idea either."

"I told you we needed fire." Xanth held onto a fistful of his hair. "How did they even get in there?"

"Yuni must have brought them here." Her brow furrowed as she inclined her head. "Though I wonder how she accomplished such a thing."

Yuni grew up in Orphia and would know the creatures well. Was there a weakness they had that let them be controlled? She racked her brain, pulling out anything she learned about them from her conversation with Luca. She formed a mental picture of Yuni standing before them, trying to imagine what she might do to corral them.

"Wait a second," she whispered. She eased the door open a crack, peeking in and motioning Xanth over. "Which one is the alpha?"

He squinted his eyes as he looked them over. "I'm not sure. None of them are black. And no one seems to be taking charge over the others."

Yuni always wore black. Perhaps it wasn't mourning attire as everyone suspected. Maybe it was because Yuni presented herself as the alpha over these beasts—and man, for that matter.

She looked at Xanth's appearance then down at her own and cursed her attire. She chose a light blue dress in a rare attempt to make herself look more attractive. Of all the days not to stick to her darker colors, it had to be this one.

There was no time to go back and change—they needed to act swiftly. She looked again at the warm glow from behind the interior door and it renewed her determination.

Maintain dominance and stand your ground. That is what alphas did, that is what she would do. She took in a deep breath, stood erect, and opened the door.

Xanth put a hand out to stop her. "You're just going to walk in?"

"Yes."

"Are you mad? They could kill you!"

She really didn't need that reminder, but her decision remained. "Perhaps I am. But I'd rather risk my life by trying than risk Luca's by refraining."

Soberness passed over his face and she pushed forward before he could do or say anything more.

The creatures were all the more terrifying up close. She walked ahead slowly but confidently. It seemed to be working, the others moved about but did not seem overly interested in her.

One in the corner revealed itself, coming far too close for comfort. She forced herself to stay put, fighting the urge to flinch or recoil. She felt each second of the terrifying impasse go by in the thud of her heart. Alphas didn't retreat, but staying still wasn't working either.

It stared at her, its tongue flicking out like a serpent. His clawed feet took one step forward...two steps...three. He was inches away. He was challenging her which meant she must prepare to fight.

She had no idea how to fight a poisonous animal, so she decided to mimic him. Reaching the pinnacle of ridiculousness in her life, she protruded her tongue and made a loud hissing noise.

He stopped moving.

She repeated the action and he took a step back. It was working.

She lunged her head forward and hissed again, careful that her feet didn't make contact with its toxic spikes. He continued stepping back and finally scurried back to the corner.

Her path now clear, she reached the second door unscathed. She let out a final hiss directed at all of them for good measure, and they gave her a wide berth of distance. Never had something that felt so foolish made her feel so victorious. Xanth let out a low whistle in admiration and she allowed a small smile of satisfaction. "You stay there and keep watch. I'm not sure how they'll react to you."

She pushed the door open with a creak and hoped Luca was the only one waiting for her on the other side.

27: Rescue

Apparently, having a companion for the first time in years exhausted Aspen, as he had fallen asleep a while ago. Luca laid on his back with his eyes shut, his emotions swirling inside him—betrayal, anger, resentment, denial, despair, anxiety. How could so many emotions mixed together leave him numb?

No, he wasn't quite numb. The sharp pang had passed, now it was like a constant dull ache that filled his body and soul. It was real enough that he could almost feel it physically.

He rolled on his side, the position no more comfortable than the former. He couldn't live like this. He wouldn't. Somehow, he would escape. But his despondency reminded him that Aspen had already tried and failed multiple times and he would likely fare the same.

Had Emily felt like this in her family's home? She wasn't bound by bars or chains, but she had never been free. She spent years emotionally confined by their rules and expectations. He may never find freedom, but he dearly hoped she would, or already had.

The door creaked open and Yuni's footsteps echoed. She was probably bringing them food, but he didn't care. He wouldn't bother himself to even look at her after her betrayal.

Emily was far beyond his reach and yet only a memory away. Those memories would provide comfort one moment then haunt him the next, but he would never stop their flow. He might kill himself in the process, but it would be a worthy way to die. He didn't want to forget all the things he loved about her.

Luca. He could even remember her voice with clarity, the way she said his name. He replayed the sound of it in his head as she teased him and laughed with him. He would invent conversations that he would've loved to have with her—getting her insight on a matter, reminiscing childhood adventures, hearing her answers to the questions he most wanted to ask about her true self. He would even fancy her saying she loved him just as much as he loved her. For he realized too late that he was truly in love with her.

Luca, are you alright?

His brows knit over his closed eyes. That question didn't follow the script in his head, and it sounded remarkably lifelike.

Opening his eyes, he saw an indistinct form on the other side of his cell. He kept blinking until the wet blur went away. It couldn't be...

He shot up and nearly stumbled over his own feet he moved so quickly. It *was* her.

"Emily," he said breathlessly. "How did you...why are you..." He looked her over quickly and then scanned the hall for any signs of Yuni. There wasn't any. "You're here." He laid his hand on hers that was wrapped around the bar, assuring himself he wasn't hallucinating. "Are *you* ok? Are you hurt at all?" Her wild hair stuck out in odd places and her skirts seemed to be wet, but otherwise she looked unharmed.

"I'm fine. Better than fine, now that I see you alive and whole." Her smile was even more beautiful than he remembered. "Now let's get you out of here." She pulled out a knife which she carefully inserted into the lock.

"But, how did you find me? When did you get back here?"

"It's a long story, one that I'm afraid will have to wait until later."

He watched her fiddle with the lock while his mind sluggishly tried to process all that was happening. "When exactly did you learn to pick locks? Did I miss that lesson in school?"

The corner of her mouth twitched. "No. I taught myself when I was about thirteen. It just seemed like something useful one should know how to do in case the need ever arose." The lock clicked, and she smiled with satisfaction. "Turns out I was right."

He stepped out as the door swung open. Before he could react, she threw her arms around him in a hug and he returned it heartily.

If he could live forever in a moment, this would be it. He closed his eyes even as tears formed in them. He buried his face in her hair, shutting out everything else around him. For a blissful moment, he could forget where he was, what had happened, and what might yet happen. All that mattered was that she was here in his arms, and he never planned on letting go of her again. He hugged her a little tighter and a sigh escaped Emily's lips—so small that he might've missed it if her head wasn't right by his ear.

She finally released him and he reluctantly did the same. He couldn't tell in the orange torchlight if her face was flushed, but she did clear her throat a little awkwardly.

"Stories later, escape now. Let's go." She turned on her heel and he began to follow her down the hall.

"Wait! I nearly forgot." He took her arm and tugged her back. "There's one more lock I need you to pick." He gestured to King Aspen who had not awoken during their reunion.

Emily gave him a wary glance but obeyed silently. It struck him that she had just trusted him enough to do so without any questions. Knowing that was hard for her made him appreciate it all the more.

"Wake up Your Majesty, we have company." He stretched his arm through the bars and poked his leg, which was barely within reach.

"Huh?" He stirred and began to sit up.

Emily gasped. "Your Majesty? As in…"

"Yuni's brother."

"Oh thank goodness," she said in an exhaled breath. "He is alive after all."

Luca made brief introductions as Emily worked on the lock and soon they were bounding down the hall. He hadn't expected the door to their freedom to reveal a swarm of devil-spiked scoundrels.

He instinctively put his hand in front of Emily, but she gently pushed it away. "It's alright. I got through them once already." She began hissing and strolled right through them as though they were harmless kittens. Luca would've laughed when she stuck out her tongue if he had not been so impressed.

If he thought her amazing before, he had to think her a complete marvel now. Whether or not she returned his feelings, he vowed never to take her for granted.

A flash of red hair entered his vision and the next thing he knew, he was being lifted off the ground. "Luca! You're alive!" Xanth exclaimed, hugging him firmly.

"I won't be for very long if you keep this up," he replied as the air was squeezed out of his lungs.

Xanth set him down and chuckled uncomfortably. "I mean…you know, it's good to see you again."

Luca laughed inside. If Xanth was trying to hide how worried he had been, he failed miserably. "You too Xanth." He clapped him on the shoulder. "You too."

"Wait, who is this?" He inclined his head toward the king.

Emily interjected. "Might I suggest we make introductions on the way, as we are still in the midst of completing our escape route?"

"Any dragons you wish to slay first?" Luca quipped, unable to resist. "Or did I miss that already?"

A genuine smile lit her face. Oh, how he missed making her smile. "No. But if you find one, I'll be ready."

Introductions and explanations were made as they traversed the cave and the murky waters. Sunlight flooded his eyes as they exited and he shielded them with his hand until they adjusted. "Where to now?"

"Well, my plan didn't involve the presence of royalty." Emily nodded to the king.

"We have our king back!" Xanth interjected. "Aren't we going to the castle so he can reclaim his throne?"

Emily was obviously hesitant, but she humbly deferred to King Aspen. "This is your kingdom, Your Majesty. What do you suggest is the best course of action?"

He pondered, and Luca really looked at the king for the first time. He was far too thin. Scraggly hair and a beard covered most of his face, but the skin peeking out was nearly as white as sheep's wool. Dark circles stood out under his eyes. The years in the dungeon had definitely taken their toll. He suppressed a shudder as he realized this could've been him in a few years' time had his friends not found him.

He let out a weary sigh. "As many times as I plotted escape, I hadn't given much thought as to how I would reclaim my throne if given the opportunity." He sobered. "I do not look like a king at all, and definitely not the one people remember. If I simply barge in through the castle doors, no one will have any reason to believe I am who I say."

"May I make a suggestion, Your Majesty?" Emily asked tentatively and he nodded his consent. "If it pleases you, we could return to San Morrina." Her wary eyes briefly darted to Luca. "It's a small village just on the outskirts of the forest. I've let a cottage there and it's somewhat isolated from the main part of the village. Yuni would be unlikely to find us. We can hide there until we form a plan and perhaps get some new clothing and a shave for you, Your Majesty."

He nodded approvingly. "That sounds like a wise plan, Emily."

Luca stared at her in disbelief. She had her own home which meant she had gotten her funds and was not under her family's control anymore. Relief poured through him. She was free.

"However we only have two horses." Emily's eyes found Luca's. "I'm afraid we'll have to share." An amused smile tugged at her lips as she lowered her voice. "Again."

Though spoken as an apology, she didn't seem to mind. He surely didn't.

"So, I suppose I should go retrieve my horse and meet you there?" Xanth asked.

Concern etched Emily's features. "Actually, I think it's best that you return home and stay there."

"What?" Xanth looked offended. "And miss out on all the action? I don't think so."

"Xanth," she said gently. "This rescue could not have been done without you, and I thank you for everything you've done. But it is safer for you to return home before Yuni learns of your part in this mission. You're enough at risk as it is."

He crossed his arms. "I'm not afraid of that," he insisted.

"I wasn't implying that you were. But think of your family, your sisters especially. If things don't go well and Yuni finds out of your involvement, think of what could happen to them."

The tension in his face eased as he sobered, the seriousness of the thought sinking in.

"Your responsibility now is to make sure they are safe."

Emily probably didn't realize what a sound argument she had just made. Luca knew how much Xanth loved his family. He would do absolutely anything to protect them.

"You're right." He addressed Emily as he gave Luca a look of brotherly affection. "Take care of him for me, ok?"

Emily just smiled in return as she gave a side glance to Luca.

The words actually saddened him, because there was more than a grain of truth in them. Emily was strong and capable. She freed herself from diabolical family members, rescued kings, conquered poisonous animals, and gave his life real meaning. The realization hit him like a heavy weight in his stomach. He wanted her, desperately needed her, but he had nothing of value to give her in return.

He could only offer himself, and she didn't need him.

28: The Return

Luca paused before dismounting, the significance of what he was about to do sinking in. For the first time in years, he would walk on the soil of San Morrina. Hiranburg held far worse memories, but being here still meant reconnecting with his past.

He slid off his horse and planted his feet on the ground. He nearly expected the pain of dredged up memories to shoot up through his soles and strike him right in the heart. But it didn't.

Maybe it was just a matter of perspective considering all that had happened in the last few hours, but returning to this part of his past did not haunt him as he always feared it would. As he looked around the village that was once his home, seeing houses dotting the landscape and hills in the distance, he actually felt somewhat wistful.

Emily scanned the cottage over quickly as she approached and Luca noted the pride in her eyes and the genuineness of her smile, though it was small. He was glad she had a place of her own that she adored.

The home was small, quaint, and charming. It would be a bit cramped for a potential family, but it was perfectly suited for a single person starting a life on their own. He hated that part of it.

He quickly chided himself for his selfishness. Her happiness is what mattered to him, even if his own was lacking.

Emily knocked and a young maid, likely not much older than himself, answered the door. "Hello Penny, I brought back some guests."

Her eyes widened when she took in the king's rugged appearance, but she said not a word as she ushered them into a small sitting room with plush chairs and an unlit fireplace. She scurried about in a fluster, trying her best to accommodate their unexpected arrival.

"I'm cooking some soup now Miss Emily, but it will be a few moments until it's ready. I'll have to add some more to the pot."

"That's alright Penny. Neither of us were quite prepared for visitors."

Penny headed out as if to leave but quickly turned back. "Oh, should I make some tea first?"

"No, you tend to the soup, I'll serve tea. Thank you."

The lady of the house preparing tea instead of the servant? That was nearly unheard of, though it didn't surprise him one bit. Emily was the industrious type, always looking to busy herself.

"Can I help?" Luca asked. If she was breaking societal norms then he figured he could too.

"Thank you, but I can manage well enough. You both have had a rough morning." She glanced at King Aspen. "Well, much more than a morning. Please, just make yourselves comfortable. I'll return shortly."

He frowned after she turned away. He couldn't even help with tea, useless as he was.

King Aspen had been quiet since the escape. Presently, his eyes were glazed over, staring blankly at nothing in particular, no doubt burdened with his thoughts and emotions. Luca thought it best not to interrupt, so he sat down with his own thoughts as his eyes wandered around the room.

It was simply decorated, likely little changed from how it was when she purchased it. It was simple, comfortable, practical, yet elegant. It was very Emily.

Emily fit well in her role as hostess. She and Penny returned and had them comfortable with tea and soup. He could enjoy the social visit and almost forget the stressful events of the day and the inevitable confrontation to come. Almost.

After briefing Penny on the situation and giving her an extremely condensed version of the events, she went to the market to retrieve clothing and shaving supplies for King Aspen. He gladly took them and began readying himself in the next room.

After collecting the teacups and bowls for Penny, Emily dropped into a chair and let out a contented sigh. She looked so different than she had that first day in Orphia. The weight had been lifted off her shoulders and she was in much better spirits. He couldn't help but admire the change, and yet her joy was not quite as pronounced as he thought it would be.

Penny left to clean up the dishes which lent them a moment of privacy. For the first time in over a month, Luca had an opportunity for a real conversation with Emily.

"You did it," he said. "You freed yourself from your aunt and uncle."

She smiled, though not brilliantly. "I did. I can scarcely believe it at times. Sometimes I wonder if it's only a dream, but every day I wake up and I'm still here."

"And are you...are you happy?"

Something in her manner shifted, and she was less at ease than before. "I am certainly much happier than I was in Uncle and Aunt's home."

Her reply felt cryptic. Being *happier* was not the same as being *happy*. He realized once again she was only showing one side of her and keeping something else concealed.

"Well, if you're happy then I'm happy," he said more for himself than for her. He hoped she was truly happy here.

Her brow knit together pensively and he wondered if she realized the deeper meaning of his words, that he was greatly concerned with her happiness.

"Thank you again for rescuing me." He changed the subject quickly. "Rescuing us, I guess I should say. You were amazing. Perhaps you should look into knighthood," he teased.

The mood didn't lighten and she didn't laugh as he expected. Emily didn't even seem to register his words. Her brow was still creased and her eyes were even more thoughtful. What was going on in that brilliant head of hers?

"Why did Yuni betray you like she did? You never explained that part."

His heart cracked. He had left for Emily, but it seemed somewhat pointless now to tell her that. He didn't want to give her any reason to blame herself when it wasn't her fault. And knowing how unneeded he was increased his fear of rejection tenfold. He couldn't tell her. He couldn't bear it. He would make up another explanation.

But that was a coward's way out, and he was so tired of being afraid. Hadn't he already decided to be brave? That he was willing to give up his home for her if she was willing to have him? The risk was worth it, if only he was brave enough to speak.

He locked eyes with her, trying to draw from her strength and courage. "I told her I was leaving." He rushed the words out of his mouth before he could change his mind. He meant to say more, but that's as far as he could get.

"Leaving...the castle?" Emily asked.

He took a deep breath. "Leaving Orphia."

"But you love Orphia. Why...what made you leave?" Her question took on a hint of urgency.

This was it. This was the moment that would change him forever. The fate of his heart hung in how she responded to a single word. "You."

She sat dumbfounded. "That part of the story was true? You came back to San Morrina...for me?"

"I tried." A humorless laugh escaped him and he put his hands in the air. "Not that you needed me. I was worried about you. I left Orphia to try to find you and see if I could save you from whatever situation you were in with your family. And look at you now!" He gestured to the room around them. "You've done it yourself. Then I end up in trouble and Xanth had to drag you back here to come and save me."

Her eyes were wide as the moon and her mouth was slightly agape. It was no wonder she was so surprised at him for thinking she needed his assistance. She probably pitied him for his misjudgment.

He let out a sad sigh. "I should've known how incapable I was of rescuing you while you were perfectly capable of rescuing yourself. Honestly, I already knew, but I had to come see you anyway." That was the primary reason he came, and she needed to know that.

He stared at his lap. If he saw pity, or worse yet, laughter in her eyes when he opened up the remainder of his heart, it might shatter completely. "I haven't felt like myself since you've left. I needed to see you again because I realized I wanted more in life. I wanted to give more of myself for someone else...for you." There, he had done it. She now had every bit of his heart, and it was up to her what to do with it.

Silence hung in the air, and not the comfortable silence they used to enjoy. It was heavy, awkward, and chilling. He felt utterly exposed at his confession and wondered if he should've made it at all.

"After all that I had said, you still wanted me?"

The fragile emotion in her voice made him look up. "Of course." He had nearly forgotten their parting argument. He put it behind him a long time ago.

Now she stared at her lap, rubbing her fingers back and forth on her other hand. "First of all, I'm sorry for that. I've regretted my words every day since I spoke them. I should've never said such bad things about you or yelled at you. You are one of the kindest, most selfless people I am privileged to know."

He didn't need an apology, but it touched him.

"Second, Xanth didn't bring me back to Orphia. I was already headed there when he told me you were missing."

A jolt went through his body. "You were?"

"Yes."

"Well, if Xanth didn't bring you then why were you..." His heart drummed with excitement at what that might mean, but he couldn't get the question out.

"Because," she answered anyway, "I wanted to apologize, I hoped we could have a second chance, and... because I missed you."

The tug of her lips, the bit of nervousness in her manner, and the sparkle in her eyes were all so genuine. This is what he had wanted. He was finally seeing the real Emily, all of her. All his cowardliness fled and he leaned forward in his chair. "I missed you too."

Then something amazing happened—she smiled. It was not the usual small curve of her lips. This was a full-on, dimple revealing, eye crinkling, heart stopping, bright smile that left him momentarily stunned. It was the most sincere smile that he had ever seen from her, and he was the cause of it.

"And to address your earlier comment, you are plenty capable because you already rescued me."

His brow furrowed as he drifted back to the conversation. "What do you mean?"

"You rescued me from myself," she said plainly.

He blinked at her. He knew this was a compliment, but he had no idea what she meant by it.

"You may not have extricated me from my problems, but you did something better—you loyally saw me through them." She shook her head. "Oh Luca, I've been self-reliant for so long. I honestly didn't think I needed anyone for anything. I push and pull away whenever anyone tries to get close enough to hurt or help me. And people leave me alone because it's not worth the fight for them. But you never gave up on me. You never forced me back when I pulled away, but you never let go. You looked past my words, saw what I really needed, and gave it to me.

"To trust another person terrified me because I thought that as soon as I did I would just be let down. But I never was with you. You taught me I can depend on someone else and don't have to fight my battles alone, though I'm still inclined to try. And that was a lesson I desperately needed to learn, but only you were patient enough to teach me." She gave his hand a gentle squeeze and then let it go. "You rescued me from myself."

The corners of his mouth lifted along with his heart. They both said they needed each other, and now they had each other.

There was more he wanted to tell her, and perhaps he now had the courage to do so. He reached out for her hand once more, placed it in both of his—

"Well, how do I look?" King Aspen's voice boomed across the room.

Luca jumped at the sound. He had honestly forgotten that other people were still in the house. He dropped her hand as they quickly stood and took a step away from each other. There would be no hiding his flushed cheeks if the warmth he felt was any indication of their appearance, but Emily formed a calm expression before turning to face the king. Seeing her slip her mask back on made him fully appreciate its absence just the moment before.

"You look like a new man, Your Majesty," Emily noted.

"I feel like one," he replied.

Indeed, any semblance of a prisoner was gone. The unkempt hair was smoothed back, the scraggly beard was cropped, and his clothes were clean and well arranged. The royal finery he was warranted may have been absent, but his straight, confident posture made him every bit the king.

King Aspen sat and he and Emily followed. "So what do we do now?" Luca asked. "How do we confront Yuni?"

"I've been contemplating the best way to do this." King Aspen scrubbed at his stubbled beard. "I feel this is as much a personal matter as it is a political one."

Luca knew where he was going with that line of thought. "You cannot go by yourself."

He raised two thick eyebrows and Luca quickly realized the implication of what he just said. "That is...I didn't mean...forgive me, Your Majesty," he stammered. "You may do whatever you wish. I just meant that I am concerned for your safety if you confront your sister alone. Especially considering what happened the last time you did so."

He shook his head. "It's alright. You are probably right, my boy. I know it's a great risk, but knowing what Yuni is willing to do"— he gestured between him and Luca—"I do not wish to put anyone else in danger."

"That is very considerate, Your Majesty," Emily added. "But the ramifications of such a meeting must be considered. As you are already aware, the future state of Orphia's crops and food supplies are bleak if changes aren't made soon. If you go unprotected and something happens to you, that in turn affects the entire kingdom. Not to mention the more desperate Yuni gets, the more sinister her actions may be."

He considered the words with a slow nod of his head. "Right again." It seems he attempted a smile but didn't have it in him. "Should we be successful, I believe I shall appoint you both as my royal advisors." He stood and paced along the woven rug beneath them. "What do you suggest?"

Emily twirled a lock of hair, something Luca noticed she did when her mind was running through a list of options. He racked his own mind, trying to come up with something useful. "What if we went to the people?" He finally felt like he had a valid idea. "Surely the people would be thrilled to know their king is alive. With the entire kingdom on our side, how could we lose?"

He paused his step as he pondered the suggestion. "There is strength in numbers, but the risk is too great. For one thing, not everyone may be as thrilled as you imagine. Not everyone liked the fact I was trying to make changes and the younger generation know little to nothing of me. Orphia is known for its peace and the last thing I want to do is divide the people by forcing them to choose sides. We could end up with a civil war on our hands." He sighed. "Of course, this is going to cause some upheaval no matter what, but I would like to keep it to a minimum. And I think the best way to do that is to act with discretion now and inform the kingdom only after the throne has officially been reclaimed."

"I can see the prudence in that," Emily added. "But I do not feel that it's wise to go alone. Luca is correct, it's far too dangerous."

Luca stood. "I can accompany you."

"As can I." Emily joined him.

A painful grip squeezed around his heart. "No," he said quickly. "You've already risked your life once, you don't need to do so again." He had been foolish enough to lose Emily twice already, by leaving her behind in his youth and by not going after her when she left Orphia. He couldn't let her risk herself again. Who knew what Yuni might do to her. The stakes were far higher, and if he lost her now, he knew they would not be so fortunate as to reunite a third time.

"I do need to. There is strength in numbers. My accompanying you makes perfect sense."

"Em, please," he pleaded. "I don't want you to be logical. I want you to be safe."

"And I want you to be safe. But I cannot assist you if I remain here."

"But if anything happened to you—"

"It would not be your fault. But if anything happened to you because I chose to stay behind it would be mine." She laid her hand on his arm. "You told me I didn't have to fight my battles alone, and you didn't let me. So what makes you think I'll let you go off and do just that?"

Goodness, it was hard to be convincing when she used his own words against him.

"Ahem." King Aspen cleared his throat and gave them a scrutinizing look, though there was amusement in his eyes. "If I may interject, I see truth to both sides of this issue. Perhaps a compromise can be arranged." His authoritative tone made them both stand at attention. "Luca and I will go to the castle together. I will make my presence known to the staff, relating the true events as tactfully as possible. Luca will serve as a witness should Yuni attempt any kind of refutation. Emily, if you insist on going, and only if you truly insist, you can stand guard nearby but remain hidden. If we need you as an additional witness, we can call on you. And if anything goes awry, you will be there to alert others for help. Does that suit you both?"

Emily gave a single, firm nod. "It does indeed, Your Majesty."

Now all eyes were on Luca, waiting for his answer. No, it didn't suit him at all. He wanted Emily safe, needed her safe. He would risk his safety a thousand times over if it meant protecting her well-being.

But as much as he wanted to indulge his overprotective side, he knew if he constantly tried to coddle her she would be utterly miserable. He had no wish to do that to her. She wasn't recklessly diving into these waters ignorant of its dangers. She knew exactly what she was volunteering for and had the wits, shrewdness, and courage to do it successfully.

Her eyes silently pleaded with him as if they were saying: *Trust me, I can do this. We can do this together.*

So now it was his turn to trust her abilities and judgment by respecting her wishes. After all the times she had trusted him when he asked, it was only fair he returned the favor.

Besides, when she set her mind to something, her tenacity rivaled the strength of a royal edict itself.

Though he still hated the idea with every ounce of his being, he nodded his head in agreement. "Fine."

***

Emily found that the beautiful backdrop Orphia provided did not at all fit with the somberness of the trio traveling there. Sunlight poured out of a cloudless sky and birds sang with a cheery lilt. The day was begging them to hope but the seriousness of their mission silenced the notion. An entire kingdom unknowingly depended on them. Her very life was at risk along with the life of the king and her dear Luca.

There was so much more to say to him, but with everything weighing on their shoulders she knew it was not the time to unburden her heart. She needed to remain as emotionally detached as possible for the coming confrontation as there was still plenty that could go wrong. The castle residents could revolt, Yuni could falsely accuse them, she could find them first and throw them back into the dungeon...or worse. That thought alone made her stomach churn.

There was no option for failure. They had to succeed. That is why no matter how many worry-filled glances Luca shot in her direction, she would not retreat. She would do everything in her power to see that they won. And if they lost, she wanted to lose together.

King Aspen held the heaviest of their burden, though it was for a very different reason. His confident stance on his horse was belied by the emotion in his eyes.

"You can do this, Your Majesty," she encouraged.

He didn't even bother trying to smile. "I just want this to be done and over with. I must reclaim my kingdom, but I hate that it must come at the cost of my only sister."

"What will happen to her?" It was probably impolite to ask, but she knew she was simply asking something he already knew the answer to.

"As king, I know what the punishment for treason must be." Emily subconsciously brought her hand to her neck. "But as a brother, I hope she responds in a way that will allow some lenience." He sighed and moisture shimmered in his eyes. "I am grasping at a thread of hope that there is still some of the good girl that I remember in her, but I fear she may be lost forever."

She let the subject drop and they continued to ride in silence. She slipped off of Onyx and found her hiding spot at the edge of the tree line. There she would be disguised by the leaves but could still keep an eye on the castle.

"I know you will be, but I must say it anyway. *Please*, be careful." Luca's voice was taut, full of emotion.

"You as well. You two are in more danger than I am."

"Em..." He swallowed, and it took him a minute to find his voice again. "If I don't make it back—"

"You will." Her voice wobbled. "You will." She was barely holding herself together as it was. A heartfelt confession from him now would unravel her completely.

His eyes searched hers with an intensity she had not yet seen. She could not allow herself to voice the words they both wanted to say, but his heart spoke through those tear-filled eyes and told her all she needed to know. She saw the exact moment understanding lit them, and she knew her eyes spoke for her heart as well. Neither said a word of acknowledgment, but they knew.

Understanding her unspoken need—as he always did—he gave her a wobbly smile. "See you soon."

And with that, they rode off. She hoped and prayed she would indeed see him again soon, safe and sound.

She kept her eyes fixed on the castle long after their forms were out of sight. If anything was amiss, she would run for help or run straight towards them if needed.

Her eyes burned and she had to remind herself to blink. What felt like an eternity was probably no more than ten minutes. Staring into the distance would not make them appear any faster. She shut her eyes a moment to give them relief.

The crunching of leaves alerted her to their return. Her heart sped up in anticipation and she looked ahead eagerly for Luca.

He wasn't there.

Neither was the king.

Every hair on her body stood, her skin prickling. The scene before her was vacant and unchanged, but her gut told her something was very, very wrong.

Her heartbeat drummed in her ears as she turned around slowly and looked directly into Yuni's scowl. In her hands was an arrow pointed directly at her.

29: Worst Case Scenario

"There you are." Yuni"s voice sent a chill down her spine. "I thought you were too smart to come back."

She summoned a courageous stance. "It's a good thing I did." She kept her eye on the arrow as she contemplated her options. Emily had nothing on her to use for offense or defense. She was a fast runner, but ducking from one tree to another would only provide minimal protection. Though the arrow was not fully drawn, she had witnessed firsthand how quickly and accurately Yuni could shoot. There was little chance of her escaping it.

In summary, her situation was rather bleak.

"Is it a good thing?" Yuni sneered. "I thought you wanted to protect Orphia. Instead, you take the chance of being followed here and letting Orphia be uncovered, putting everyone at risk."

"The only things to be uncovered are your secrets," she said firmly, trying to keep her talking. The more Yuni talked the more distracted she'd be. "That is the true reason you are so protective of this place—to save your position."

She narrowed her eyes in disapproval. "Everything I do is in the citizens' best interests."

"Including throwing innocent people into prison?"

Her grip tightened on the arrow and Emily realized she was getting too caught up in her passion. She needed to tread carefully. "Why?" Emily asked quickly, hoping it would provide her some time. "At least tell me why you felt the need to lock them away."

"Because they don't know what's best for Orphia or themselves," she replied without hesitation. "Orphia has enjoyed peace under our family's rule for generations, but my brother wasn't content with leaving things that way. Luca was until you came along. You turn his head and start filling it with your naive ideas. Who knows what damage would be done if he was off running free in the world. The harm he would bring to himself, the questions he would raise by returning with you. It would ruin us and them!"

Strange, Yuni did not once mention keeping her power. And she gave her answer too readily for it to be a impulsive fabrication. Could it be in some twisted way she thought she was playing the hero?

She stared into Yuni's eyes. Her grip on the arrow was firm but she noted the fingers trembling very slightly. The lines of her face were tight but her eyes did not bear a bloodthirsty malice.

The one weapon Emily did have was her mind. Maybe, just maybe, Yuni could be reasoned with. At the very least, maybe she could distract her enough that she made a mistake that would give her an opportunity to escape. It was her only hope.

"Then why allow Luca here in the first place?" Emily asked. "He came from the outside world, why did you risk it with him?"

Yuni's expression was firm but hesitant. She could almost see her mind working, formulating a careful response. "He was the perfect heir," she finally replied. "Men always take precedence in the throne, unfair as it is. I am expected to produce an heir, but to do that I must marry. When I marry, my husband becomes king and I am nothing. Luca was the perfect solution. The kingdom is safe and I can ensure he will continue in our family's traditions and will not take the throne until I see him fit. Until then, I can keep ruling Orphia peacefully." Her expression hardened once more. "Then you come along and ruin him and now I'm left to find a new heir."

Yuni was wearing her mask again, Emily could tell. But why? What truth was she trying to conceal?

Family. Her parents. That was the common thread in her replies. That is what was important to her.

"I don't think that's it, at least not the whole of it," Emily ventured. "You could've killed Luca instead of locking him up if he was so expendable. And your brother and me for that matter." Emily swallowed as she noted the sharp point of the arrow's tip still pointed at her. "But you didn't. I don't think you are as heartless and evil as you're trying to appear to be."

Yuni kept glaring at her.

"I lost my parents too, you know. I was even younger than you were when it happened to me. Pain and grief express themselves in different, sometimes illogical ways."

She stiffened. "How do you know about that?"

"You're not a cold-blooded killer, Yuni." She ignored the question. "I think you're hurting. You want to do what you think is right by your parents. You think you're doing the greater good, but you can't bring yourself to hurt anyone." Goodness, she hoped what she was saying was true. "It doesn't have to be like this. You can care for your brother and Luca and still allow them some freedom."

Yuni maintained form with the arrow but her grasp relaxed.

"You can't bring your parents back, but having other people you care about can ease the pain. Don't give up what you have. Don't push them away." She slowly inched herself towards the denser forest, hoping Yuni wouldn't notice. Her eyes had taken on a distant look, almost like she was in a daze. "Don't do anything you'll regret." Another step...then another...just a few more...

A snapping twig pierced the silence, shaking Yuni out of her reverie. She growled at Emily. "Enough!"

She let go of the arrow right as a large form barreled toward Yuni. The arrow whooshed through the air, imprecise but headed in Emily's direction. Instead of the arrow, something solid plowed into her and knocked her backward. She hit the ground hard as she heard fabric rip but felt nothing pierce her. All of this happened simultaneously—almost too quick to register—and she lay there breathing heavily.

Quickly and gratefully realizing she was still alive, she sat up to see that the king, with remarkable speed and strength, had accosted Yuni. He had his arms around her as she writhed and struggled to free herself. But why was he alone? If he was here, then where was—

"Luca!" Emily cried out as her eyes fell on his limp form. He laid face down in the grass with his arm draped over her.

She scrambled to her knees to get a better look at him. Redness seeped from his torn sleeve. "Luca?" Emily asked frantically. "Luca? Can you hear me?"

He didn't respond.

She pressed her ear to his back and was relieved to hear him breathing. He was unconscious but still alive.

She tore a piece of cloth from her dress and used it as a makeshift tourniquet to slow the bleeding on his arm. She then bent down to look at his face. Her trembling fingers pushed back a few soft curls, revealing another wound where he hit his head. Even her delicate touch caused his face to pinch in pain.

"Luca?" Even at a whisper, her voice was quivering.

He answered her with a muffled groan. His brown lashes fluttered slightly as his eyes barely slit open then immediately closed again.

A light thud brought her head up and reminded her of Yuni's presence. She was on her knees and had gone slack in her brother's arms. He kept fast hold of her, but his grip was not as tight as it was previously. Yuni no longer fought him. She didn't even move. Rather, she seemed on the verge of fainting. The crossbow lay on the ground forgotten and her horrified eyes were on Luca.

"What...what have I done?" Yuni murmured.

She didn't protest or say another word as King Aspen led her away. Her eyes never left Luca's arm where her arrow grazed him—her arrow that potentially could've killed him.

"I'll bring a doctor back immediately," the king whispered as they passed.

The forest was eerily silent as she waited. She did whatever ministrations she could until help came. When there was nothing else she could think of to do, she reached for his limp hand and squeezed it just as he had done many times to comfort her. Her thumb went back and forth along the back of it while unbidden tears rolled silently down her cheeks.

30: Ever After

Luca's head hurt. Someone screamed his name, but the voice sounded like it was underwater. Hazy recollections floated around in his mind, none of them staying still long enough to link together. Someone with dark hair peering at him. Horse hoofs. The vague feeling of being carried. Someone holding his hand, running their finger along the back of it. He could feel that even now.

He pried his eyes open, sunlight flooding them and cutting through his foggy mind. He blinked a few times until he recognized the desk ahead. He was in his bedroom.

The hand squeezed tightly around his own. He followed it up to find that it belonged to Emily.

"You're awake," she said gently.

Seeing her triggered a clearer memory of her pallid face with Yuni's arrow flying toward her. It made his stomach clench. But now she was here, alive and well, looking down at him with those glimmering eyes.

"Are...are you ok?" Luca asked quietly.

She smiled. "I am supposed to be asking you that. But yes, thanks to you I'm perfectly fine."

He went to brush a wayward hair from her face. His arm burned at the movement and he gasped in pain.

"Careful." She stilled his arm. "You've got a bad wound there."

"You'll likely have a bad headache as well," a man, apparently a doctor, spoke from the other side of the room.

"You had a hard fall, but I think you'll recover just fine." He smiled. "I'll let the king know you're awake."

"Wait! Where is he? Where's Yuni?" Luca looked between the doctor and Emily, unsure who would explain.

"They are both in the throne room downstairs. He wanted to be here with you, but had to see to more pressing matters first."

"Yuni confessed to everything," Emily added. "And shed some further light on the motives of her actions."

"Yes, but I'm afraid Emily will have to relate the details. His Majesty insisted on knowing the moment you were awake, so I must go inform him." He nodded as he headed out the door.

Emily didn't watch his departure, but simply continued the explanation. "Apparently Yuni made a deathbed promise to her mother to continue their family legacy and see to the welfare of her brother and the rest of Orphia. She said the changes her brother was trying to make frightened her, and she felt she was protecting everyone from the outside world."

Luca wasn't sure how to feel about that. "Do you think she's sincere?" Despite all that she did, he hoped she was. He despised her actions, but he also wanted to believe that all those years she spent caring for him were out of genuine care and concern.

"I do," she said after a moment of reflection. "It doesn't excuse her actions by any means, but it does seem her motives were good, even if her reasoning was extreme." She pulled her chair closer to his bedside. "She also hasn't stopped crying since returning to the castle."

"Really?" Had he ever seen Yuni cry? He couldn't recall if he had, though he was sure she must've cried sometimes.

"Yes. And she has continually inquired about you. Knowing she could've taken your life with her arrow shook her terribly." Emily rubbed at her wrist absentmindedly. "At least you know that her love toward you was not hypocritical."

His heart softened toward her just a little. He could never condone her actions, but it helped him let go of any residual anger. "What will happen to her?"

"Considering her confession and cooperation since returning, the king feels the death penalty need not be enforced." Emily's shoulders relaxed a little as she answered him. "But she still committed treason, kidnapping, and attempted murder. She will be stripped of her royal status and detained elsewhere. After discussing the matter with his royal advisors, myself, and the doctor, it was decided for her to be assigned to community service. She will be monitored and restricted in her doings, but the doctor feels the activity will give her a sense of purpose and perhaps help her mental and emotional state."

"Well, it seems like I missed quite a lot while I was unconscious."

Emily's gaze turned despondent. "I was worried you weren't going to wake up."

Luca smiled in an attempt to cheer her up. "But I did, and the doctor says I'm going to be fine."

"I know, it's just..." She visibly swallowed, trying to compose herself. Goodness, she looked like she was on the verge of tears. Was he worse off than he thought? "Oh, I'm so sorry." She hung her head, as if ashamed to look at him anymore. Or perhaps it was to hide tears that were threatening to escape. "You were right, I shouldn't have come with you. You almost died trying to protect me. If I wouldn't have been there—"

"Stop," he said gently. He wasn't about to let her blame herself over this. "The very same thing could've happened to me even if you weren't there. I'm not at all sorry you came."

She peered through her lashes. "You're not?"

"No." He offered a lopsided grin. "You know, call me crazy, but I'm actually glad I got hit with the arrow."

She looked at him full on, her brow pinched together. "You can't be serious."

"I am."

"Then perhaps you hit your head harder than we thought," she teased.

"No, my mental faculties are quite in order." He was happy that he pulled her out of her sadness, but sobered again as he thought of his next words. "I'm glad it happened because it meant I finally got to be your hero."

The twinkle in her eyes melted into a warm fondness. "Luca, you already were." She leaned in closer to him. "Heroism isn't being bold and brash with an insane act of bravery. Heroes, the truest ones, are regular people who care about others. They are kind and regularly put others' interests ahead of their own. They never give up on the ones they care about." She grabbed his hand again. "You prove to be my hero daily in your own gentle and compassionate way. The fact that you risked yourself for me only confirms the person I already knew you to be." She gripped his hand tighter. "It took almost losing you for me to realize that I was falling in love with someone who had always been my hero."

"Well, I learned from the best." He inclined his head towards her. "You've always been brave, selfless, and everything else a hero should—" His breath froze in his lungs and he thought his heart might stop beating altogether. "Wait, did you just say that you...you love me?"

She gave him a nervous smile as she nodded in confirmation.

That was all the encouragement he needed.

Before his nerves could stop him, he leaned up and kissed her. His lingering insecurity and hesitation, the remains of masks and walls they both hid behind for years, all melted away in the sweet euphoria of this long-awaited moment.

"Em," he murmured as he pulled away, "I fell in love with you a long time ago, I just didn't know it. I was drowning in love for you before I realized I had even fallen."

Her eyes sparkled with a joy he had never seen before, and he had great fulfillment in knowing he put it there. He hoped he would always be able to bring her that kind of happiness.

"I have one more brave thing to do, and it may be the hardest yet. Em, will you...will you marry me?"

Her eyebrows raised in surprise, but she quickly replaced it with a sweet smile. "Oh, Luca," she said, her voice warm and soft, "I can't."

His smile fell. That's not at all how the conversation ended in his head. "But...I thought—" She cut off his protest with a kiss of her own. Also unexpected, but he didn't mind that part so much.

"I can't marry you without being properly courted first." She offered a mischievous smile. "But if you ask me again in a few months I think I'll have a different answer for you."

He shook his head in amusement. "Always the voice of reason." He chuckled. "But I can consent to those terms. I will gladly court you, my dear, for however long you wish."

"Not too long."

A squeaky floorboard brought their attention to the doorway where Xanth stood frozen in mid-retreat. Realizing he had been seen, he gave them a little wave and smiled nervously. "I...uh, heard you were awake and wanted to bring you this"—he held up a book— "but you were...you two were...busy. I wasn't sure if I should wait or leave and, um..."

Luca couldn't help laughing at his flustered friend. Poor Xanth was red all the way up to his hairline.

"You know what, I'll just leave it here." He took a half step forward and set the book down on the floor. "And now that I've made things awkward I'll just see myself out." He fled down the hallway.

"He's never going to leave us alone, is he?" Emily asked in good humor.

"I'm afraid not. He's a terribly loyal friend. We come as a sort of pair."

"Oh dear. That does change things." She made an exaggerated look of pondering. "But I think I'll take you anyway."

"I'm glad for that."

She helped him sit up in bed and he winced as his bandaged arm shifted. "I almost forgot about my arm."

"It may very well leave a scar."

"Well that would be appropriate," he remarked. "One scar to remind me of my rescue, and one to remind me of yours." He nodded to his other arm that bore his childhood scar.

"It seems we've always needed each other. It just took us this long to figure it out."

With his good arm, he smoothed the hair behind her ear. "True, but the lost time will fade in comparison to the forever ahead."

"Forever," she said thoughtfully, as if trying the word on her lips for the first time. Then she smiled in satisfaction. "I can't wait."

Epilogue

"Keep your eyes closed," Luca said as he gently guided Emily by the hand.

She gave a little snort of amusement. "You do realize even if I open them I will still be unable to see with the blindfold?"

"I know, but I don't want to take any chances."

"Alright." She smiled. She suspected he was showing her an early wedding gift, as the big day was only a few weeks away.

The months in between had been quite busy. Amidst their courtship, Orphia was becoming publicized and King Aspen was arranging trade agreements. Luca had reacquainted himself with San Morrina and even Hiranburg. To his surprise, he was warmly welcomed back into the community. Some of his old roommates even apologized for how they treated him. It gave him newfound confidence that she knew had been lying just beneath the surface. She loved seeing him that way.

He was also nearly smothered by Amira, whose shock at his being alive *and* being Emily's rescuer nearly gave her a heart attack. She quickly recovered and waxed poetic about how romantic their story was.

"Can't you tell me where we're going?" Emily asked impatiently.

"I could, but then it wouldn't be a surprise. And it would be a lot less fun."

"For you," she muttered.

She could practically hear the smile in his voice. "Exactly."

Several paces later, their steps slowed and she could feel the rocky terrain under her feet. "You're taking me to the river, aren't you?"

"Guessing isn't allowed! Just wait and you'll find out soon."

She complied though she now knew that's exactly where he was taking her. She had not yet figured out why.

They stopped and he untied the blindfold. "Ok, open!"

Sure enough, the River of Fallen Stars was before her. She looked around, trying to see what she was missing. It looked the same as it always did.

"Well?" Luca prompted.

"It's beautiful as always. But we were just here a few days ago. I can't see anything different."

He peered over her shoulder to catch her eye. "Ah, but it is different. A few days ago this was just a river. But now"— he pulled out a rolled-up paper from behind him—"it's the location of our future home."

She snatched the paper from his hands and unfurled it to see the house plans contained inside. It was hard to tell on paper, but it seemed to resemble her cottage in San Morrina. "We can build here?"

"King Aspen just gave me the approval for it. Obviously, it won't be ready in time for the wedding, so we will have to live in the castle in the meantime. But neither of us have had a real home in so long that I thought it would be nice to have a place that is just ours."

She gaped at the plans in her hand. The thoughtfulness of this man continued to astonish her. Her gratitude rendered her speechless.

"Do...do you like it? Because if you don't, we could always remain at the castle if you wish."

"Luca, I couldn't wish for anything better than to live with you in this delightful home you've planned for us. I love it!" She threw her arms around his neck and he spun her. "I love it nearly as much as I love you."

"Well that's a relief," he said. "I don't know how I was so fortunate to be gifted your love, but I will try to do all I can to be deserving of it."

She brushed one of his curls back and kissed his cheek. "You are more deserving than anyone else in the world, my Luca."

The sun began to set and the colors reflected in the river, tinging the blue water with a vibrant pink and orange hue. He put his arm around her as they sat on the riverbank, looking over the water as they talked of their future. They spoke of wedding plans, what their house would look like, and their ideas on how to support the people of Orphia as a couple.

Watching the sun continue to fall into the night, she leaned against his shoulder and he placed a gentle kiss on her head. They spent the remainder of their time in contented silence as the glittering waters came to life.

Their journey had not been easy, and it would not likely ever be. Life was seldom easy but living it was not as daunting as it once seemed. Perhaps living "happily ever after" did not mean a problem-free eternity, but instead, creating happiness and finding it in each other no matter life's circumstances.

Their pasts still haunted them at times. Trials would surely come ahead. But whatever the future brought, they would no longer fight it alone. They were both fallen stars, and they had found belonging with each other.

When they sat like this—side by side with fingers intertwined—they could take on the world.

Author's Note and Acknowledgments

It was fun to give free rein to my imagination while creating the kingdoms of Kalopsia and Orphia. Though the places and creatures are obviously fictionalized, much of the inspiration came from real-world things. Some examples are the Bioluminescent Beach in the Maldives, Rainbow Mountain in Peru, Cave of Crystals in Mexico, Swing At The End Of The World in Ecuador, the Technicolor Squirrel, and—perhaps the best—the Pink Fairy Armadillo. I have also personally enjoyed mora berries while visiting South America. So while I hope my book provides a wonderful world for you to run away to, it's good to know that sometimes reality can provide just as beautiful of an escape.

This is my debut novel as an indie author, so if you liked it please leave a quick review on Amazon or Goodreads. Even a short one or a star rating is appreciated! Seriously, it will make this author's day. And who knows...maybe it will inspire me to write a sequel. ;)

Of course, no book would be complete without a thank you to the people who helped make it happen. So thank you to everyone who read my first story and cheered me on to keep writing, to Mom who read my early draft and liked it despite its rough edges, to the early readers and reviewers, and to everyone who plucked my book out of thousands of others and chose to read it. You guys are awesome.

This book was dedicated to all of my honorary siblings, but there are a few who deserve a special mention. Jordan—my "Bubba" since birth, Teresa—my childhood best friend, Courteney—my travel buddy, Cheyenne—my "S" sister, and Matt and Becca—my fellow Disney fans. And to the countless others whose names could fill every page in this book—my life wouldn't be the same without you all, thank you.

About the Author

Madison grew up in a small town in Florida, surrounded by her loving family. She has always enjoyed getting lost in the fictional worlds of movies, literature, and her own imagination. Her favorite stories are clean and sweet with happily ever afters. She enjoys traveling, drawing, going to the beach, spending time with her friends and family, and playing with her dog, Sprinkles.

https://madisonmcauley.weebly.com

Also by Madison McAuley

Stand-alone Regency Romance:

Finally, Forever Yours

Fallen Stars Series:

The River of Fallen Stars

The Shore of Sun's Afterglow

The Garden of Changing Blooms